Hidden Tribe

Scott Harper & Desirée Lee

Hidden Tribe

Copyright © 2016 Scott Harper & Desirée Lee

Published by Umbral Press
PO Box 671
Dorris, CA 96023
http://www.umbralpress.com

ISBN-13: 978-1939378064
ISBN-10: 1939378060

Cover designed by Diadem Designs

"This book not only held my interest, but was written in a way that used documented factual information about the creatures to help tell the story, and clearly shows that the authors did their research and didn't just follow the Hollywood cookie cutter image of a Bigfoot as a vicious monster loose in the countryside destroying everything and everyone in its path for no apparent reason."

Fortean researcher Thomas Lee Curtin Jr.

CHAPTER 1

Iktomi crouched low to the ground, his massive bulk hidden behind the wide trunk of a broken pine tree, and clusters of ferns. He remained motionless, rendering himself all but invisible, listening.

The dual sounds of the deer's racing hooves in the clutter of vegetation, and its pounding heart, told Iktomi the exact location of the prey. Mingled with the noises of the deer's panic were the footfalls of Toylona, as she gave chase through the dense forest.

At precisely the right moment, Iktomi leapt from cover, relieving his mate, and taking over the pursuit. He bristled his hair from head to foot, adding perceived size to his already considerable largeness. The deer bleated its terror and dismay, angling away from Iktomi as he lunged.

Exhausted though it may have been, the deer sprang forward, charging away, struggling to increase the distance between them. Iktomi refused to allow the prey to escape. The healthy young buck would feed Iktomi, Toylona, and their offspring for two or three days. He gave chase, using his long, powerful legs to their maximum advantage.

When the deer's zigzag path took it around several trees which forced Iktomi to slow his pursuit, he inhaled deeply. Lungs filled with air, Iktomi jumped clear of the trees, bellowing. His chest vibrated with the combined force of the roar, and the infrasound underlay.

The moment the sounds struck the deer, it froze in place, sides heaving with exhaustion and terror. Iktomi

1

pounced on it instantly, grabbing it beneath the chin. One quick twist and pull broke the prey's neck, killing it.

Iktomi froze, looking around. Toylona stood nearby, also motionless. Together they listened. All remained quiet. Their hair gradually smoothed back down as they waited. Eventually, Iktomi grabbed the carcass with one huge hand, and flung it over his shoulder. He joined Toylona, and they began retracing their steps toward their lair, and their waiting young.

Halfway back, a series of high-pitched clinking noises drifted through the woods to them. Again, they froze, crouching low. Toylona sniffed the air, wrinkling her nose.

Iktomi caught the scent, too. "Human," he grunted quietly. "Female."

Any human who overheard the words wouldn't understand the language. Still, it would give away their present location. Always best to avoid humans. Still, they didn't often venture so far into the thick woods. The presence of one, seemingly alone, so far into the forest stirred Iktomi's curiosity.

"Go on back," he told Toylona, still keeping his voice low. "Take the food to the children."

She nodded, relieving him of the deer, holding it as easily as he had. "Be careful," she warned before slipping away into the dense vegetation.

Iktomi watched her go, and then followed the clinking sounds. His broad, thickly-padded feet made almost no noise when they touched the ground. He took great care to avoid treading upon dry leaves, or fallen twigs.

A pair of pines that had grown together made for excellent cover. Peering through a gap between the slightly angled trunks, closing his eyes to the merest of slits, so as to minimize the chances of the being spotted due to light reflecting from them, Iktomi saw her.

The female worked at setting up the human equivalent of a camp. Crouching down, she used a small metal cudgel to drive metal spikes into the ground. Her lean body hunched forward as she struck blow after blow. Each impact sent up a high-pitched metallic clink. A breeze stirred the long, light brown hair that spilled over her back and shoulders.

Iktomi stared at her hair. It always astounded him when he realized how little hair humans possessed. His own people were covered with it from birth—fine and light at first, but then quickly darkening and thickening. The small, near-hairless beings always struck him as very alien.

Still...

Iktomi's eyes narrowed. He fought to keep a growl from rising up in his throat. Physically repugnant, and weak they may be, but humans had conquered the world. Nearly everywhere his people had roamed once upon a time now crawled with humans. And still they spread, building and expanding their territory. Their actions robbed his own people of their preferred wooded terrain.

Try as they would to avoid human contact, sometimes it happened. Typically, it happened when a young one, inexperienced, still learning to hide properly, ended up being spotted. Most humans left them alone. Yet some trekked into the deep forests seeking them. Iktomi himself sometimes played games with them, listening to their pale imitations of his people's great roars, shrieks, screams, and whistles his people used to communicate, and responding from different locations. Excited, the humans would exhaust themselves chasing him from one ridge to another until he tired of the play, and hunkered down quietly to await the invaders' departure.

He watched the female as she continued her task. Had one of his people been sighted in the area recently by humans? Could that be what had lured this one out?

"I also need to gather wood for my fire," she muttered aloud. Iktomi heard her clearly, although he didn't understand her words. "I shouldn't have spent so much time getting here. Then again, most of the people who knew I planned this expedition would tell me I shouldn't be out here at all. They'd say I'm just wasting my time, and money."

He glanced around, not seeing another human. Why did the female speak? She didn't appear to be aware of his presence.

She sighed, and went on.

"They'd also tell me that I shouldn't be talking to myself. But, what do they know? How much time alone do they spend in the woods? None; that's how much."

The female wrapped a bright yellow artificial vine to the metal spike, securing it. Iktomi observed her closely. The line seemed to provide support for the fabric cave she erected. Moving in an awkward hobbled crouch, the human made her way to the next spike. She secured another artificial vine to it. As she worked, she spoke again.

"Anyway, sasquatch seem to be drawn to the sound of women's voices. Anything I can do to help bring one closer to me is a good thing. Right? Right. I'm glad I agree with myself. I talk to myself in the forest for the same reason I use brightly-colored ropes, and bright metal tent stakes—anything that might catch the attention of a sasquatch, and make it curious is a good thing."

Finishing with the lines, she stood, brushing her hands together. She then began pulling things from a container made of tan fabric, and metal tubing. Iktomi watched as she walked to a tree, and secured something to it, and then gather stones into a ring. She placed some chunks of wood into the ring.

"In the morning," she continued, "more cameras will go up in the area. I also want to scout around for tracks. There've been a lot of sightings in this region over the past few years. If I'm lucky, there's a family group here. Tomorrow night, I might try some call wood-knocking. Rock-clacking is good anytime, too."

Iktomi wished he knew what her words meant. Again, he glanced around, searching for some sign of another human. He saw no one.

The human drew out a box so small it nearly fit into the palm of her hand. From it, she removed a short wooden stick tipped with red. When she scratched the red part on the side of the box, fire sprang into being with a sharp, pungent smell.

Iktomi winced at the sight and scent of the flame. Fire often destroyed areas of forest. Yet humans used it calmly, and on a regular basis from what he and others he had communicated with had witnessed.

The female grabbed up some dry leaves, tucked them under the wood, and lit them with the burning stick in her hand. Fire fed on the dead leaves, slowly taking hold of the wood.

She then removed more items from the fabric and metal container. When she opened a couple of those, Iktomi smelled food. His stomach rumbled. He wanted to return to Toylona, and their young to partake in the deer. Still, the presence of a human represented a danger to them that could not be taken lightly. He remained in position, holding still so as not to draw attention to himself, and watched.

The human placed a flat, round piece of metal into the fire. She then placed the food onto it, relying on the metal device's upward-curving sides to keep the food from falling into the flames.

After several minutes, she used a long piece of metal with spikes on one end to remove the food. She placed it on a disc of some artificial material, opened a container of water, and began eating.

Iktomi watched until she finished, and cleaned up. Done, the human dowsed the fire, and retreated into the artificial cave she had put together.

Darkness would arrive soon. Iktomi waited another few minutes. When the human did not exit her shelter, he turned away, retracing his path back toward the place where he and Toylona had parted company. From there, he followed her faint trail back to their lair. As he moved, he took care to erase signs of their passing. Special care always needed to be taken with such things. But with a human in the immediate area, the need for such vigilance had become far greater.

Their current shelter, built from two toppled trees

draped with mossy limbs and grass, held himself, Toylona, and their three offspring comfortably. Iktomi uttered a short whistle to alert them to his presence before slipping inside to join them.

Toylona had already gutted the deer. She and their young had pulled the choicest pieces out, and began eating. As Iktomi entered, Toylona handed him part of the deer's liver. Iktomi ate it quickly, hungrier than he had known himself to be.

"Is there a human?" Toylona grumbled a few moments later.

"There is," he replied. "Female, as the smell indicated."

"Alone?"

"She seems to be. But she talks as if to another."

Toylona shook her head at the oddness of human behavior. "What is she doing?"

Iktomi accepted part of the deer's heart when one of the children offered it. "She made shelter, and fire."

Toylona shuddered at the mention of fire, as did the young ones. "She stays a while, then?"

"From the look of it." Iktomi ate the section of heart, and followed it with some berries from a pile beside them. "Stay hidden, and quiet. Keep the children with you."

Toylona's dark eyes narrowed beneath her brow ridge. "If there is only the one, why must we stay hidden?"

"She sets up devices like other humans have done. I think she is here to find us. Keep hidden."

Toylona lowered her head in acquiescence. "Will you keep watching the human?"

"Yes."

"Be safe."

"Always," Iktomi grunted. "It is you and the children I worry for."

"There is only one human," Toylona reminded him. "We will be safe."

Iktomi gazed at the young ones. They ripped dripping chunks from inside the carcass of the deer, eating quickly.

"They are young," Iktomi muttered. "They are inexperienced. See to it that they do not leave any sign for the human to find."

"I will. If she finds anything, she may well bring more humans."

"That is what I fear," Iktomi agreed.

"When will you go back to her?"

"Tomorrow," Iktomi grunted. "Before I left, she had eaten, and gone into her shelter. I expect her to be there for the night. In the morning I will go back."

Toylona slid over, snuggling against him. Her warmth felt good. He held her close. Before long he felt himself dozing as the children continued to eat.

CHAPTER 2

Birdsong filled the morning air as Iktomi crouched low to the ground behind the dual pines he had used as cover to observe the human female the evening before. Within a few minutes of his arrival, sounds drifted to him from the artificial cave the human had erected the night before. Iktomi froze, holding his breath, rendering himself as close to immobile as possible for a living creature.

The sounds of her movements from inside the shelter grew steadily more pronounced. Moments later, an unusual noise, sounding to Iktomi like a faint stuttering snore, came from the artificial cave. As the sounded ended, a pair of flaps folded up, revealing the female as she emerged into the morning sunlight. She wore the same odd fabric coverings over her body as she had the day before. She stretched, yawned, and looked around before moving to the tree where she had secured the boxy object with a wide, flat artificial black vine the day before.

Reaching up, she removed it from the trunk, carrying it inside of her shelter. Iktomi's keen ears picked up a series of quiet clicking sounds, and a few frustrated grunts from the human. Eventually, she came back outside, and returned the box to its former place on the tree. She stood, looking around. Iktomi held still, pretending to be nothing more than part of the trees he hid behind. Her gaze passed right by him, uninterested.

Sighing loudly, she set about making a new fire in the manner as she had done the previous evening. Once the fire had been prepared, she put food in the curved-sided metal slab, and placed it over the flames. Before long, Iktomi watched her eat, and extinguish the fire. After a bit of tidying up, she again ducked inside of her false cave.

Iktomi grew weary of watching her. If she didn't do something more interesting soon, he would leave to forage with his family. The smells of the human's food made his stomach rumble. Still, he didn't want to leave her in their territory unsupervised. Humans were nothing if not dangerous and destructive. He thought it best to keep an eye on her at least until he had a better idea of why she had trekked so deep into the forest.

When she emerged from the shelter again, she wore two more layers of artificial coverings on her upper body to insulate herself against the cool mountain air. She carried one of the longer variations of what Iktomi and his people had learned that humans called "guns" with her. She also wore the metal-and-fabric pack that she had used the evening before. Iktomi caught a whiff of the pungent, unnatural fabrics. His nose wrinkled involuntarily, grateful that his own people had been blessed with thick layers of hair from head to toe, thus negating the need for such smell, and silly-looking things.

As she moved out of her camp, Iktomi followed her stealthily. She withdrew a small round object from the coverings on her body. Iktomi caught a brief glimpse of what looked like a black pine needle quivering in the center of the device, wavering between two of the markings that encircled the outer edge of the thing. The female glanced back and forth between the object she carried, and the landscape around her a few times. She then set out at a steady pace, covering the uneven ground quickly.

Given her humanness, Iktomi found himself impressed at how steadily she progressed. Rocks, roots, and other such obstacles didn't slow her in the slightest. She went over and around them almost as smoothly as one of his own people would.

Iktomi trailed her from a slight distance. He kept her in sight, yet lagged behind far enough to ensure that he would be able to easily hide himself in the landscape should she turn to look behind her. During the times when he lost direct visual contact with his quarry, he could still track her simply by the careless signs she left in the dirt, and the combined scents of her human body, and artificial skins—all of which were glaringly out of place in his environment.

As the day grew warmer, she stripped off the additional layers that covered her upper body, securing them around her slim waist. Clad in only a thinner covering that left most of her arms and legs bare, the human paused long enough for a short meal—this one eaten without the preparation of a fire—and to check the round needle device again.

"If I haven't found anything within the next hour or so, I'm turning back for camp," she said, speaking to no one again, "I'll try another direction tomorrow."

Iktomi watched her check over her resting spot, gather up a couple stray pieces of her debris, and then continue on her way. Again, he followed, careful not to get too close.

The human had only gone a short way when she stopped, letting out a quiet gasp. She stared at the ground, brushing some fallen leaves aside with her fingertips.

Frowning in curiosity, Iktomi crept closer. His stomach clenched upon seeing what she had discovered.

A line of footprints cut across a mostly level place on mountainside. None were too distinct, being old by the look of them, but they were there. And they had most definitely caught the attention of the human female—particularly the three clearest ones.

"Sneaky," she muttered. "Walking on the large rocks, and fallen logs when you can."

Laughing delightedly to herself, she slung the pack from her shoulders, setting it upright on the ground. She opened the top flap, and began removing several objects, the first of which proved to be a rounded metallic thing. She drew a long, flat, bright yellow strip of metal from the it, laying it alongside first one track, then the second, and then the third. She placed it length-wise, and cross-wise over each of the three.

"Sixteen-inches-long," she muttered to herself. "Six-inches-wide across the ball of the foot. Three-and-a-quarter inches across the heel."

Again, Iktomi wished he knew what the sounds that she made meant. He watched as she took from the pack a pale, flat wooden strip decorated with the same type of markings as the yellow metal strip had been. She placed the wood alongside one of the footprints, and removed a small black device from her pack. This new thing smelled foul and oily to Iktomi from where he stood. He wondered how the human could tolerate it before realizing just how weak the human sense of smell must be.

The female pressed a spot on the oily black device several times. Each time Iktomi heard a corresponding click, and the human stepped around to view the tracks from a new perspective before pressing the place on the tool again.

Replacing the clicking tool in the pack, she next withdrew several small pieces of rigid material. These smelled faintly of wood, but that fragrance could only just be discerned through the medley of acrid chemical stenches mixed with it.

Iktomi continued watching as the human gently pushed the new items into the ground, each turned up to stand on one narrow edge, hemming in each track.

His stomach sank when Iktomi realized her intent. He, and others of his people he had spoken with, had witnessed a number of variations on this process. She planned to make copies of the three footprints. The material she had just placed would form edging to keeping the semi-liquid substance Iktomi expected next from running too far.

As he anticipated, the next things she withdrew from the pack were a bowl of the same oily-smelling substance as the clicking tool had been—only this time a brilliant shade of pink, rather than black—a clear container of water, and a bag from which came a peculiar powdery smell.

The human opened the package of powder, pouring

some into the bowl. Adding water, she broke a short section of stick from a downed pine branch nearby, and used it to stir. From time to time she added more powder to the mix.

Apparently satisfied with the concoction, she carefully tipped the pink bowl over the first footprint. Maneuvering it back and forth slowly, she gradually poured a measure of the snowy-white, thick liquid into the confines of the barrier she had set up around the track. Finished, she moved to the second, and then the third prints.

Once she had finished, she returned the bowl, package of powder, and the water into her pack, withdrawing something wrapped in a shiny, crinkling covering if their place. She carefully peeled away part of the glimmering wrapping, and slowly ate the contents. As she chewed, she gradually turned in a complete circle, scrutinizing the landscape. Iktomi hunkered down, holding still, slitting his eyes. As before, her gaze passed right over him.

Iktomi chortled inside. Humans were so easy to fool. With their poor eyesight, and almost nonexistent sense of smell, eluding them typically proved to be almost too easy. However, the repercussions of the human having found the tracks disturbed him. Would she summon other humans? Would she linger in the area longer to try and find more tracks? Or, more annoying and potentially dangerous still, stay to try to find one of Iktomi's people in the flesh?

She washed down her food with a drink of water, placed the debris in her pack, and returned to the footprints. After standing still for a time, staring down at the work she had done, the human retrieved her pack. She withdrew slender lengths of metal, and bent them into arches. She placed both ends of each arch in the drying white substance she had filled the prints with. Two pieces of metal went into each—one at the front, and the other at the rear.

Afterward, she stood, waiting some more. She passed the time by looking around once again. As always, Iktomi stayed low and still. Despite looking right at him at least twice, the human showed no signs whatsoever of having realized his presence.

Finally, after letting a while pass, she knelt, removing sheets of semi-transparent, waxy material from her pack. Using the metal pieces she had implanted into the track copies, she lifted the full-formed replicas from the ground, and used a sharp-edged pinching hand tool to snip off the metal just above the point where each piece met the white substance. She then carefully wrapped each of the three footprint copies in the waxy material, and eased them into her pack.

"Back to camp for a better look at you three," she quietly said. "Hopefully, the one who left your impressions in the ground is still in the area."

After checking the needled device once more, she turned back toward the site of her artificial cave. Iktomi followed her until she had returned, staying long enough to be fairly sure that she had no plans to leave again anytime soon. The human appeared to be too busy examining the replicas of the footprints, using both natural sunlight, and a handheld artificial light source, to want to do anything else for the foreseeable future.

Turning, Iktomi walked carefully away, taking a meandering route back toward Toylona, and their offspring. He took great care not to leave fresh prints, and avoided stepping on leaves, twigs, or other forest ground covering when possible. The human had already found far too much. Toylona had to be told. They had to make plans to hide their young ones until the human had left the area. Iktomi feverishly hoped that she did not summon other humans. Too often, when one of them made a discovery akin to what he had seen the human female make, other humans arrived in the area very soon after.

Iktomi found his family safely ensconced in their shelter. He gave the standard quick whistle to alert them to his arrival before pushing his way inside. He kept the notice briefer than usual, unwilling to risk being overheard by anyone else.

"Well?" Toylona grunted to him the moment he entered.

Iktomi settled in, all three of their offspring snuggling comfortably against him. He hugged them to him.

"She found tracks," he answered his mate.

Her eyes grew wide. "Ours?"

Shrugging, Iktomi rumbled, "Large enough to by mine. But I've not been to the place where she found them for a while. The prints she found weren't very fresh. But they weren't very old, either."

"What do we do?"

Helping himself to a handful of gathered berries, he replied, "I keep watch. You take our young somewhere safe."

"Where?"

"Further up. Higher into the mountains."

Toylona watched their offspring worriedly. "Are there other humans around?"

"None that I have seen, but that could change."

Nodding, Toylona gave a dismayed grunt. "She found tracks. She will probably bring others soon."

"Maybe."

"When it is dark, I will lead the young ones up higher. We will go to our old den up there," Toylona told him.

Iktomi grumbled assent. "Take care not to leave prints. Or to allow hair to become snagged on bushes. Anything she finds will only encourage her to stay. And increase the chances of her bringing other humans to our territory."

Toylona nodded again.

"What will you do," Iktomi asked, "if another is living in our old den site?"

"Warn them of the human," Toylona replied. "And then look for a new place to hide high in the mountains."

Iktomi hugged the young ones to him even tighter. "Good. I will check the old den site for you first. If you are not there, I will find you. Be careful."

"You be careful. Are you going back out now?"

Nodding, Iktomi said, "I have to. There is much daylight left still. There is no telling where the human may go, what she may do, or what else she may find."

"Frighten her away if you must."

"No," Iktomi argued. "Such actions are typically only temporary. And then even more humans arrive to hunt us. It is better to hide, and wait for her to grow frustrated, and leave on her own. We do not even know if she is here to hunt us."

Toylona showed her teeth. "Even if her intent did not start off as a hunt, she has found proof that we are here. From what you say, it sounds as if she will hunt us now. Again, I say, frighten her away if need be."

"If it comes to that," Iktomi agreed before pushing his way back outside.

CHAPTER 3

Iktomi crouched behind the conjoined pines again, watching the human female. As she seemed so apt to do, she had, once more, begun speaking to herself while she stood before an odd device. This one appeared to be a slightly larger variation of the oily black thing she had clicked at the footprints. It balanced atop a trio of slender black artificial sticks.

"While these tracks aren't the best," she said, "they're the first ones I've found in years, and not for lack of looking, either! Unfortunately, the footprints were too old to get any real detail. So, no dermal ridges, or anything like that from these. Still, they're clear enough to tell that these were made by a living foot."

She lay the copies of the tracks on the ground, in the order she had found them—right foot, left foot, and then another right footprint. Removing the device from the sticks to which it had been mounted, she fiddled with it while focusing on the brief trail.

"Note the toes, which are curled a bit, digging into the earth. This is a common feature in many sasquatch prints that have been found. One theory is that the creatures grip the ground with their toes to gain additional traction.

"Also notice the outline and shape of the tracks. Look closely at the two prints made by the creature's right foot. We can see how the foot flexed and moved from one step to the next. This is evidence of anthropoid morphology, rather than a hoax. Anyone faking such tracks would be far more apt to use a simple wooden cutout, or something similar, strapped to their feet. Such an appliance would be too rigid to demonstrate such flexing and motion.

"It's too bad I didn't find these prints sooner. Had they been fresher, and clearer, they may well have contained dermal ridges. A number of such footprints have been found over the years. Sadly, I've never personally discovered any of those."

She paused, standing still, aiming the device in her hands at the footprints. Iktomi watched closely, attempting to divine her purpose. However, her actions continued to mystify him.

The faint snapping of a twig caused him to slowly crouch lower. Iktomi sniffed the air tentatively. The piquant stink of a second human—this one male—caused his hair to ruff up involuntarily. Making a conscious effort to smooth it back down, he held still otherwise.

Leaves scuffed as the newcomer approached. He seemed to want his advance to be clandestine. A glance at the female told Iktomi that she remained oblivious to the other human's presence. Iktomi refocused on his progress as an acorn skipped off the side of a stone. Like most humans, this new one didn't seem to be nearly as stealthy as he obviously wanted.

Another twig broke, much closer to the female's camp. Finally, she became aware of the nearness of the second human. She froze briefly, before moving slowly to return the device in her hands to the top of the odd trio of sticks. When more leaves crunched, she held her breath, and picked up her gun.

She inched close to the black device again. "Something is in the woods, near my camp," she whispered. "What I'm hearing sounds like two feet—something bipedal—as opposed to a deer, or some other four-legged animal."

She inhaled deeply, sampling the air.

"I don't smell the tell-tale stench of a sasquatch, though. I've smelled that before. It's rank; it's like skunk concentrate, especially if one has urinated in the area recently. Whatever is approaching my camp, I don't think it's a sasquatch. Still, their stink seems to be a defense mechanism. They appear to be able to create it at will. Mountain gorillas have glands under their arms from which they can emit pungent secretions when they get excited. A lot of sasquatch encounters don't include report of such a stink. What I'm hearing right now may or may not be a sasquatch. Yet I've seen no other signs of human habitation in this area. Although I've only been here for a bit more than twenty-four hours, so that isn't saying much."

She fell silent, waiting. The gun remained firmly in place at her shoulder.

"Alexia?" a masculine voice called several moments later. "Is that you over there?"

Iktomi saw the female tense as her head angled sharply. Her body language told him that not only did she know the male, but she didn't like him in the least.

"Just a warning shot," she muttered. "Something to send him on his way."

"It is you!" the voice said. "I thought so."

"Mr. Wessler," she answered through teeth that were firmly gritted. "What are you doing out here?"

The new human stepped into view through the trees partway around the camp from Iktomi.

"Call me Dane," he said, smiling broadly, displaying his even, white teeth.

The male stood noticeably taller than the female, had dark blonde hair, and appeared only a few years older than she. He wore variations on the same type of body covering that she wore. Iktomi had seen such things on most of the humans he had witnessed in the forests—thick, warm things that completely covered the arms and legs, with heavy foot protection. Once more he gave silent thanks that his own people had no need of such silliness.

"What are you doing out here, Mr. Wessler?" the female asked.

Grin broadening, he strode into her camp. "Same as you." He pointed at the trio of footprint copies. "I see you've already had some luck. Where did you find those?"

"That's confidential."

"We're on the same side," he told her, gazing at the tracks.

"Where are you camped?"

"Why?" He turned to her, grinning in a way that Iktomi thought of as happily. "Are you thinking of visiting me?"

"No; just the opposite. I want to know where your camp is, so I know which area to avoid. I'm trying to do serious work out here. Having a clown trampling around, making noise, is going to be detrimental to that."

"Noise? Are you referring to my guitar?"

She nodded, quirking an eyebrow in irritation.

He chuckled. "A lot of researchers have had some success in eliciting responses from the Forest Gods by playing music."

"I don't care what you do—as long as you do it far from me. Again, please, why are you out here?"

"There've been a lot of sightings in this area over the past few years," he replied, crouching to take a closer look at the tracks. "I plotted out the ones I knew about on a map. This valley is right smack in the middle of a cluster of locations where the Forest Gods have been reported. It makes sense that if they're all around here, they're in this valley, too. Even if none of them are living here full-time, they must crisscross through it to get from one side to the other. Far as I know, there's nothing here they'd want to avoid badly enough to trek all the way around the valley over and over." He stood up, facing her again. "When, that is, they're here."

"Here?"

"On this plane of existence," he explained.

"You're still supporting the supernatural sasquatch theory?"

"How else do you explain the lack of definitive evidence supporting their existence?" he asked.

The female sighed in response. Her reaction, unfamiliar

though Iktomi might be with humans, spoke eloquently of her frustration.

"Lack of evidence?" she asked. "We have thousands of footprints that have been discovered. We have hundreds of photographs, and audio recordings. We have dozens of video recordings. Several handprints have been found. A few of the handprints, and even some of the footprints, have exhibited dermal ridges. Some of those prints have also been shown to display some form of injury or handicap that the creature apparently suffered from—attributes that would take an extensively detailed knowledge of anatomy, anatomical morphology, and several other fields to pull off. Not to mention that those knowledge bases would all need to be understood equally well by the hoaxer.

"We have a large number of hair samples, some of which scientists have been able to sample DNA from. Testing on those have sometimes come back showing that the being the DNA came from wasn't human, or chimpanzee—but some unknown species that is, evolutionarily-speaking, somewhere in between them! More recent studies of sasquatch DNA have shown not only that, but suggested that sasquatch are descended from human ancestors, and some unknown species.

"On top of all of that, we have hundreds of thousands of eye-witness reports of these creatures. Taken all together, it's a pile of evidence that would be the proverbial open-and-shut case in any court, anywhere in the world! People are sentenced to execution every single day on what amounts to a tiny, tiny fraction of the evidence that we have documented to support the existence of sasquatch as a living population!"

As the male held up his hands, and the female stopped talking. Iktomi wished yet again that he could understand their speech. If he knew what they were saying, he might be better able to gauge what level of threat—if any—these two posed to his family, and to himself. Based solely on the passion with which the female seemed to speak, Iktomi couldn't help but to feel extremely wary of them.

"You don't need to convince me that they're real," the male said. "I know they are. I just don't think they're terrestrial."

The female snorted in distain, but didn't make a verbal comment.

"Think about it," the male told her. "If sasquatch were from here—Earth, I mean—why hasn't anyone ever found remains?"

"You know the answers to that."

"Tell me anyway. Please? Let me hear what you think."

The female sighed deeply. "These creatures live in the wild, not our modern human society. When an animal dies in the wild, scavengers get to the body quickly. In a matter of a few days, all that's left are bones. Other scavengers grab those, scattering them. It's entirely possible that people see sasquatch bones on a regular basis, but simply find one random piece of the skeleton, chewed on, and left by other animals, and simply don't recognize what they're seeing.

"It's also possible that sasquatch bury their dead. They know about humans. They've learned how to avoid us. These things are masters of their environment. They're like ninja in that regard. They go out of their way to hide footprints when they can. They will freeze in place, and can easily be mistaken for a tree, or a stump—if they're crouched down. They've especially been known to do that in poor lighting.

"With the lengths they go to in order to avoid detection, it's entirely possible that their dead are disposed of in such a way as to not leave remains for us to find. For all we know, they eat their dead. Doing so would make perfect sense from their point of view. They'd be getting rid of the body—rather than leaving one somewhere to be found by humans—and gaining the protein from the food."

Grinning again, the male said, "Sasquatch are gods. They're beings from another dimension. Why do they pop into this world from time to time? That I don't know. But I do know they should be revered and worshipped, not hunted." He gave her gun a look that Iktomi didn't fully understand.

"The gun isn't for a sasquatch," she retorted. "You know I'm one hundred percent no-kill where they're concerned. It'd still be short-sighted and irresponsible of me to come out here unarmed. There are other things out here besides sasquatch. You know I want definitive evidence—other than a body—to drop at the feet of the scientific community. I want these creatures protected by federal and state laws. I don't want them harmed."

"I still say you're wasting your time trying to find physical evidence of creatures that aren't here most of the time," the male said. "Even when they are here, they might not be fully here. A lot of reports state that they vanish instantly."

"We're looking for solid, corporeal beings, Mr. Wessler—not ghosts."

"I never said they were ghosts."

"Why are you out here?" she asked. "You say I'm wasting my time. So why are you out here?"

"You are wasting your time. You're roaming the woods, looking for something that probably isn't even here at this exact moment. I, on the other hand, am trying to get them to come pay me a visit."

Frowning, she retorted, "Which they can't do if you're not in your camp. Why don't you get back there?"

"Have I overstayed my welcome?"

"No. You were never welcome here in the first place. Now go, and let me work."

He chuckled, shook his head, and wandered away. Iktomi watched him, and also kept an eye on the female. She glared after the retreating male, gun still in hand, albeit lowered. Her poise made Iktomi wonder if she would use the weapon against the male should he return. She held her ground for a time even after the sounds of the other human's feet scuffing in the forest debris had faded to silence.

"Idiot," she murmured before turning back to the trio of copies she had made of the footprints. After staring at them for a couple of minutes, she turned back to the device perched atop the sticks, saying, "Dane has me so flustered that I can't concentrate now. I suppose it's time to eat."

Iktomi frowned, puzzling at the significance of the device. The female talked to it as she had previously spoken to herself. He cocked his head, continuing to observe her as she lit a fresh fire, and set about preparing her food.

As she worked, strains of music floated through the air. She froze briefly, staring off in the direction of the sounds. A low growl issued from her as her teeth gritted.

Iktomi watched her anger build the entire time she readied her meal, and ate. The music seemed to enrage her. Iktomi found that he liked it. While vastly different from the clacking of rocks, and twigs, or thumping of hollow logs that his own people did, the unusual sounds pleased him. Curious, he wanted to find their source. He forced himself to remain still, however. Until he discovered more about the female's reasons for being there, he needed to watch her.

Of course, he needed to watch the male, too. But he couldn't be in both places at once. And Toylona needed to remain with their offspring. Without at least one parent there to keep them subdued, their children would likely run playing through the forest, leaving footprints everywhere for the humans to discover. Likely, they'd leave plenty of other sign, too. Not to mention the noises they would likely make.

Given the female's passion and anger, she struck Iktomi as the more dangerous of the pair. He decided he would keep watch on her. At least for now. Maybe her path would cross that of the male again. Until the male showed indications of being as potentially dangerous as the female, though, she had to remain Iktomi's focus. Still, the music called to him. The source had to be human. Could it be coming from the male?

Finished eating, the female quickly cleared away the mess. She then snatched up her gun, and strode into the deeper woods. She did so with an abruptness that caught Iktomi off guard. He eased from his hiding place, trailing behind her.

Gradually, the music grew louder. Iktomi realized the

female also sought its source. To Iktomi's satisfaction, that proved to be the encampment of the human male. He sat upon an artificial construct consisting of some oily material strung upon a metallic frame. In his hands he held the device upon which he made the music. The instrument had a wide body, with a long neck. What looked to Iktomi like very thin vines were strung taut from one end to the other. As the male's fingers played over them, these vines vibrated, creating a wide array of tones. Taking up position behind a wide tree around which a grouping of tall ferns clustered, Iktomi again settled in to watch.

"Dane, will you please stop," the female asked.

"Why, Alexia?"

Dane? Alexia? Iktomi had heard them speaking these words before. They stood out among the others. Something about the inflection used with them. It reminded him of when he said his own name, or that of his mate.

His eyes widened. Could Dane and Alexia be names? He worked his mouth as he thought. Could the female he had been watching be called Alexia? Could the male be Dane? Iktomi decided this to be true.

Alexia. Now he had a name for his primary quarry. Dane. Now he had a name for his secondary quarry.

"I can't work with the noise, that's why," said the female—Alexia, Iktomi reminded himself.

The male—Dane—picked up the tempo. "I'm playing for the Forest Gods, not you."

She rested one hand on a slender hip, holding the gun with her other. "If you won't quit playing guitar, will you please move your camp further from mine?"

"I like it right here," he replied, and gave her a cheery smile.

"Fine. I'll move my own camp in the morning, then."

Dane strummed a series of lively chords, nodding thoughtfully. After a moment his grin widened. "I like you, Alexia. Because I like you, it bothers me that you're out here camping alone. If you move your camp, I just might have to move mine, too—closer to your new location. I think someone ought to be nearby in case you run into a problem, and need help."

"Seriously?" she asked, staring at him in astonishment so clear that Iktomi picked up on it easily. "You're stalking me in the woods to ruin my attempts at data collection?"

"As I've said, I don't think the Forest Gods should be bothered."

"And you're not bothering them with your guitar?"

"They haven't objected. I think of my music as an offering to them. I go into the woods to play for them. It's a way of getting nearer to their divinity."

"You're nuts."

"I have a differing point of view than you," he replied. "Nothing more."

Turning away, she said, "Do me a favor, then, and keep your point of view away from me, and my camp!"

She strode away, furious. Iktomi debated briefly whether to stay, and watch Dane play the instrument. However, Dane seemed far more peaceful. Alexia appeared to be the one to be concerned about. Reluctantly, Iktomi slid from his hiding place, trailing Alexia.

"Maybe I could break camp, and slip off somewhere without him knowing," she said, speaking to herself once more. "He'd find me," she grumped. "He's a man on a mission. He'd find a way to track me. With him out here, maybe I should just pack it in, and go home."

She ran a hand through her long hair in frustration. "No. I won't let him ruin this. I only just got out here, and I've already found tracks. I won't let him chase me away."

She doubled her pace back to her camp.

CHAPTER 4

Iktomi lay curled on the ground not far from Alexia's encampment. He had slept there, rather than trek higher into the mountains in search of Toylona and their offspring, only to retrace his steps back a short time later. The music played by Dane had continued long into the night. Apparently, Alexia had found it disruptive, for she had lain awake in her artificial cave for most of the night, talking to herself. Iktomi had forced himself to remain awake as long as she, in case she chose to leave her camp for a time.

Now, he awoke to the odd stuttering snore that indicated the opening of her shelter.

"I had planned on some wood-knocks last night," she grumbled to herself as she stepped into the morning sunlight. "I let Dane upset me so much that he made me forget my plan. Tonight, then—Dane, or no Dane."

Iktomi rolled quietly to his feet, stretching. His stomach rumbled. He hoped she would leave her camp soon. Trailing her through the forest would afford him the opportunity to forage.

Alexia removed the device she kept mounted to the tree nearest her shelter. She did something to it that made it click faintly over and over. All the while she stared intently at the back of device, frowning.

"Nothing," she muttered before securing the odd thing to the tree once more. "It's as if they know to avoid trail cameras. Sasquatch are far more intelligent than most people give them credit for. Some researchers think sasquatch can somehow sense the minute electrical currents from these cameras. Maybe; we know next to nothing about this species."

She stepped back into her shelter, only to emerge again moments later with two more of the devices. She worked quickly, securing them to separate trees further from her shelter.

Finished, she built a fire, and set about making food for herself. Iktomi's stomach rumbled again loudly at the smells. He thought about slipping away to find a meal for himself. Ultimately, however, he forced himself to wait. He didn't want to chance missing Alexia if she set out from her camp.

No sounds drifted in from Dane's camp. Iktomi wondered if he still slept, or if his morning activities were simply quieter than Alexia's. He missed Dane's music, and hoped to hear more of it later.

Iktomi's musings were cut short when Alexia performed a quick clean-up after her meal, grabbed up her gun, and set out. Iktomi followed discretely behind, picking leaves and berries here and there. The foliage, drying out in preparation of the cold, snowy season, lacked the succulent juiciness he preferred. Still, it helped to fill his empty belly.

Alexia hadn't gone far when Iktomi heard and smelled Dane approaching, angling toward her from his own encampment. Soon after, Alexia appeared to hear him, too, for she stopped, snorted in irritation, and turned to face the direction from which the other human came.

Dane began to whistle cheerfully soon before stepping into sight. "Going for a hike?" he asked.

"Yes. You're up early after being up so late last night."

A look of mock remorse settled onto his features. "I do hope I didn't disturb you."

"Not at all."

Feigned relief overtook his tone. Iktomi felt proud of himself to be able to detect the falsity, despite not knowing what the words themselves meant. "I'm so glad. Hey, I noticed you didn't do any call-blasting last night."

"I never do call-blasting—ever," she said tersely. "We

don't know their language. That means we have no idea what any given recording of them means. One researcher might get an audio recording of a sasquatch screaming, and howling. Later they, or another researcher, might use that recording for call-blasting. But what if the sasquatch that had been recorded knew the researchers were there? What if it had been shouting to other sasquatches in the area, saying, 'Hey, guys, listen up! There are humans here, looking for us! Whatever you do, keep quiet, and avoid this place for a while!' By call-blasting that recording, you'd be warning every sasquatch in earshot that you're there, alerting them to stay away."

"You don't know that's what they're saying," he pointed out.

"That's my point," she told him. "We've no idea what they're saying. Why risk broadcasting a warning like that? Or, worse yet, a challenge? What if you call-blasted a series of shrieks that amounted to 'I'm bigger and tougher than any other sasquatch in these woods. Don't believe me? Come over here, and I'll prove it!' What then? You might wind up with an angry, territorial sasquatch coming at you, planning to throw you off of its home turf. Yes, you'd be getting one in close to you. The question is do you really want a creature that's probably two feet—or more—taller, and a few hundred pounds heavier, angry with you?"

"I see what you're saying."

"Good," she said, relaxing a bit. "A lot of researchers don't seem to. Now, I have work to do. Please stay away from me."

Dane turned, walking away. Alexia watched him, as Iktomi observed them both. Dane angled back toward his own camp. Alexia stared after him, frowning deeply, until long after he had vanished from sight.

She then continued on her way, withdrawing a stack of thin pieces of something that smelled of wood and chemicals from her pocket. The fragile layers were held together by a coiled metallic spiral along one edge. Alexia took out an oily-scented stick, and used it to made strange markings on one of the leaves in the stack. Iktomi watched, puzzled, again wishing he had a better understanding of humans.

****

Toylona sat on a comfortable mat of pine boughs. Her three offspring romped and played a few feet away. She watched as the two youngest wrestled, taking turns tumbling over each other. The oldest sat a little way from his siblings, banging a pair of rocks together, practicing one of their peoples' main ways of long-distance communication. Toylona let him work, knowing that they were far enough up the mountain from the human Iktomi had under watch so as not to be heard by her.

She and Iktomi were constantly amazed at how quickly the young ones grew. Already, their hair had darkened, and their faces had lost the roundness they previously held. Their once-spindly limbs began filling out with muscles. Their heads were already forming into peaks, especially that of the oldest. The time for his naming would soon be upon them. It didn't seem possible.

When the odd crinkling sound hit her ears, Toylona beckoned to her young, and froze. They held still, but their sides heaved from the exertion of their play. All three of them stared at her, ready to take their cues from her actions. She slowly held up a hand, motioning for them to remain quiet.

The strange sound came to her again.

Toylona indicated that the young ones should stay where they were. She then rose smoothly to her feet, and crept forward, listening.

"I can't believe how quiet it is out here," a female human voice said. "We haven't seen a deer all day."

Toylona nibbled her lower lip. A human. Female, and speaking. She wondered if this was the same one that Iktomi had been observing. He had told her that she spoke as if to others, even when alone. She looked around, but saw no sign of Iktomi. Inhaling deeply, she sought out his unique scent. She could find no sign of it, either.

"Siskiyou County is over-hunted," a human male voice said. "We should've gone somewhere else. Studies have shown that the buck-to-doe ratio in this area is way off."

Fear caused Toylona's hair to bristle. Humans! Two of them, at least. A male, and a female. Waving for the offspring to keep still, she eased forward for a look at the intruders.

"Next year we'll go somewhere else," the female said.

Toylona could see them further down the side of the mountain. The pair of them sat together on a jumble of rocks. They appeared to drinking water from clear containers that smelled of oil, and crinkled from time to time—the source of the sound that had alerted her to their presence.

The male nodded. "If it was early enough, I'd suggest going somewhere else this year, too. But it's already late September. We only have a few days of deer season left."

Toylona didn't know enough about humans to judge how much of a threat they might pose to her and the young ones. She saw long guns lying next to each of them, though. She bared her teeth at them in a silent snarl. If they had those, they were a danger.

The female downed the last of her water, closed the container, and stowed it in a metal-and-fabric pouch that she then slung onto her back when she stood up. "Ready to move on?"

The male put his own rubbish away. "Whenever you are."

He stood, and they took up their guns.

"Which way?" the female asked.

Toylona peered at them, keeping them under close observation. Their strange coverings they wore on their bodies, limbs, and heads had mottled patterns of various shades of greens and browns. Due to the shading, it would be easy to lose sight of them. Of course, their smells would lead her right to them even if they should happen to be out of her line of sight.

The male consulted a small, round device withdrawn from a pouch worked into the covers over his body, and motioned to the north. "That way, Ursula."

The female slid down a two-foot slope to more level ground.

Behind Toylona, her eldest offspring resumed clacking his rocks together. She turned to him, motioning for him to stop.

"They're moving away," he told her. "I can hear them going downhill." He brought the rocks together again.

Toylona grunted softly, agreeing with him. She turned her attention back to the humans. "They could still hear, though. Keep still until we're sure they have gone."

The banging of the rocks continued behind her as her offspring ignored her order.

The male followed the female down the incline in a barely-controlled slide. Just as he steadied himself, preparing to dust himself off, the female grabbed his arm lightly. The way she touched him told Toylona that the humans were mated.

"Did you hear that?" the female whispered.

Keeping his own voice low in response, the male asked, "Hear what?"

"That noise."

He shook his head. "I didn't hear anything."

The male started to move, but his mate held him tighter, keeping him in place.

"Listen," she instructed.

"To what?"

"Just listen."

He held still, and Toylona wished she knew what their strange speech meant. She didn't like that they had paused while her offspring continued making noise with the rocks. She turned back to him.

"Quit. Now," she told him firmly.

He only shrugged. "Why? They're only humans. It isn't as if they can find us."

"They can if you keep making sounds to let them know we're here. Stop it!"

"What am I listening for?" the male human asked, his voice carrying clearly to Toylona.

"Wait," the female ordered, holding up her free hand.

Behind Toylona, the oldest of her offspring resumed banging the rocks together. The sound set Toylona's teeth on edge now.

"What is that?" the human female whispered. She pointed up the slope in the direction of Toylona, and the young ones.

Toylona's hair bristled again. She spun, knocking the rocks from her offspring's grasp. "They can hear you!' she said, her voice low, but furious. "You're telling the humans that we're here! Keep silent!"

The human male's voice drifted to them, saying, "I'm not sure. Probably another hunter trying to build a campfire."

"With what? Flint and steel?" his mate replied, unease evident in her voice.

Defiantly, Toylona's eldest took up the rocks again. "They're just dumb humans," he argued, smashing the rocks together harder than before.

"That isn't another hunter. If it is, they're doing something I've never done while hunting," the human female said from below.

"Like what?" her mate answered.

"I've no idea."

The male said, "Let's go take a look," and Toylona heard a click that she thought came from a gun.

"I don't know if we should," the female responded.

"I do," her mate said.

Toylona hunkered down, beckoning the youngest two nearer to her. She then shot a furious glare at the oldest. "Keep quiet!"

Ignoring her, he brought the rocks together again.

Toylona listened as the sounds of the humans' scuffing footsteps started up the side of the mountain toward herself and the young ones. She reached out, snatching the rocks away from the oldest offspring. When he started to make a reply, she clamped one hand over his mouth. With her other hand, she tossed the rocks away, putting them out of his reach.

"The humans are coming this way," she hissed at him. "You've told them right where we are!"

"Whatever is it, it sounds like it's up there," Toylona heard the male say from below.

"Let it stay there," his mate said. "There are no deer out here. Let's just turn back. Let's go home. We'll try someplace else next year."

"Not yet. I'm curious as to what's making that sound. Why would someone be sitting up there, banging rocks together? If it's like you said, and someone is having trouble lighting a campfire, we can help them."

"Guy..."

"Maybe someone lost their matches," he went on. "Maybe they're trying to create sparks by smacking stones together. Let's go see if we can be of assistance."

"I just want to leave." The female let out a small whimper.

"Ursula, I've never seen you like this," he soothed. "What's wrong?"

"I just want to get out of here."

"What are you so afraid of? Come on," he said.

Toylona heard the footsteps growing nearer. Not knowing what else to do, she pointed toward the tallest tree within sight. "Go. Climb. Hide!"

The trio of young ones scampered to the base of the tree, and scurried up it. Within moments they were well-hidden high up in the branches. Toylona grunted, satisfied. She then turned to face the unseen humans. Their smell, and the sound of their footsteps told her they were fast approaching. She inhaled deeply, filling her lungs, before cutting loose with a long series of shrieks, and chatters aimed at the unseen invaders, telling them to leave the area. She knew they wouldn't understand her language any better than she knew theirs. But she hoped the intent behind the words would be clear to them.

The footsteps halted instantly. "What is that?" the male whispered, sounding nervous. "It sounds like an angry chimpanzee."

"Guy, please! Let's go!"

"We have rifles," he muttered. "Whatever it is, if we have to we can—"

Toylona screamed at them, the cry shifting over to a full-throated roar. Panicked outcries came from both humans. Toylona heard them scurrying back down the mountainside, slipping and sliding more than running.

She turned, and waved the young ones down from the tree. They returned to her side, and she cuffed the eldest hard on the shoulder. "From now on, when you're told be to keep still, you listen. Understand?"

"Yes."

"Good. Let's go."

She turned, leading her children away from the fading sounds of the departing humans. They had heard the noise made by the young one. After coming closer, Toylona had been forced to frighten them off. Such things happened in the past with others of their people. When it did, it almost always meant more humans arriving soon after. Toylona wanted her offspring long gone from the area before that occurred.

CHAPTER 5

Iktomi grunted softly to himself, wondering what Alexia's actions were intended to accomplish. She used a tiny pair of metallic pinchers to gently remove something from the tip of a pine branch that hung down to about even with her shoulders. Her hand wavered, as she untangled something from the needles. As she used the pinchers to slip her discovery into a small clear pouch, Iktomi finally realized what she had found—several coarse strands of dark brown hair.

His stomach sank. Hair from one of his people. More evidence of their presence found by this human. One more reason for her to linger, and continue her search.

By now he had no doubts whatsoever that her reason for being deep in the woods centered around his people. Whether she sought them personally, or simply clues pointing to their presence, he didn't know. But he knew she had come there because of them.

Alexia tucked the pouch away in the larger metal-and-fabric sack she carried on her back when away from her camp.

"Footprints and hair so quickly," she told herself. "This place is the proverbial goldmine!"

Iktomi followed her for a while, until she paused, focusing on the sky. Iktomi looked, too, but saw nothing unusual.

"If I start back to camp now," Alexia muttered, "I can make it back before dark. I'll have time to examine the hair. On the other hand, if I stay out longer, I just might find more hair. Or prints. Or maybe even something better. They're definitely in this area. On the other hand, I don't have the equipment with me on this trip to do a thorough analysis on the hair; only my microscope. Still, even that could tell me something."

She hummed softly for a few moments, looking around at the surrounding forest, and mountains. Finally, she turned away, beginning to retrace her steps forward her encampment. Iktomi tailed her, barely keeping her in sight.

Should he turn aggressive with her? Such tactics might chase her out of the region for the time being. But, almost certainly, either she, or other humans, would be back in the area soon, trying to find him. Also, even if he ran Alexia off, that still left Dane. Whereas Alexia struck him as aggressive, and possibly a threat, Dane seemed very gentle. And Iktomi liked the music the human male played. Dane seemed content to sit in peace, creating the music. Only Alexia seemed concerned with bothering his people.

For the moment, Iktomi opted to simply continue observing Alexia. He could always change his plan later, if she gave him sufficient cause.

Upon returning to her camp, Alexia smiled broadly, and sighed happily. "No sign of Dane."

She retreated into her fabric cave, and Iktomi heard the sounds of her working inside. However, he couldn't see her. Not, he mused, that he would understand her actions even if he could.

After only a few minutes, music drifted in from the direction of Dane's camp.

Alexia grunted in irritation. "Dane," she muttered darkly. "Fine. Whatever. It'll be dark soon. I need to get into position. These samples can wait until tomorrow."

Iktomi heard her moved things around inside her shelter. It seemed to him that she did so more roughly than needed.

When she exited the artificial cave, her expression spoke eloquently of her ire, and she carried her gun. The large carry pouch she took with her when leaving her camp hung in place on her back.

Moving to the side of her encampment clearing furthest from Dane, she slung her weapon over one shoulder, and climbed a tree. Iktomi pondered her reasoning as she settled comfortably into a spot where three large branches divided.

Easing back, Alexia let out a long sigh. "This works. Why can't all trees be this comfortable?"

She withdrew food and water from the pack, eating and drinking. All the while Iktomi watched her, and listened to Dane's music.

Finished, she put away her trash, and took out two thick lengths of wood. Each appeared about as long as her forearm. She held one in each hand, remaining still for a few seconds, before bring them firmly together.

A loud knock issued from the impacting pieces of wood. The abruptness of the sound caused Iktomi to flinch.

Alexia paused, apparently listening. Iktomi stayed hunkered down, waiting. Humans sometimes did this, he knew. They realized that such smacking of branches was a method used by his people for communication. They mimicked it in the forests, and sometimes tricked a listener into making a response. The responders were typically young ones, inexperienced, and not wary enough of humans. But not always.

Iktomi listened with her, but Dane's music, a breeze stirring the trees, and a few insects braving the chill evening were all that he heard.

Alexia brought the chunks of wood together again before going quiet once more. Again, Iktomi listened, dreading hearing a like reply. The human female had already found too much. She had become too insistent upon finding more. An answer to her knocks would only serve to encourage her, and make it that much harder to get rid of her.

"Come on," Alexia whispered. "I know you're out there. Give me a sign. Knock back. Howl. Whoop. Shriek. Scream. Screech. Throw a rock at me. Do something."

After a third failed attempt to elicit a response, she

heaved a sigh, and shoved the wood back into the carry pack.

"They probably can't hear me over that noise Dane is making!"

She leaned back, falling silent. She watched the sky as it grew darker, keeping still. Iktomi sat, waiting, listening to Dane's music. But she just held still, making no noise.

After a while, Iktomi gently shifted position, wanting to keep her in sight, but also wanting to better listen to Dane. Time passed, and still Alexia showed no inclination to descend from the tree.

Iktomi wondered what he would find if he made the brief journey over to Dane's camp? Would the male human be sitting in the same location as before, conjuring music from the odd instrument? He itched to find out. Doing so, however, would mean leaving Alexia—the more dangerous of the two—unwatched.

He peered up at the tree. She remained in place, seemingly waiting for something.

Iktomi's stomach gurgled. He rose, deciding to pay Dane a visit. He would able to forage a bit on the way there, and back again.

Upon arrival, Iktomi hid behind a wide tree. Dane rested in the odd, metallic-framed seat, strumming the instrument. The human male wore a large smile.

Wood knocks sounded from the direction of the other camp. Iktomi thought of going back, but decided to stay. If Alexia had resumed knocking, she had probably stayed up in the tree.

Dane's playing gradually became softer and softer. Disappointment flared in Iktomi; he wanted more. Dane rose, ceasing the music, and slipped into his fabric shelter. Iktomi started to rise, about to leave, when the human came back out. He carried with him a small device that reeked of metal and oil. After placing it in his seat, he touched a spot on it.

Iktomi started when the same music Dane had been playing came from the little device. Grinning, Dane waited for a moment, and then touched the device again. The sounds coming from the device grew louder. Nodding, Dane glanced toward Alexia's camp, turned and slipped from his own.

Scowling at the deceit, Iktomi revised his opinion of Dane. Why keep the music going, even when he left his camp? Iktomi had seen the look the male had cast in the direction of the female's camp. Had he set the artificial music source up to fool her? If so, why?

He skulked after Dane, watching him closely. The human seemed to be up to something. Iktomi just didn't know what yet. However, his instincts told him that whatever Dane had in mind boded ill for Alexia.

It seemed he had guessed right when Dane stopped in the thickest section of trees within sight of the clearing where Alexia had erected her shelter. Dane stood still, watching the female's camp.

Iktomi cocked his head, trying to figure out Dane's reason for being there. Did he have romantic interests in the female? Were his unusual actions part of a human courtship ritual? Or did Dane pose a threat after all—not to Iktomi's people, but to Alexia? If that turned out to be the case, what would Iktomi do? Should he step in to save Alexia? Or stay out of it, and allow whatever unfolded between the intruders to do so without his involvement? Or had the knocks Alexia continued doing every few minutes attracted Dane's curiosity?

The question was rendered moot when Dane slipped away from the other's camp. He moved silently—for a human—venturing deeper into the forest. Once well out of view of Alexia's encampment, Dane withdrew a small tubular object from the fabric covers on his body. With a faint click, the object shone a bright beam of light ahead of him. Iktomi recoiled slightly at the unexpected brightness, but continued after his quarry.

Iktomi recognized the path he took as the same Alexia had taken before, when she hung up her series of strange devices on trees here and there. Dane reached the first of them, and removed it from its place. Frowning, Iktomi watched him fiddle with something on the back of the box. Whatever he did created a quick series of quiet beeps. Grinning, Dane replaced the device, and moved on.

One by one, he stopped at each as he came to them, repeating the ritual. Were the things Alexia had hung a threat? Did Dane intend to help fight that threat? Or did his manipulation of the things have another reason?

Iktomi shook his head to himself. Without knowing what the items were meant to do, he had no way to determine anything. Dane might be trying to help Iktomi's people. Or he might be trying to help Alexia. If so, though, why the deception with the music? Not for the first time, Iktomi found himself glad of not having to deal with humans and their odd behaviors often.

He tailed the human as he looped, and zigzagged through the forest. Each time Dane spotted one of Alexia's devices he removed it from its perch on the trunk, fiddled with it, and returned it.

After hours of this, he finally wandered back to his camp. Iktomi paused, debating over watching Dane further, or looking in on Alexia. Another short series of knocks from her direction let him assume that she remained in the tree. Iktomi relaxed, eyeing Dane.

The human male checked the object he had left lying on his seat earlier. Music still issued loudly from it. Seemingly satisfied, he retreated to his artificial cave, sealing it behind him. Iktomi waited, but Dane did not reappear.

Finally, he turned toward Alexia's camp, returning to her. He arrived just in time to see her packing away the pieces of wood she had been using to knock. She braced herself on a wide limb, slung her gun and carrying pack over her shoulders, and climbed smoothly down from the tree.

"I hope his fingers bleed," she whispered, her annoyance plain even to Iktomi.

Audibly grinding her teeth, she retreated into her shelter, closing it behind her. Left with nothing else to do, Iktomi waited, listening to the music from Dane's camp. He marveled at how the tunes emitting from the object on Dane's seat sounded lifelike enough to pass for the music Dane made with his fingers on the instrument he had played before.

As he waited, he considered returning to Toylona, and their trio of offspring. He missed them, and missed their shared body heat as they would huddle together during the night. However, sunrise would not be too far off. He doubted he would have returned to the humans before then if he left. Should either of them venture off into the woods before he got back, he would either be forced to allow them to wander unobserved, or spend the time catching up. Which would leave the other unwatched for that much longer.

In the end, he curled up at the base of the same pairing of pine trees he had used for cover at Alexia's camp since discovering her presence. Lack of a woven bed of slim branches, covered with pine needles, moss, or grass bothered him. But such a thing would give her direct evidence of his having been there. For the sake of the safety of his people, he would suffer through another lonely, cold night by himself, and without a proper bed.

CHAPTER 6

"Help us!" a human female screamed.

Iktomi sat up instantly, keeping low to the ground, blinking sleep from his eyes. The sounds of underbrush, and twigs cracking and snapping sounded out, loud in the otherwise early morning silence of the deep forest.

"Help! Help us!" the voice called again.

Iktomi forced himself to focus on what he could hear and smell. The voice was, as his first impression upon being startled awake had told him, human and female. The voice differed from Alexia's. From the scents reaching him, there were two humans—the female, and a male companion. Both were very frightened. The barrage of noise they made alerted him that they were rushing headlong directly at him. What were yet more humans doing out here?

Iktomi leaped up, kept low, and rushed for cover in a cluster of ferns that grew densely around the base of a huge tree. His new position put him further from Alexia's encampment, but far enough away from his old hiding place to avoid the newcomers as they ran by.

The wan moonlight gave him plenty of illumination to see the new humans. They were older than the ones he had been keeping under watch. Given his lack of knowledge regarding humans, he couldn't be sure, but judged them to be not far from elderly. They wore the same types of body coverings that Alexia and Dane wore, only patterned with designs that blended into the trees around them. They also carried nothing with them. Their lack of guns allowed Iktomi to relax.

"Someone, please!" the new male shouted as he and the new female rushed into Alexia's camp.

A stuttered snoring sound came from Alexia's shelter as she unsealed it. Emerging, she gazed tiredly at the new arrivals, her gun clutched tightly.

"What happened?" Alexia asked. "And who are you?"

The new male attempted to wrest the gun from Alexia, but she twisted away hard, maintaining ownership of it. The newcomer's attempt at acquiring the gun caused Iktomi to scowl heatedly at him.

"Bigfoot!" the new female said.

"What?" Alexia's voice rose nearly to a shout.

"Bigfoot!" the other female said again, more loudly. "We've seen one!"

Excitement surged through Alexia. "Take me to it!"

"No!" the unknown male bellowed. "You have to help us get out of here!"

"Calm down," Alexia told them. "Sasquatch don't typically hurt people, unless you've hurt them first. Did you?"

"No," the other female said. "We ran when we saw it. But it came at us screaming!"

Making hand gestures as silent pleas for them to settle down, Alexia inched all the way out of her shelter. "This happened tonight?"

"Yes!" the male bellowed.

"Sit down," Alexia said. "Tell me what happened."

"We're not sitting," the man said gruffly. "We're getting out of here. You're taking us out of here now."

He grabbed Alexia's gun, wrenching it from her grasp. Spinning, he swept it around the edge of the clearing. Iktomi flattened himself on the ground, struggling to keep from growling at the abruptly aggressive human.

"No," Alexia replied to the male. "I'm not. Give me back my rifle, calm down, and tell me what happened. Please."

"We want to get out of these woods," the new female said.

"What are your names?" Alexia asked.

"I'm Ursula Dunmead," the other female replied, touching her chest. "My husband's name is Guy." She motioned to the male.

"Guy and Ursula. I'm happy to meet you. My name is Alexia Hollander."

Iktomi frowned. Alexia had spoken her name. He pondered what he had heard from the new female in conjunction with her actions. Ursula? Guy? She had indicated herself and the male as she had spoken those words. Iktomi decided these were names, like Alexia and Dane. He also realized that Guy and Ursula were mated, given the way they moved around each other.

"Forget the introductions," Guy shouted, "just get us out of here! Now!"

"Not at night," Alexia replied calmly. "Even if there was a real danger—and I assure you, there isn't—we'd be better off waiting until morning."

"You don't know that!" Guy said.

"Yes, I do. Trust me."

Ursula seemed to be relaxing a bit. She looked at Alexia thoughtfully for a long moment. "Guy, maybe we ought to listen to her."

Alexia motioned to their clothing. "You're hunters?"

Guy didn't bother to answer. He continued scanning the tree line with the gun.

Ursula replied, but stood with her mate, watching the dark trees.

"We'd never hunted in northern California before," the older female told Alexia "We've heard about the hunting here in Siskiyou County. We wanted to check it out for ourselves. The hunting has been too good for too long, though. We've barely seen any deer since we got here. We've been moving deeper and deeper into the woods. Several hours ago, we heard something."

"Howling?" asked Alexia.

The other female shuddered. "Not at first. What we heard to start with sounded like a couple of rocks being banged together."

A flutter of excitement worked its way through Alexia's voice. "That's common. Sasquatch do that quite often."

Iktomi listened closely, wishing he understood their words. Apparently, whatever had frightened Guy and Ursula so badly simply invigorated Alexia.

"We thought someone might need our help," Ursula said. "We started to move closer to the sound to investigate."

"And what happened?" asked Alexia.

"It started chattering and screaming at us. We ran," Ursula told her.

"Did you see it?" Alexia's voice quavered with enthusiasm.

"Just a brief glimpse," Ursula told her. "We're lucky it didn't chase us."

Guy shuddered. "We'd have never have outrun it."

"No," Alexia agreed. "You wouldn't. An adult male sasquatch typically stands around eight-feet-tall. It's been estimated that they can run at speeds up to thirty-five miles per hour. Some researchers are confident that a healthy, adult sasquatch could hit speeds of up to forty miles per hour. If those estimates are even close to being correct, there's no way a human could outrun them. Given, too, that the sasquatch knows this terrain, and you don't..."

Still playing the muzzle of the gun over the tree line, Guy said, "We just ran. We didn't bother to look back. We didn't know for sure if it had followed us, and was just too quiet for us to hear. The direction we first ran in happened to be further from our camp. Once we realized that, we didn't want to try and go back. We were afraid we'd run into it again. Or others. If there's one bigfoot out here, there could be more. I mean, there has to be a population of them. It's not just one animal wandering around, being seen over and over. Right?"

Ursula took up again. "Our rifles kept snagging on brush and twigs as we ran. We were too scared to make a stand, if it came to that. We were too afraid that we wouldn't kill it, even if we managed to hit it. Rather than carry the guns, and be slowed down by them, or risk one going off accidently, we dropped them. Without the guns we ran faster."

Guy told Alexia, "We ended up being lost. We just kept running until we found your camp."

"Hang on," Alexia replied.

She ducked back into her shelter. When she came back out, she held two small devices that emitted bright light. One swung from a slim handle in each of her hands.

"You two take a lantern. I'll keep the other," she told the newcomers. "You're positive you saw a sasquatch?"

"Yes," Guy said instantly. "There's no way it was anything else!"

"What you're telling me isn't unheard of." Alexia kept her tone low, soothing. "It's called a demonstration charge. Animals do it all the time—especially large ones. Male silverback gorillas are notorious for it. Had the sasquatch wanted to catch you, it could have. Had it wanted to hurt you, it would have. From what you're telling me, I think that it simply wanted you two out of its territory. It saw you as intruders. It took action to get rid of you. There are a lot of reports on file of stories very similar to what you've just related to me."

"Whatever," Guy retorted. "Just get us out of here! Lead us back to civilization. I'm finished with hunting!"

"Me, too," his wife agreed.

"No," Alexia said. "I'm staying out here for a few more days."

Guy finally took his gaze from the trees. He turned, staring at her, incredulous. "You actually want to stay out here with that thing?"

"That 'thing' is why I'm out here! I'm trying to collect evidence of the existence of sasquatch."

"Why?" Guy asked, seemingly stunned.

"To get them—as a species—protection from people who would harm them."

She focused on her gun—still in the hands of the male—

and reached for it. When Guy drew away from her, Alexia stepped forward quickly, yanking the weapon from his grasp.

Iktomi relaxed. Whereas Alexia struck him as more aggressive than Dane, Guy seemed far more hostile than Alexia. The thought of the gun in Alexia's hands didn't bother him nearly as much as seeing it in Guy's possession.

Alexia continued, saying, "Once the general public knows that sasquatch are real, a lot of ignorant people are going to want to kill one just to have that trophy. Even if they're protected, people will still poach. Then there are the logging companies. Logging is a multi-billion dollar a year industry. You think the ruckus over spotted owls caused an upheaval, and upset a lot of people? Just wait until science accepts the existence of a previously unknown great ape species in North America! Sasquatch will be given a very special place on the endangered species list. Their habitat will be closely guarded, and protected. And that habitat is the same resource that the logging industry makes its billions from every year. Given those facts, the logging industry is a major threat to sasquatch—and vice-versa."

"So?" Guy grunted.

Alexia's eyes widened. "So a lot of people researching sasquatch think that the logging industry already knows about, and accepts, sasquatch as a reality. Some of those same people also think that the logging industry has gotten into the proverbial bed with the United States government to ensure that the general public never find out about sasquatch. There are even reports on file to suggest that government agents, or mercenaries, or someone is actually going into the woods armed with a lot of very powerful weapons. Their goal is to carry out extermination missions with the aim of causing sasquatch to go extinct before proof of their existence can be put in front of the general public. The logging industry doesn't want sasquatch in the woods. They want those selfsame forests for themselves to destroy, and profit from. Sasquatch as a species need to be protected from those evil people!"

Guy stared back at her. "We need some of those people here right now!"

"No," Alexia retorted through harshly gritted teeth, "we don't."

"Just get us out of here," Ursula pleaded.

"I'll give you directions to the nearest town," Alexia continued. "But I'm not leaving. Certainly not now, knowing that there's one in the immediate area."

Both newcomers shook their heads. "You can't do that!" Guy shouted. "You have to help us get out of these woods!"

"I will help you; I'll give you directions. I've told you that."

"You need to do more!" Ursula said. "We don't have weapons!"

"If you don't try to hurt a sasquatch," Alexia told them, "they're not apt to try and hurt you."

"But earlier—" Guy began.

Irritated, Alexia waved a hand, cutting him off. "As I've explained, you weren't in danger. It only wanted to frighten you away."

They stood, glaring at her. In the silence, strands of guitar music floated into camp once more. Alexia groaned.

Guy and Ursula looked around.

"What is that?" Ursula asked.

"My unwanted neighbor," Alexia told them. "He's out here because of sasquatch, too. Our theories are vastly different, but, ultimately we both want the same thing— protection for sasquatch."

The newcomers stared at her for a few seconds, as if she were insane.

Finally, Alexia yawned. "I'm going back to bed. You two can camp out here if you like. Once the sun is up, I'll give those directions I promised. It's too dangerous to be wandering in the woods at night—even with a lantern. You two are lucky neither of you broke a leg rushing through the woods at night."

"As if we'll be able to sleep anytime soon," Guy snorted.

48

"Especially out here!"

Alexia shrugged. "It's your call. Either way, you're welcome to hang out here for the next few hours. Feel free to build a campfire if it'll put you at ease. If you do, just be sure at least one of you stays awake to watch. This area is in a bad drought. We don't want a campfire getting out of control."

Alexia retreated into her shelter once more. Guy and Ursula simply stood still, alternating between watching the forest, and staring at each other in fear.

Iktomi kept frozen, not wanting to risk any movements on his part being noticed. As he waited, he listened to Dane's music, wondering if Dane had taken up the instrument again, or if the sounds were from the device on his seat.

CHAPTER 7

Alexia's breathing, and stirring movements from within her shelter told Iktomi that she didn't sleep after Guy and Ursula entered her camp. The sun had barely begun rising when she opened her fabric cave, and stepped into view. Guy and Ursula leapt from beside the cold remains of Alexia's fire from the previous evening, converging on her.

"Who wants breakfast?" Alexia asked.

Guy shook his head. "We only want out of here."

"Will you please reconsider?" Ursula asked. "We have no idea where we are. We have no idea how to deal with that thing out there! You seem to."

Her mate shuddered, and glanced around, fearful. "Once I'm out of the forest I'm never coming back. I never thought I'd give up hunting. But then, I never thought I'd encounter a bigfoot, either. These things aren't supposed to be real!" He wrung his hands, reeking of fear. "They're just stories, legends, and myths! How can bigfoot be real?"

Alexia winced. "I don't like that term."

"What?" Guy asked.

"Bigfoot," Alexia answered, grimacing.

Ursula frowned. "Why?"

Voice hardening, Alexia said, "It symbolizes the dumbing-down of our culture. That word was coined by a journalist upon seeing plaster casts of sasquatch tracks in nineteen-fifty-eight, after the prints were found by a road construction worker. Whatever made the tracks had very large feet. So the journalist started using that stupid name. Historically, the creatures are known by an array of names—

there are dozens of them. Sasquatch is the most recognizable here and now. It's a modernization of the word 'sásq'ets'. The original word is from the language of one of the Canadian First Nation tribes. Please call them something with more dignity than an extremely unimaginative name derived from their foot size."

Ursula opened her mouth, as if to speak. Alexia held up a finger, cutting her off.

"Before you ask, I don't like to hear the term 'Abominable Snowman', either. That's term isn't even what the people indigenous to that area call those creatures. Their term is 'yeti'. A newspaper reporter mistranslated it. Notice a trend where the media is concerned with these types of beings?"

Ursula folded her arms. "I had been about to ask what all this has to do with our current circumstances. How does help us get out of here?"

"It doesn't. I'm just trying to educate you."

Guy stared around them at the forest. "Educate us on the way out of here. Even with whatever directions you give us, we're so lost right now we might not find our way. Besides, what if we run into another bigfoot?"

Iktomi remained still under the cover of the ferns, and the large tree bole. He wanted to move, but didn't count on the humans' preoccupation with whatever they were talking about to prevent them from noticing him if he did. Instead, he remained in place, watching, listening, and waiting.

Alexia glowered at her visitors for long moments before saying, "All right. I'll lead you out."

"Thank you!" chirped Ursula.

Guy sagged with relief. "Yes, thank you."

Alexia turned toward her tent. "Breakfast first?"

"No," Guy answered. "We just want to get out of here."

Alexia froze, halfway toward reaching for something inside of her shelter. Slowly, she retracted. "Okay. Give me ten minutes, and I'll be ready to go."

Guy frowned. "Why ten minutes? Why can't we leave

now?"

"Because I need to use a tree."

He stared at her for a moment before his face reddened in obvious embarrassment. "All right," he mumbled, turning back to his mate.

****

"Humans are everywhere around here now!" Toylona very quietly huffed at her offspring as she made sure all of them—especially the eldest—were safely hidden. "Are we going to have to retreat even deeper into the forests? Is there no escaping them?"

The new human—a female far younger than the previous two she had seen—obviously didn't belong in the woods. She tripped over rocks and roots every few steps. Each time she swiped her long, pale yellow hair out of her face, it fell right back across her eyes, partially blinding her. She stank of fear; it caused her to stand out almost as much as the brilliant pink of the coverings she wore over her body.

She tripped again, caught herself against a tree trunk, and breathed heavily. "I hate it out here," she pouted. She examined her hands, groaning at the sight of broken fingernails. "I really hate it out here."

Toylona examined her own dark copper-colored nails. Their edges were sharp, and strong. Looking back at the human female, she felt a wave of pity for the pale, weak creature. Humans seemed inferior to her own people in every way. The only thing humans appeared to have in their favor looked to be the devices they created. And those struck Toylona as so strange that she couldn't see the use of most of them.

Moving on, the human female kicked several pinecones out of her way. "At least it's daylight again," she said, seemingly comforted by the sound of her own voice. "Bad as the woods are in the day, they're a million times worse at night."

Toylona thought back to Iktomi's comments about the first human he had begun watching, and her habit of speaking to herself. Did all humans do that when alone?

The human paused again, scratching at the bright coverings she wore over her body, obviously uncomfortable. She pushed her hair back again, only to have it flop into her face once more. She stamped her foot down hard in frustration.

"I don't know why I spent the money on these stupid clothes!" She sighed. "Yes I do. I did it to try and impress him. Has it been worth it? No. And I'd much rather have food and water right now. I haven't had anything since yesterday evening. Is he even looking for me? He'd better be!"

She moved ahead a few more steps, carefully picking her way over a snarl of roots.

"Last night, I'd have felt better with a gun—even though I have no idea how to load or shoot one. Right now, though, I think food would be better."

Deep in the woods to her left, a fox uttered a short yip. The human gasped, looking in the direction of the sound. When a second little bark echoed, she turned and ran.

After only six steps her foot caught on a protruding root. She pitched forward, landing on her stomach on the soft, mossy ground. The impact knocked the breath from her lungs.

She rolled over, clutching her foot and ankle. The touch made her gasp. She wiggled her way to the tree, and used its trunk to try and regain her feet. The instant she put weight on the injury, it gave out, pitching her back to the ground.

A third small yip drifted from the denser forest, and the human began screaming.

The shrill noise made Toylona wince. Her young ones covered their ears.

"Humans are stupid," her eldest commented.

Nodding, Toylona had to agree. Some of their people took an interest in humans, and their intrusions into the forest. Toylona didn't. She would be perfectly content to never have to see another one, or even have another one to set foot in the territory she, Iktomi, and their offspring called home.

In times long past, she had heard it said, humans lived in much closer harmony with the land. Then, encounters between her people and theirs were more apt, according to the stories, to be cordial. Now, humans seemed terrified of the wild. Time had transformed them into creatures who relied on all manner odd devices, and the strange coverings they wore all over their bodies. They seemed to have lost all touch with nature. They surrounded themselves with artificial things, and grew afraid when those were lost to them.

The human female continued screaming, long and loud. Her outcries took on a hysterical pitch, undulating through the air. Toylona's sensitive nose detected the pungent smell of urine as the human lost all control of herself in her fear. A scent underlying the smell of the urine itself told Toylona that the female bled a little, too. The particular aroma of the blood let her know that the female had entered a time of the month when mating would prove effective in producing offspring.

Over the din of the screams, and the scent of the female's urine, Toylona didn't even hear or smell the human male. Her first awareness of him came abruptly when he crashed through the forest to crouch at the female's side. The unexpected arrival of still another human started Toylona badly. The long gun he carried only added to her unease. She hunkered back, closer to her offspring. Silently, she urged them to remain still and silent.

"What's wrong?" the male asked.

"I fell," the female replied, holding her ankle. She sniffled a bit. "I should say I fell again."

He glanced around. "What was chasing you?"

Her nose wrinkled. "Nothing was chasing me. But I did hear something off that way." She pointed to her left.

He fought to keep the disgust from his voice, but it still crept through. "You started screaming your head off like that

54

because you fell?"

"And there's something out there!" A small yipping sound echoed in the trees. The female pointed again. "There! See? Hear it?"

"That's only a fox," he told her. "It's nothing to be frightened of." He held out a hand to her. "My name is Heath Varlas. Let me help you."

She held out a hand to him. "Heath? I'm Tabatha Jordan. Thank you for helping me."

He pulled her upright, and she winced, limping, barely able to keep her balance.

"You hurt your ankle, Tabatha?" he asked.

She nodded. "I've twisted it several times out here. This time is the worst, though."

Toylona paid careful attention to them, trying to determine how large of a threat they posed. Given the way they spoke the words "Tabatha" and "Heath", she suspected those were names. She began thinking of them with those titles. Heath carried a gun. He also seemed far more at ease in the forest than Tabatha. To Toylona, both of those points marked him as the far greater danger of the pair.

Heath pulled one of her arms around his shoulders, steadying her. He carried his rifle in his free hand. "Why are you out here?" he asked as he helped her to a tree stump to sit. Expertly, he started to check her ankle and foot. "I mean, no offense, but you're wearing a pink flannel shirt, pink camouflage pants, and neon pink hiking boots. I've never seen anyone out here dressed like that who actually belonged in the woods."

"I'm trying to impress some guy," she sighed. "I don't think it's going very well. He's into the woods, and hiking, and all of that stuff. I wanted to share his interests. I came out here with him on a camping trip."

"Where is he now?" Heath asked, gently massaging her ankle.

Tabatha shrugged. "Last night, I had to..." She blushed, and lowered her voice. "I had to...um...use the...um...little girl's tree..."

"Uh-huh," Heath grunted, impatient. "And you wandered too far from camp? You got lost?"

"Right!" she chirped. "It's happened to you, too?"

"No," he replied through gritted teeth. "I just took an educated guess."

"Oh. Is my ankle, like, broken, or something?"

"No. You just twisted it a bit. You should be able to walk. Stand up."

Heath backed up three steps. Tabatha braced herself with her hands, flinching when her fingers pressed on a patch of moss on the stump. After making it halfway to her feet, she let out an astonished gasp, and plopped back down.

"Ow!" she exclaimed when her bottom impacted with the wood. She winched, staring up at him with pleading eyes. "I can't walk yet. Don't just leave me out here. Please!"

"What am I supposed to do with you?"

"Don't you, like, have a camp around here?"

Heath sagged. "Yes."

"Can't we go there?"

"What about your boyfriend?"

"He can find me later. He knows about the woods, and junk. He can, like, follow our footsteps, or something."

"It might be better if we tried getting you back to your own camp."

"We can't. I don't even know which way it is now. After getting lost last night, I wandered around in the trees, trying to get back. I yelled for him, but he never found me. I never heard him calling back, either. I think I'm really lost. Can we please go to your camp?"

Heath nodded, unhappy. "Only for a short time, though. Soon as you can manage, we need to go find your own camp."

She held up her arms, nodding.

He frowned. "What?"

"Carry me."

"What? Why?"

"I can't walk. You'll have to carry me."

Heath watched her for a time. All the while, she stared back, expectant. Her arms remained in the air. Finally he acquiesced, and slung his gun over his arm by the thick vine-like thing attached to it. After running his fingers backward through his short, dark hair, he helped her to her feet. Soon as she stood upright, he scooped her up, one arm beneath her knees, the other behind her shoulders.

Tabatha wrapped her arms around his neck. She nuzzled close, and smiled against his throat. A burst of pheromones from her told Toylona that Tabatha felt a strong urge to mate with Heath.

Heath turned, tracing his steps back the way he had come.

"You're strong," she whispered. "I like that."

He didn't bother to reply.

"Are you out here alone?" she asked.

"Yes," he grunted.

Her eyes widened with obvious interest. "You're not married?"

"No."

"Girlfriend?" she asked.

Heath frowned. "No."

She hesitated. "Boyfriend?"

"No."

She snuggled closer. "You're alone?"

"Yes," he replied, eyebrows drawing together.

Tightening her arms around his neck, she said softly, "Not anymore. No one should be alone out here. It's horrible."

"I like the woods," he replied, his tone flat and disinterested. "I always have. Once you learn how to live out here, it isn't frightening."

"It is to me."

"You haven't learned how to survive in the forest, either."

Vegetation hid them from Toylona's sight. However, she

still heard them easily.

"I've done okay," Tabatha huffed.

Again, Heath didn't bother to comment.

"How did you learn?" she asked.

"I grew up in the Pacific Northwest woods. My parents, and a couple of uncles taught me how to live out here."

"You do have a home, though. Right? A real home, I mean; not just a tent in the woods."

"Yes," he said, sounding as he were trying hard not to snap at her. "I come out here a lot, though. I like the woods. Usually," he added pointedly, "I don't have to deal with other people out here."

"You don't like people?"

"As a whole, no."

"Why?"

"Most people strike me as being self-centered, and ignorant," he replied.

"Yeah. Don't you just hate dealing with people like that?"

"Yes," he grunted. "I very much do."

Tabatha continued her chatter nonstop until she and Heath were finally far enough away to be lost to Toylona's hearing.

"What do we do?" her eldest child asked. "Everywhere we turn there are more humans."

"I know." She stroked his head briefly before moving on to give comforting touches to the other two as well. "We need to find your father. He needs to know of these two humans, as well as the other pair we saw. He'll probably want to move us elsewhere; for the time being, at least."

CHAPTER 8

Iktomi stayed close enough to hear Alexia, Guy, and Ursula, even when he lost direct line-of-sight with them. Their voices, as well as their smells—human body odor, the smells of the coverings they wore, most of the food and drink they consumed, and a myriad of other scents that wafted from them, but didn't belong in the woods—made it too easy to follow them.

Alexia carried her gun hung on her shoulder. Her metal-and-fabric carry pack rode on her back. Ursula seemed to pay no attention to the gun. Guy, however, cast pointed looks in its direction at regular intervals. Iktomi had no doubts that the older male wanted possession of the weapon back. He hoped Alexia continued denying it to him.

"Sasquatch aren't likely to hurt you," Alexia told the older couple. "Nearly all of the instances on file of one attacking a human are cases of self-defense on the part of the sasquatch. The very few that aren't... Well, humans can and do murder for the sheer thrill of it. Chimpanzees do, too. It stands to reason that a race like the sasquatch would have the occasional aberrant individual, too. Always assuming, of course, that they would even view the killing of a human as murder. If they didn't, though, why don't more of them lash out at as? Most encounters are peaceful, ending with the sasquatch merely walking away into cover if it realized it's been spotted. The overwhelmingly vast majority of them seem to be extremely peaceful. They only want to be left alone. Paradoxically, I want them left alone, yet am out here looking for them. Why? To find evidence—short of killing one—to convince mainstream science of their existence, so that lawmakers will pass laws making it illegal to harass, or kill them."

"They aren't that peaceable. One attacked us," Ursula said.

Alexia shook her head. "No, it didn't. It only wanted you out of its territory. We've already gone over that. If the sasquatch you encountered had wanted to harm you, it would have. As a whole, they're a peaceful race. They know about us—humans, I mean—and they typically go to great lengths to avoid us."

"How many of them are there?" Guy asked. "I've been hunting my whole life. I've never thought bigfoot were real. I've certainly never seen a bigfoot before."

"Sasquatch populations," Alexia said, "have been estimated up to five thousand in the United States. Possibly more."

"Five thousand of those things?" Guy's voice had taken on a hushed tone of amazement.

"Possibly," Alexia answered. "There has to be enough to maintain a viable breeding population. For years, people have occasionally reported seeing small—between two- and four-feet-tall—beings that looked like tailless monkeys. The reports usually hold key similarities. They usually talk about the long limbs, and large eyes. Listening to the reports, it sounds as if people were seeing gibbons. You know what those are?"

"Some sort of monkey," Guy said.

"Close," she corrected. "They're actually a type of ape. They're from southeast Asia. Anyway, that's what these sightings reports sounded a good deal like. Only within the recent past did researchers start realizing what these thing probably are."

Ursula walked a bit faster, inching closer to Alexia. "What are they?"

"Juvenile sasquatch," Alexia replied. "In nineteen-ninety-seven, footage was shot in upstate New York. No one realized what had accidently been captured in the background until only a few years ago. You can see what looks like two sasquatch at a tree. One is an adult—it looks like your stereotypical sasquatch. But there's a second, smaller figure in the film. It leaps off the shoulders of the adult, into the tree, and then climbs and jumps all over the place. It looks like the small gibbon-type creatures people had reported for years! That was when researchers really started to put two and two together, and realize what those other anomalous creatures are!"

"That sounds frightening to watch," Ursula commented, glancing around.

"It's fascinating, actually," Alexia told her. "It's an excellent piece of evidence that we're dealing with a living population of some cryptid, rather than a long string of hoaxes and misidentifications."

Guy frowned. "Cryptid? What's that?"

Alexia smiled. "The word 'cryptid' comes from the ancient Greek. It means 'hide' or 'hidden'. We refer to animal species that mainstream science doesn't yet accept or recognize as cryptids—sasquatch, yeti, lake monsters, chupacabra, things like that."

Guy's frown deepened. "Chupa—what, now?"

"Chupacabra," Alexia repeated, her grin growing. "The term is Spanish. It translates to mean 'goat sucker'. It's the name for a type of cryptid that seems to have originated on the island of Puerto Rico, but has since spread to America. They got their name because they usually target livestock. Goats are what they're mainly known for attacking, but they do go after other animals, too. They leave a pair of puncture wounds in the throat of their victim, and the victim's body will typically have been drained of blood. Chupacabra attacks have been likened to vampire attacks many times.

"If chupacabra are real, you don't want to run into one," Alexia continued. "They're typically described as being around three-feet-tall, with a hunched-over, bipedal posture. They have large, red eyes that glow, and needles on their backs that look like porcupine quills. Their hands and feet have claws. They have fangs that people claim the chupacabras use to exsanguinate their victims. According to some reports, chupacabras are excellent jumpers. Others say they can glide, with membranes beneath their forelimbs, like what flying squirrels do. Other witnesses claim to have seen chupacabras just flat-out flying."

Ursula shuddered. "No. I never want to meet one of those things."

"Bigfoot are bad enough," Guy put in.

"Sasquatch are benign," Alexia said. "In this region, anyway. In the south-eastern part of the country, there are what seem to be a whole sub-species of sasquatch. Those can be aggressive toward humans. What we have in this area generally go out of their way to avoid us."

Shaking his head, Guy said, "The one that came after us didn't."

"We've already been over the reasons why," Alexia reminded him again. "Stop beating a dead horse."

"Have you ever seen one?" Ursula asked. "A bigfoot, I mean."

Alexia nodded. "I have, yes. Twice. The first time I was only a small child. My parents and I were camping during the summer, here in the Pacific Northwest. We saw one from a distance of a hundred yards, or so. It looked to be picking berries."

Guy snorted. "Berries?"

"Sasquatch are omnivorous," Alexia explained. "They eat meat, and vegetable matter, both."

Ursula kept watch on the woods around them. "What about the other one you saw? What was it doing?"

"Just walking by," Alexia said quietly. "I was an adult then. I had gone out hiking alone, and had stopped for a rest. Everything went quiet and hushed. A few moments later, a twig snapped. I held my breath, knowing that something was walking toward me. A few seconds later, a sasquatch passed between two trees maybe, twenty feet away. It didn't even seem to notice me. I heard its footsteps as it went on its way. It took several minutes for the birds and other wildlife to start making noise again. Other animals typically go quiet when a sasquatch is nearby. Whether that's out of fear, respect, or for some other reason, we don't know."

Guy continued looking around, nervous. "You said they're omnivorous. How do you know?"

Alexia animated her tone. "They've been seen many times picking and eating fruits, vegetables, and berries. They've also been seen doing what looked like digging for roots—or maybe grubs. Sasquatch have also been known to steal fish from peoples' nets, lines, and coolers. There are also accounts on file of hunters bringing down large game—deer or wild hog—only to have the kill picked up, and carried off by a sasquatch."

"So they scavenge the meat they eat?" Guy asked.

Alexia watched him closely. "Some. They also hunt."

"They've been seen doing that?" Ursula inquired.

Nodding, Alexia said, "Several times, yes. Groups of sasquatch will work in teams to bring down deer. They run in relays. One sasquatch will chase the deer, directing it toward the next sasquatch. When the deer passes that one, the second sasquatch will herd it toward third, and so on.

"Eventually, the deer gets tired; it slows down. When that happens, the sasquatch currently chasing it can catch it. The deer is brought down, and it's legs are broken to keep it from getting up, and running off again. Then its neck is broken, killing it."

Ursula and Guy both winced, seemingly more nervous than before.

Alexia continued, saying, "The deer's carcass is then torn open at the belly. People who have seen this claim that sasquatch use their fingernails to do that. People who have gotten a close look at them describe sasquatch fingernails as hard, and fairly sharp. They're basically like chisels, and are said to be a coppery color. Anyway, once the kill is opened, the first thing they seem to go after is the liver."

"High protein content," Guy muttered.

"Right," Alexia agreed. "Sasquatch have been known to raid farms, and carry pigs away. They've also been known to go after dogs. Sasquatch have also been seen digging at rabbit burrows. They seem to enjoy a fairly wide range of meats, in addition to the vegetation they eat."

Guy shuddered. "If I hadn't seen one of these things with my own eyes, I wouldn't believe a word of what you're telling us."

"Everything I've told you has been documented," Alexia said. "Once you get home, feel free to look it up."

"No, I don't think I will," Guy retorted. "Once we get out of these woods, I don't plan on ever setting foot somewhere I might run across another of those things. I already know they're real. I don't need to go digging up reports, or other evidence."

Ursula nodded. "What's their range? Where can we go where we aren't going to be in a place where they're seen?"

After taking a deep breath, and slowly releasing it, Alexia said, "You'll be hard-pressed to find such a place. Sasquatch are found all over the United States. Some areas seem to have much higher concentrations of them, of course. Here in the Pacific Northwest, you're smack in the middle of the densest number of sightings in the country. But everywhere you go in the United States, you'll find reports of either the classic description of sasquatch, or something similar. A lot of people used to laugh off reports of sightings from Ohio. Over the past few years, though, there have been a large number of accounts from there. Ohio now doesn't rank too far below the Pacific Northwest in the number of sightings there."

"What about Hawaii?" Ursula's voice trembled a bit.

"On the Hawaiian islands, there are reports of something the natives call Menehune," Alexia replied. "They don't look like the stereotypical sasquatch. They're said to be a race of hairy, dwarf creatures; kind of like a pygmy sasquatch."

Guy grunted in exasperation. "And you've already

mentioned the ones in the southern part of the country."

Alexia nodded. "In Florida, they're known as skunk apes, because they smell so bad. Skunk apes are said to smell worse than a traditional sasquatch. With the heat and humidity down there, I can fully accept, and understand that."

"New England?" Ursula asked.

"Of course," Alexia said. "In New England, and the Midwest, you'll find mostly reports of typical sasquatch. Though in the Midwest, you'll sometimes hear of reports that sound more like the southern off-shoots."

"Why the off-shoots?" Ursula wanted to know.

Alexia stepped over a gnarled tree root, pointing it out to her companions. "There are a number of theories," she answered. "The most prevalent one is that the population down there is more isolated. That isolation would make for a large amount of inbreeding. That, in turn, would lead to mutations. Many of the tracks found in that region are of prints with odd numbers of toes—commonly four, but as few as two. Sometimes six-toed tracks are found. Such mutations of the feet are one common sign of inbreeding in other species. Aggressive tendencies is another, and that's something else we see frequently in reports coming from the southern region of the country."

"What about Arizona?" Ursula asked. "The northern part of the state is forested, but what about the low desert? Any sasquatch reports from there?"

"A few, yes. They're becoming more common, too. I think they're being forced to move into territory they wouldn't normally be in to find food. Human development has done that to animal species over the entire world."

Guy let out a frustrated huff. "If there's nowhere in this country we can go, and not have a chance of running into another one of those things, what about other countries?"

"Good luck finding one," Alexia told him. "Canada has a very large number of sasquatch reports. Similar creatures have been reported in Mexico, Central and South America, and Russia. China has the yeren. Tibet has the yeti. Australia has a creature very similar to sasquatch which locals call yowie. From time to time, reports of creatures that might be sasquatch, or something akin to them, come from the United Kingdom, too.

"Sumatra, which is an Indonesian island, has the orang pendek. The name translates into "short man". The orang pendek is much smaller than a sasquatch. Typically, they're reported as having red or orange hair, about the same color as orangutans. Not long ago a group of biologists working over there went public, claiming they had been in possession of an orang pendek body for seventeen years. During that time, they've been amassing research on it. They plan to publically release their findings—hard evidence, they claim, to prove the existence of the orang pendek.

"Then we have what might be some type of sasquatch creature in South America, too," Alexia continued. "They're called the mapinguari. However, there's some debate there. Some researchers think that the mapinguari are actually a breed of giant ground sloth that have survived extinction, and lived through to the present day."

Guy swore under his breath. "So what you're telling us is that, wherever we go, unless we stay inside our home all the time, there's a chance that we might happen upon another of these things?"

A small grin overcame Alexia's face. "Honestly? Even then you might run into one."

"What?" the older couple both gasped at once.

The abruptness of their outcry startled Iktomi. He slowed his pace, lagging a bit further behind. Apparently unaware of his presence, the trio of humans continued to walk and talk.

"In several states, and in several other counties," Alexia answered Guy, "there have been reports of sasquatch, or a given region's counterpart, breaking into peoples' homes. Please allow me to officially coin the term 'sasquatch burglar'."

"You're serious, aren't you?" Guy's distress level kept

growing.

Alexia nodded. "It's becoming more and more common, too. I think it goes back to the same point I brought up when talking about sasquatch in the deserts of Arizona. People have infringed on their territory so much, that they're forced to do unusual things in order to survive. Also, sasquatch seem to be intelligent, and very, very curious. Even when they don't break into a house, they'll sometimes be seen peeping in through a window."

Ursula shuddered. "I want to move to Mars."

"As I keep telling you," Alexia said, "they're peaceful beings. There's no reason to fear them."

"Says the person with the gun," Guy retorted.

Ursula shushed him.

"I'm just saying," Guy pointed out.

"Quiet!" his mate hissed. "I heard something ahead of us!"

CHAPTER 9

The three humans paused, waiting and listening. Iktomi halted, keeping low to avoid being seen if one of them happened to look back. A moment later, dead leaves rustled, and the humans tensed. Guy reached for the rifle, but Alexia stepped away from him, keeping the weapon out of his reach. The sounds and scents from them prevented Iktomi from detecting anything beyond the group.

Muted voices drifted to them soon after. Iktomi silently lamented the arrival of still more humans.

"What is that?" Ursula whispered. "Can those things talk?"

Alexia whispered back, "Sasquatch do seem to have a spoken language. We just haven't been able to figure it out yet. Although they are also mimics, and have been known to walk through the woods, near humans, mumbling to themselves, imitating human speech. It seems to be a sort of audible camouflage. People hear that, and think other humans are nearby. While, in reality, it's a sasquatch passing them."

Guy made another grab for the rifle.

Alexia jerked the weapon away from him. "I don't think that's what we're hearing now," she admonished. "I think there are people over there." She stood taller, took a deep breath, and shouted, "Hello? Who's there?"

Glaring at her, Guy made shushing noises.

"Hello?" a distinctly male voice called back. "Keep talking. I'll zero in on your voice!"

"My name is Alexia Hollander," she shouted back. "I'm out here on a research project. Two other people are with me.

I'm also warning you—I'm armed with a rifle!"

"That's fine," the unseen male called back. "I'm not a pot-grower. I'm a hunter. My name is Heath Varlas. I have a young woman with me. Her ankle is injured. Her name is Tabatha Jordan. Do any of you know her?"

Alexia grimaced, her teeth clenched tightly. She shot a quick look at her tense companions. Both of them shook their heads.

Turning back to face the direction of the footsteps, Alexia shouted, "Sorry, but no. None of us knows her!"

The new arrivals stepped into view just as Iktomi caught a familiar scent that caused his heart to leap. Toylona!

He looked around, seeking his mate, as Guy said, "We thought you were another bigfoot at first."

The newly-arrived male glanced sharply at him, eyes widening. "You say 'another'. You've seen one?"

"Did we ever!" Ursula cut in.

Toylona slipped from behind a nearby tree, her eyes wide as she locked gazes with Iktomi. He waved her to him. She lay flat on the ground, crawling to him on her belly, using the vegetation between them and the humans as cover.

"Where are our young?" he asked Toylona quietly, wrapping an arm around her.

"Safely up the mountain," she replied. "I'll rejoin them soon. They have strict orders not to wander from the safe area where I left them. I came looking for you to tell you about those two humans." She pointed directly at Guy and Ursula. "On the way, I ran across those other two. I think the names of those first ones are Ursula and Guy."

Iktomi nodded. "They seem to be mated."

"Yes," she agreed. "And the others are Heath and Tabatha. They're not mated, but Tabatha wants to be. Her most receptive time of the month is upon her; she's ready to mate"

"Thank you," he whispered back. "Why are they here? Are they looking for us?"

She shrugged. "I haven't been able to determine. Watch,

listen, and see what we can learn."

"What happened to you?" Alexia asked Tabatha.

"I fell," Tabatha told her. "I hurt my ankle, and can't walk now." She clung tighter to the man carrying her, smiling. "I'm lucky that Heath found me."

Heath made a strange face, as the younger female snuggled more tightly against him.

Tabatha blinked, pulling her attention away from Heath, focusing on Guy. "Wait," she said. "Did you just say you saw bigfoot?"

"More than that," Guy told her.

Ursula stepped closer to the girl. "One of them came at us."

Tabatha's eyes widened. She glanced around, abruptly nervous. "They're real? Like, for real, real?"

Ursula nodded.

Guy's hands made twitching motions, as if trying to grasp an invisible gun. "They are, yes."

Tabatha gulped audibly, and snuggled more tightly against Heath, who rolled his eyes.

Iktomi noticed Alexia watching Heath closely. Something about him had captured her interest, but in a far different way than it had captured Tabatha's.

Heath looked back at Alexia. He blinked, and averted his gaze. "I found Tabatha a mile or so from here. We're still some distance from my camp. Are any of you camped closer?"

Ursula nodded. "Alexia's camp is less than half a mile from here."

Guy grabbed Alexia's arm in a hard grip. "You can't take them back to your camp! You have to get my wife and I out of here. You promised!" He turned to Ursula, adding, "What are you doing? We need to get out of here!"

Ursula motioned to Tabatha. "She's hurt."

"Let Heath take care of her! We're getting out of here!"

"It's a moot point," Alexia said coldly, staring at Heath. "You stay well away from my camp."

Ursula stared at Alexia in shock. Even Guy gave her a surprised look.

Heath grinned, uncertain. "Why? What did I do?"

"When I first heard your name, I knew it sounded familiar. When I saw your expression upon hearing that there's a sasquatch in the area it dawned on me who you are. You're not going anywhere my camp."

Ursula stepped closer to her. "Who is he?"

"A hunter, like he says," Alexia replied. Her hot glare never wavered from Heath. "He's also very interested in sasquatch, but, he's firmly in favor of killing one. He wants to gun one down—at least one—and dump the body at the feet of the mainstream scientific community."

"It's the only way to prove they really exist," Heath replied calmly.

"No," Alexia told him, every bit as calm, "it isn't."

Ursula put a hand on Alexia's shoulder. "None of that matters right now. The girl is hurt. She needs help. Yours is the closest camp."

Guy moved to stand beside Heath. "I take it you have more guns in your camp."

Heath nodded. "Of course."

"And you're willing to shoot these things?"

"I am."

Guy stood straighter. "Excellent. My wife and I will lead you back to Alexia's camp. You can leave the girl there, and then take us to your camp. We can borrow guns for the hike out, and you can lead us to somewhere safe."

Heath frowned. Before he could speak, Ursula stepped to her husband's side.

"I like that plan," she told Heath. "Alexia promised to lead us to safety, but she won't give us guns to protect ourselves."

"Sasquatch aren't a threat!" Alexia nearly screamed.

Ignoring her, Ursula went on. "She doesn't seem to care about protecting us. She wants to find one of those monsters so she can protect it."

"I have work of my own to do out here," Heath said. "Which way to camp?"

Alexia's fists tightened at her sides. Her teeth gritted, and her breathing quickened.

"Tell you what," Guy said as Tabatha clung even more tightly to Heath. "If you do what my wife and I are asking, we'll help you shoot any of those things we see on the hike out. All right? You can keep the body. You can keep any recognition, fame, or money that goes along with it. All we want is to get out of here!"

"Three guns are better than one," Ursula chimed in.

Heath grinned broadly, showing straight, white teeth. "It's a deal."

"Good," Guy said. "Her camp is this way." He turned, beginning to retrace their steps.

Alexia rushed after him. "You can't just dump an injured girl in my camp, and expect me to take care of her! I have work to do!"

"And I have to get my wife to safety," Guy retorted, not slowing.

Iktomi led Toylona off to one side. They looped quietly around until they were behind the humans once again. Slowly, they followed, keeping within earshot.

"I'll stay here, and keep an eye on the humans," Iktomi said softly. "You had best get back to our offspring."

Toylona appeared sheepish. "Especially since Guy and Ursula saw me when I was forced to frighten them off after our eldest alerted them to our presence."

Iktomi gave her a startled look, his stomach sinking. "That's probably why they're so frightened."

"Probably."

"This isn't good," Iktomi lamented. "So many humans here. Alexia, at least, is looking for us. Now you tell me that two of the others saw you."

"I had no choice."

"I understand. But this still isn't a good thing."

Toylona hung her head. "While I go back up the

mountain to our young, what will you do? With so large of a group of humans, you don't dare try to frighten them away now."

Shrugging, he replied, "I'll keep following them. What I do next will depend upon what they do."

"What if they split up? There are five of them."

"Six. There's another near Alexia's encampment."

She sagged. "Six humans. Potentially six different paths to try to go on at once. It's impossible."

"I know."

"So what will you do if they don't remain together?"

Iktomi thought for a moment, before answering, "If they divide their group, I'll just have to follow the one, or ones, that seem to pose the greatest threat."

"Guy and Ursula had guns when I first saw them. Heath and Alexia have guns, too."

Nodding, Iktomi reasoned, "Tabatha seems the least threatening."

"By far!" Toylona laughed. "She screamed, terrified, when she heard a fox."

Iktomi chuckled. "Dane doesn't seem threatening, either. But there's more to him than I first thought. Go back to our young. I'll do the best I can here."

Toylona hugged him, and then started away. She turned back, saying, "I'll ensure that they are safe. If I can find another to watch over them I will. Then I'll return to help you watch the humans."

He started to reject her offer, but then nodded. There were simply too many humans in the area. Before, he had been concerned with having two, and trying to choose which to watch at a given time. Now he found himself with six.

"All right. But take care of our offspring first," he instructed.

"I will. And I'll return as soon as I can."

Iktomi stood, watching his mate retreat back into the forest. He waited until all sounds of her passing had vanished before tailing the humans once more.

Soon, it became apparent that they were returning to Alexia's camp. Iktomi felt a detour to Dane's encampment would be prudent. It had been too long since he had looked in on the other human.

He angled off into the woods, careful not to make noise, or leave footprints. Just a quick check on Dane, he told himself, and then he would cross to Alexia's camp to see what the rest of the group happened to be doing by then.

CHAPTER 10

Iktomi stood in deep shadows. Dane's artificial cave waited a short ways in front of him, but there were enough low-hanging tree limbs to afford him cover if the human emerged unexpectedly. He sniffed the air, but detected no sign of the human. Everything remained quiet, with no trace of Dane's music. No sound emerged from the shelter. After a short time, Iktomi concluded that Dane had left the area.

He turned around slowly, quiet from sheer habit, wondering which direction the human had gone. Should he return to Alexia's camp, and await the arrival of the others? Or should he try to find Dane? The rest of the humans had been journeying back toward Alexia's camp. Dane could be anywhere, and doing anything. It had already been too long since he had seen him. Iktomi needed to know what Dane had gotten up to. Especially in light of the deception he had played with the music.

Cautiously, Iktomi ventured from the protection of the trees. He eased into Dane's encampment, senses alert for any indication whatsoever of human nearness.

Dane had clearly gone for the time being. He would be back, Iktomi reasoned. If he meant not to return, he would've taken his things with him. But where had he gone?

Iktomi examined the ground. Dane's footprints—exhibiting the odd ridge pattern left by the undersides of the ridiculous coverings he wore on his feet—marred the ground everywhere. Due to the intense clutter, it took him a little time to pick out the freshest set of tracks. He followed them, surprised to discover that the path led toward Alexia's camp.

Music filled the air, Iktomi followed until he found Dane sitting on a seat, very much like the one he used in his own camp, in the middle of the clearing where Alexia had set up. The human happily strummed the odd instrument he liked. Iktomi held back, careful to remain hidden. The others would arrive soon, but he had no way of telling just when. He double-checked his position to make sure he remained clear of the path he expected them to follow when they came in.

Dane played on, apparently ignorant of Iktomi's close proximity. After a very brief time, the music lowered in volume.

"I probably should not have erased the images from her trail cameras," Dane muttered. "I feel badly about that. But, at the same time, if she did manage to obtain a decent photo of one of the Forest Gods, all kinds of people would flock to the area. Most of them would only be interested in trying to kill one of the beings—either for scientific purposes, or for the sheer callous stupidity of trophy hunting. It might not take that much. A single blurred image, or a shadow passing in front of the camera could do it. I can't take the chance. The Forest Gods are too important."

Iktomi shook his head, amused anew at the penchant for humans to speak when they thought themselves to be alone and unwatched. The thought reminded him of the need to remain alert due to the predicted arrival of the other humans. He turned slightly, looking around. His arm brushed a thin branch beside him. A tiny twig broke.

Dane jolted fully upright at the sound. Iktomi froze, holding his breath, watching the human. Dane had obviously heard the sound. Hopefully he attributed to the other humans.

After a few moments, Dane resumed playing his instrument. Iktomi relaxed. When Dane stood without warning, turning in his direction, Iktomi almost panicked. Instead, he quickly turned away, ducking deeper into the trees.

Yet Dane's started gasp told him that he had been

spotted. The human's heart beat so strongly with excitement that Iktomi could hear it faintly.

"Thank you," Dane whispered, tears in his voice. "It's an honor to have had you so close. It's an honor to have seen you. Thank you."

Iktomi retreated further before turning back. Dane still stood by the seat, the instrument forgotten in his hands. His eyes were wide. Streaks of moisture marred both of his cheeks. Given the distance, and the cover, between them, Iktomi doubted that Dane could see him now—even if the human looked directly at him. He hunkered down slowly, forcing himself to remain calm. If Dane moved toward him, he would leave the area. Otherwise, he would remain, and try to learn more from the entire group of humans. Assuming, of course, that the others had meant to return. But why else would they have turned so quickly to retrace the path back?

Dane stood for a long time, watching the woods. Only gradually did he begin to move again, before slowly maneuvering his seat around to face the spot where he had seen Iktomi. He settled into it, and began to play the instrument again. Now, though, the music had become very faint.

Iktomi realized that Dane deliberately kept the sounds low so as to hear better. As he watched the human, Iktomi relaxed. Dane had made no aggressive action. In fact, he had made no move to follow him at all. Maybe his original estimate of Dane had been correct. Maybe this human posed no threat to his people.

Iktomi remained still and silent. After another short time had passed, the scent of more humans caught his attention. Dane seemed not to notice them until they were entered the clearing.

"Alexia!" he shouted, leaping up from his seat.

She scowled at him. "What do you think you're doing?" She stalked directly toward him.

"One was here!" Dane practically shouted.

She frowned at him, hands on her hips. "What are you

talking about?"

"One of the Forest Gods," he breathed. "One of them came here a few minutes ago."

The middle-aged couple pressed forward. "Are you talking about a bigfoot?" the man asked.

Dane nodded vigorously. "Yes. One of them visited here."

"Where did it go?" Ursula asked, her tone quavering slightly.

Dane lifted a hand, as if to point. Ultimately, he hesitated, giving Heath a long, hard stare. Slowly, Dane's brow furrowed, and his eyes narrowed to slits. "Heath Varlas?" he asked, tone bitter.

The other man nodded as he knelt to gently lay the girl he still carried on the ground.

"Get out of here," Dane ordered Heath.

Alexia snorted. "I should tell you the same thing, Dane. This is my camp!"

"You've been invaded by the enemy," he replied.

Alexia sagged. "I know."

Heath stood, turning to Dane. "Which way did the sasquatch go?"

Indignant, Dane shouted, "I'm not telling you!"

Immediately, Heath turned to the older couple. "Guy, Ursula, spread out. If one was here, there'll be tracks. Find them."

"No!" Dane shouted, rushing at Heath.

Heath caught Dane, held him for a moment, then shoved him backward. Without a word, he joined the other two in the woods just beyond the clearing. The trio fanned out, examining the ground.

Dane turned to Alexia. "What do we do?"

Forlorn, she shook her head. "I don't know. I guess we just hope that either it didn't leave tracks to be followed, or else it manages to lose them somehow."

"I have something!" Guy shouted. "Here!"

"No," Dane whispered. "That's where I saw it!" He

started toward Heath.

Alexia caught his arm, pulling him to a halt. "Don't."

"What? Why?"

"We have no legal grounds for trying to stop him," Alexia said sadly. "We do anything to him, he can turn around and sue us. Something like that would just make us look bad. He'd by the victim; he'd be the martyr."

Tears welled in Dane's eyes. "We can't just stand here!"

"Sasquatch are experts at avoiding humans. That's why they're so hard to find. It's amazing that one walked so close to camp in broad daylight," she explained. "You know these things, Dane! You know them as well as I do." She tightened her grip on his arm. "Odds are those three will track it for a short time, and then lose it. The sasquatch will have stepped on rocks, dry ground, logs, and anything else it can use to avoid leaving prints. If it knows it's being followed, it'll probably be careful not to leave any broken undergrowth behind, too."

"What if they do get within sight of it?"

Before she could reply, Guy called back to them, "We're heading out! You two take care of the girl!"

Dane fumed. Alexia did the same. "What do we do?" he asked her.

Tabatha cut in, saying, "How about helping me into that chair, and getting me some aspirin?"

Dane shifted his focus to Tabatha only gradually. Even then, he cast stricken looks after the three who had departed. As Dane helped Tabatha up, and into the seat Dane has been using until a short time ago, Iktomi realized that the others had found some sign of his presence that he had left behind.

Quickly, he slipped away, deeper into the woods. He couldn't leave, though. Despite not knowing the language the humans spoke, Iktomi could tell from the tones of their voices that something had changed. Once he had managed to elude the trio stalking him, he would circle back, and try to learn more from the others.

He moved with strides that were longer than normal,

eating up distance with each step. The increased pace also meant less chance of leaving a print for the humans to find. When he could, he trod upon hard surfaces—tree roots, rocks, and the like—to lessen the odds of leaving a track, as well. When an opportune branch presented itself, something low enough and sturdy enough to work for his needs, he would leap up, grab it, and swing forward. Such swings allowed him to coverer longer sections of ground than walking, and completely eliminated the possibility of leaving a footprint.

What were they going to do? Six humans were in the area. Six that they knew of, anyway. With so many around, there could easily be more. Toylona had been forced to let two of them see her as she drove them away from their offspring. Dane had spotted Iktomi. Alexia had discovered footprints and hair from at least one individual. Things had gotten far out of hand very quickly.

As he hurried through the forest, he wove a jagged, zigzagging path, trying to confuse any indications of his passing that he inadvertently left. After a while, he took to a tree, climbing as high as he could, until the limbs became too thin and weak to hold his great weight. He envied the young he shared with his mate. Any one of them, even their oldest, would've been able to scurry up the tree faster, and climb higher.

He waited, alert for any sign that the trio of humans were still trailing him. He wanted to return to Toylona, collect her and their young, and simply leave the region. However, doing so would endanger the rest of their people who lived in the area. Far as he knew, they didn't know about the humans. Banging on trees, or vocalizing to alert them would only bring the humans after him. They had certainly come to seek his kind. They would know what they were hearing.

No.

His only options were to either try and find each one who needed to be warned of the humans individually, or to keep watching the humans. He decided to opt for the second.

If things grew worse, he could always change his mind.

Once enough time passed for him to be confident that he had lost his pursuers, he slowly descended. Stopping at the base of the tree, he listened again. No sounds reached his ears to indicate humans nearby. He heard only the normal sounds of the forest—birds, insects, the breeze in the trees, a beaver gnawing on wood nearby, and a small stream babbling as it ran its course.

Circling around, wanting to give a wide berth to the three humans who had set out after him, Iktomi headed back toward Alexia's camp. He hoped that she, Dane, and Tabatha were still there when he returned. If not, he thought it unwise to risk trying to find them in the woods just now. With the others searching for him, he ran a great risk of them picking up his trail again.

CHAPTER 11

"My ankle, like, really hurts. Do you have any painkiller?" Tabatha asked.

"This isn't my camp," Dane replied. "It's hers." He gestured toward Alexia.

"I have aspirin, yes," Alexia offered. "Give me a moment."

Iktomi eased into his former place behind the twined pines as the brief exchange took place.

Alexia ducked into her artificial cave. Iktomi heard her rustling around inside briefly. When she emerged, she carried a clear container of water in one hand. Her other hand curled into a fist.

She held out her fisted hand. Tabatha reached for it. Alexia uncurled her fingers. Two tiny white round things that Iktomi assumed were seeds of some type dropped into the younger female's palm. Alexia handed her the water.

"I'll grab you a snack, too," she said. "Taking medication on an empty stomach isn't usually a good idea."

Tabatha's stomach gurgled. Her face reddened, and she smiled, sheepish. "Thanks. I haven't eaten in a while."

"You said you were lost in the woods all night," Alexia reminded her, heading back to the shelter.

Dane focused on Tabatha. "You haven't eaten since yesterday?"

She nodded, removing the top from the water container. After popping the white things into her mouth, she took a long swallow of water, downing nearly half of it in one drink.

"What happened?" Dane asked.

"Wandered out of camp to...um...potty. I went too far. I got turned around, and lost."

"Where you with anyone?"

"A guy."

Alexia stepped in, handing Tabatha a rectangular chunk of food. It smelled the same as several of the things Iktomi had seen her eat before. "Have a protein bar. It'll keep the aspirin from upsetting your stomach, and probably just make you feel better in general."

"Thank you," Tabatha told her. After consuming half the food, she shifted her attention back to Dane. "I came out here with a guy I wanted to date. I agreed to spend the weekend camping with him."

Dane nodded. "You've never camped before, have you?"

"Is it that obvious?"

He grinned faintly. "I'm afraid it is. Why do you say that you wanted to date him? You sound like you've changed your mind."

She finished off the food before saying, "He's really into, like, the outdoors. I'm so not. He's hot and all, but I don't think I can deal with this."

Inching closer to her, Dane said, "Being outdoors isn't a bad thing. You just need to know what you're doing. If this guy just let you wander off, get lost, and hasn't been able to find you, it sounds to me like he doesn't know what he's doing."

"Really?"

Dane nodded.

"You know what you're doing out here?"

"Yes, Dane," Alexia cut in, her tone pointed, "what are you doing?"

His cheeks reddened. Slowly, he drew back from Tabatha, standing. "I'm just making sure she's all right."

"She's fine," Alexia replied. "We ought to be focused on the others. If we can do anything to discourage them from taking a shot at a sasquatch, we should."

Dane nodded, moving a few steps further from Tabatha.

The young woman watched him, pouting.

"They really are out here?" she asked.

"They are," Dane told her.

"You saw one?"

"I did, yes. Just moments before the rest of you showed up. It was right over there." He pointed to the spot where the Iktomi had stood when Dane has seen him.

The realization that the trio were speaking of him sent a shudder through Iktomi. He had long since come to the conclusion that Alexia sought his people. So Dane and Tabatha did, too? Or had Dane simply felt a desire to tell the females of Iktomi's appearance at the encampment earlier? Stories circulated from time to time of members of his race who had spent so much time observing humans that they had managed to pick up on a little bit of their odd, jabbering language. Iktomi wished for assistance from one of them now. Lacking it, however, he simply watched, and listening, hoping to learn what he could.

"What are they?" Tabatha asked. "Apes?"

Alexia cut in again, saying, "No one really knows. Some of their physical traits and behaviors are classic primate ones—such as the way their thumbs have been reported to work. According to witnesses who have made note of it, sasquatch thumbs aren't as opposable as ours are. Casts made of their handprints back those observations up. At the same time, they're very obviously more evolved and intelligent than any other known ape species on the planet aside from humans. DNA has been gathered several times—from hair, blood, and even fecal samples—but the studies done haven't been universally accepted. Recent studies have suggested that sasquatch share a common ancestor with modern man, but those same test results also turned up evidence of an unknown ape species that would have had to have mated with early humans to produce the result."

Tabatha stared up at Alexia, her brow furrowed in confusion. "Huh?"

Dane knelt by the seat again, before Alexia could reply.

"It isn't important."

"You only say that," Alexia told him, "because of your own personal beliefs concerning these creatures."

Tabatha inclined her head fractionally toward Dane. "What do you think they are?" She batted her eyelashes a couple of times.

Amusement swept through Iktomi at the scent of Dane's personal pheromones. Tabatha's own fragrance changed slightly, too. He suspected that Dane would take Tabatha off somewhere to mate with her soon. Alexia's own scent and body language radiated ire. Iktomi wondering if the reason were jealousy, or something else.

Dane shook his head. Reluctantly, he stood, yet remained next to her. "I'll tell you later. For now, Alexia is right. If we can do anything to help our friend out there, we need to. None of us wants to see him get shot."

Alexia stepped closer. "You know the creature you saw was male? You got that good a look at it?"

Shaking his head, Dane said, "I just chose a pronoun. It could just as easily have been female. I didn't see breasts, though."

Tabatha giggled. "Bigfoot breasts?"

"Of course," Dane told her. "The best, most famous video recording of a sasquatch ever was taken in nineteen-sixty-seven in Bluff Creek, California. That took place in Humboldt County, which is the next county south-west from where we are now."

She frowned up at him. "I'm, like, totally lost. What county are we in here?"

"Siskiyou," Alexia answered.

"Anyway," Dane cut in loudly, "that video was a bit less than two-minutes-long. But the guys who filmed it weren't far from the being. In the film, you can see that they recorded a female. You can see her breasts moving as she walked."

Tabatha stared up at him with wide eyes. "Wow."

"Right," Dane enthused. "Wow. In those days, the technology to hoax something like that only existed in big-budget films. I'm not sure that level of costuming and make-up existed even in Hollywood. Besides, if someone were trying to fake something like that, why would they go to the trouble of putting together an anatomically correct female with pendulous breasts?"

"Right," Tabatha breathed, staring up at Dane in utter awe.

"That film footage is so good," he went on, "that you can see the muscles moving beneath her hair as she walks. She can see her feet flexing, too. With modern day video enhancements, you can even see her eyes and forehead moving."

"So it couldn't have been faked?" Tabatha asked.

"Not likely," Dane replied, bouncing on his toes in excitement. "That level of fakery would be almost impossible for a layman to pull off today. In nineteen-sixty-seven, I'd have to say it would have been utterly impossible."

Alexia cleared her throat. "Can we get back on track, please? Heath and his new best buddies are out there. We know there's a sasquatch in the area. So do they, and they want to kill it. Is there anything we can do to stop them, or change their minds, without giving them grounds for a lawsuit?"

Dane and Tabatha stared at each other. Tabatha merely shrugged. Dane turned back to Alexia.

"What if the only things we can do would give them grounds for a lawsuit?" he asked. "Are you willing to cross that line if need be?"

She stared back at him, eyes wide, holding her breath. He arched an eyebrow, waiting on a response.

****

"I can't believe this!" Heath bellowed. "We were practically on top of a sasquatch, but we had to detour back to my camp to get guns for you two!"

Guy snorted loudly. "Without us being armed, you were

the only one with a gun. Do you really want to track a bigfoot like that?"

"My husband is right," Ursula said.

"We still gave up our best chance at finding it!" Heath raged. "They're very difficult to track. We were right there! Now that we've looped back, the trail is cold. It's gone! It hid signs of its passing once it was a short distance from Alexia's camp! I should not have let you two idiots talk me into the detour!"

"We had to," Ursula said. "Guy and I can't be running around unarmed. Not with those things out here!"

Heath grunted, not bothering to make a real reply.

Toylona stayed low, watching the three humans. She might not know much about them, but their posture and tones told her that none of them were happy. Heath seemed furious at Guy and Ursula, and, while they seemed at peace with each other, both appeared angry with Heath.

After hearing them arguing in the woods, she had backtracked to find them, putting off the planned return to her young. As she followed them, she saw scattered signs of Iktomi's passage through the area. Upon realizing that the three humans had been hunting her mate, anger surged inside of her. She thought to simply kill them, and be done with it, despite Iktomi's wishes not to harm them. Only the presence of their guns had stayed her.

Now, she merely kept low, tailing them.

Traces left by Iktomi had vanished. She suspected he had taken to the trees to avoid leaving marks on the ground. The humans seemed too dull-witted to think of that. Not once did they look up. They focused only on the forest floor, and each other.

"Stupid," she muttered softly to herself. "It's a wonder that humans can survive without someone to care for them, as if for newborns."

Heath waved a hand at the older couple. "Spread out. I'll stay in the middle. You two take the sides. Stay within easy sight of each other."

Ursula and Guy angled away from Heath. They stayed within reach of each other. Had they not, Toylona might have tried to pick them off one by one. She knew Iktomi would not be happy, but she thought it better to incur his temporary anger than to allow the humans to continue posing such a blatant threat to her family. However, she saw no way of taking one without putting herself at risk from the guns of the other two. So, she held back, following, watching, and listening.

"What happened to it?" Guy asked after a time. "Any ideas?"

"They do this," Heath said, his teeth clenched. "They just seem to vanish. They're masters of their environment. It could be anywhere by now."

Ursula looked around, openly nervous. "Do you think it's watching us?"

"Doubtful," Heath told her. "It saw Dane. It knows there are people here. It's probably a couple of miles away by now, maybe even further."

"Could it be the one we saw before?" Guy asked.

"Maybe. There's no way to tell."

"How many of them are out here?" Ursula inquired.

Heath shrugged. "This area has a large population of them. These things are experts at hiding, though. We could be surrounded by them right now, and, unless the breeze blew their stench to us, we'd never know it."

Guy and Ursula crowded closer, casting frightened looks around.

"Why did that one chase us off when we got close," Guy asked, "yet this one walked almost right up to Dane, calm as can be?"

"You just answered your own question," Heath replied. He peered around into the trees as he spoke.

"What do you mean?" Guy followed Heath's gaze, holding his rifle halfway to his shoulder.

Heath sighed, frustrated. "Think about it. You two heard it, and walked toward it. You may well have spooked it. If it was engrossed in whatever it was doing, it might not have known you were there until you were almost on top of it. Yet, in Dane's case, the sasquatch approached him. It had control of the encounter."

Ursula frowned, puzzled. "Why would one get that close? Why would it allow him to see it?"

"They're curious. Sometimes they get too close, and are seen when they don't want to be. Or, maybe, they just get overconfident. Maybe it was a young one, lacking much experience, and didn't realize it was letting itself be seen at first. There's no way to know."

They stood quietly for a few minutes, checking the ground.

Finally, Ursula whispered, "What do we do now? Do we just give up, and let it go?"

Heath shook his head. "No. Not after being so close. We never should have taken that side trip to my camp. Come on."

He led the way forward, waving for them to spread out again.

CHAPTER 12

"I still don't see a way of stopping Heath and the others," Dane said. "Not by any legal means, that is."

Tabatha still remained on the lone seat. Alexia and Dane sat on the ground, facing her. Iktomi crouched low behind his pines, watching, yet remaining wary of the other three humans. It wouldn't do for him to be so involved in watching the ones before him that he allowed the others to sneak up on him.

Alexia picked a dead brown leaf off the ground, and fiddled with it. "We haven't heard any gunshots. My guess is the sasquatch gave them the slip."

"Can we take that chance?" Dane retorted.

Tearing bits from the leaf, slowly reducing it to the network of woody veins, Alexia shrugged. "Why take drastic action if we don't need to?"

"What 'drastic action'? All we've done is sit here and talk!" Dane shot back.

Alexia spun the remains of the leaf in her fingers. "Exactly. I don't want them to kill a sasquatch, either. Believe me, I don't! I want these creatures protected, not murdered. If we go running after Heath, we're only going to be goading him into shooting if he gets the chance."

"He already plans to!" Dane shouted.

Nodding, Alexia said, "How many hunters have planned to do just that? How many have changed their minds once they've gotten a sasquatch lined up in their sites?"

Tabatha leaned forward. "Why would they change their minds?"

Dane shifted to focus on her. "Because of how human these beings look," he explained. "There are a lot of stories on file of people being ready to shoot, but then not being able to pull the trigger because of that."

"Sasquatch," Alexia told the younger female, "are, by and large, very peaceful. And, as Dane said, they bear a certain resemblance to humans in a lot of ways. People tend to stop before squeezing the trigger, wondering if what they're looking at really is human. Some don't shoot for moral reasons. Others stop at the last second simply for fear of going to prison for murder."

Tabatha crossed her legs, massaging her injured ankle. "What will you do if Heath shoots one?"

"Nothing legal," Dane growled.

Alexia waved his words away. "My point is that Heath might not be able to bring himself to shoot. Despite his talk, he might not be able to do it. On the other hand, if we go chasing after him, trying to interfere, he may well pull the trigger on a sasquatch simply to spite us. Doing nothing right now might be the best action we can take."

"I don't like it," Dane said.

Raising her eyebrows, Alexia asked, "You think I do? All I wanted were a few peaceful days out here alone to try and gather some evidence. Now look! The woods are crawling with people—half of them wanting to kill the very animals I want to quietly study!"

Tabatha winced. "I shouldn't be here."

"You can't walk yet," Dane soothed. "Alexia doesn't mind you being here. Do you?" He turned to Alexia.

She sighed. "No. It isn't as if I'm getting any work done, anyway."

Dane stood. "I still don't think we ought to just sit here, and hope. We need to be out there doing something."

Alexia tossed the remnants of the leaf aside. "Like what?"

He eased toward the perimeter of the camp. "I don't know for sure. I do know that I can't just hang out here, waiting and hoping."

Dane turned, striding away into the trees. Iktomi tensed, but the sound of the human's footsteps led steadily away from his place of concealment. Iktomi wondered if he should follow Dane, or keep watch on the females. He opted for the latter, still viewing Alexia as more threatening due simply to his certainty of her desire to find his people. Besides, the pheromones emitted by Tabatha captivated him even more so than the music Dane liked to play.

Alexia scrambled to her feet. "Dane, wait!"

He ignored her, vanishing into the maze of moss-coated trees.

Sighing, Alexia turned to Tabatha. "I can't let him go off like this. He might get himself shot if he runs up on Heath. Can you walk yet?"

"I'm not sure." Tabatha put her foot back on the ground. She stood slowly, and made her way toward Alexia. "It still hurts."

"But you can walk on it."

"It hurts."

Alexia gritted her teeth. "You can deal with the pain, and come with me—now—of you can sit here alone, and wait for us to get back."

A look of fear crossed Tabatha's face. "How long will you be gone?"

"I've no idea," Alexia replied, her tone harsh. Turning away, she snatched up her gun, and set off after Dane.

"Wait!" Tabatha cried out. "I'm coming with you!"

Glad of the chance to still keep all three of them under watch, Iktomi eased from his hiding place as the females went after Dane. He made sure to remain well back from them, barely moving forward at all due to Tabatha's slow, limping progress. He needed to be able to slip away noiselessly in the event of the other three humans getting too close in their hunt of him.

****

"Is that from that...thing?" Ursula asked. She kept her voice low.

Toylona had lagged far enough behind, out of caution, that she only just heard the human's voice. She increased her pace, catching up to them, yet taking great care to make no noise.

Heath nodded, breathing through his mouth. "One has been here recently. The scent is fading." He matched her tone, speaking in the merest of whispers.

Guy covered his nose with one hand, clutching the gun in his other. "Fading? This bad, and you say it's fading?"

"It stopped here," Heath explained. "It lingered, maybe hoping that if it stayed quiet for a while we wouldn't be able to track it as easily."

Ursula gave Heath a scowl. "If they smell this rank, why didn't we notice anything from the one we saw before?"

Shrugging, Heath replied, "Some reports don't make mention of any smell. In fact, a lot of them don't."

"So what are we tracking—a bigfoot that doesn't like to bathe?" Guy asked.

Heath waved a hand at him a way that Toylona interpreted as being impatient. "Keep your voice down! Some people think these things can emit the smell at will."

"Like a skunk?" Guy asked.

Ursula eased closer to Heath. "It knows we're tracking it by now. It must. If that's the case, why would it leave a stench like this to tell us we're on the right track?"

"It could be meant as a warning," Heath replied. "Come on. It might still be very close by."

"A warning," Guy mumbled. "Something that big and powerful gives us a warning, and you want to ignore it."

Heath lifted his gun, drawing attention to it. "We have rifles. We have the upper hand here."

Toylona bared her teeth at the weapons they carried. Again, she wondered if it would be best to simply kill the humans, and be finished with them. All three were obviously a danger. Guy—and Ursula to a lesser degree—reeked of fear. That, combined with weapons, made for an extremely dangerous mix.

Heath led them forward at an even more cautious pace. Every few steps, he stopped, listening. Birdsong and insects were the only sounds.

Guy held his gun at the ready, peering through the odd top-mounted tube on the weapon. "What if we can't find it?"

"Then we come back out tomorrow, and pick up the search again," Heath answered. "We know at least one is in the area."

Ursula shook her head. Her expression grew even more uneasy. "That isn't what we agreed on. Our deal is that you lead my husband and I out of here. We said we'd help you shoot one of these things if we happened across one. We never agreed to stay out here longer, and help you keep hunting. We've already gone way above and beyond our end of the bargain."

"We're too close to give up now," Heath replied.

Lowering the gun, Guy said, "My wife is right. I was getting caught up in the idea of shooting that thing. We didn't agree to this, though. Which way to civilization?"

Heath glowered at them, and they both backed off a step. "It's too late in the day to reach the nearest city. Do you really want to hike through these forests at night, knowing what's out here?"

"No," Guy replied instantly.

Ursula echoed, "No."

Heath smirked at them. "I didn't think so. We'll keep looking a bit more now, while we have the light. We might be wise to scout around a bit at night, too. Sasquatch are primarily nocturnal."

"What is this one doing out during the day?" Guy asked.

The other male shrugged. "Who knows? I said 'primarily nocturnal', if you'll recall. Some researchers theorize that sasquatch adopted that habit simply as a way of avoiding humans better. We're mostly active during the day, so they started moving around mostly at night. You two heard one doing whatever it was doing, and tried to walk right up on it, though. You disturbed it. The one we're following approached Dane for whatever reason. It may well be the same creature, wanting to scout out all the humans in the area after feeling threatened by you two."

"We only want to get out of here," Ursula told him. "There's no reason why it should still feel threatened by us!"

"You're in its territory," Heath pointed out. "If a sasquatch wandered into your living room, you'd feel threatened by it. Right?"

Ursula only nodded.

"Even if it just wanted to leave, but couldn't find a way out?"

She nodded again. "I see your point."

"There could be a family group here, too," Heath went on. "This thing might be guarding a mate and offspring. Some researchers think that sasquatch hide out in caves, or other shelters, during the day, keeping together as a group. They think that a guard is placed outside the hiding place. The job of the guard in these cases seems to be warning the others who are resting about human presence, and chasing those humans away."

"Just like what happened to us," Guy said.

"Right," Heath told him. "That rock-clacking you two heard might well have been a signal from a guard to a hidden group that there were humans—you two—nearby. Then, when you moved closer, the guard did the second part of his job."

Ursula shuddered. "These things sound very smart."

"They are. They're extremely intelligent," Heath said. "That's a huge part of why they're so hard to track and find. Come on; we're wasting time."

He forged ahead, the other two keeping with him, walking a few steps to either side of him. Toylona remained in place until the humans were hidden from view by the vegetation, following them by scent and sound.

CHAPTER 13

Iktomi slipped silently through the dense moss-covered tree trunks, and vibrant orange and red foliage. Alexia and Tabatha were a short distance ahead. He could still hear Dane, despite the human's attempts at silence, ahead of the females. Tabatha limped along, whimpering with each step. Alexia shot the younger female hostile glares every few moments.

Ahead, Dane ceased his forward movements. Alexia and Tabatha caught up with him before long. Iktomi, glad of having all three of them within sight again, kept back, watching and listening.

"I'm serious, you guys," Tabatha whined, her voice pitched high. "I'm in real pain here! I shouldn't be up walking around!"

Alexia stopped, gritted her teeth, and turned to the younger woman. "Keep your voice down, please. We don't want Heath and his new best friends to know we're after them. Okay?"

Tabatha nodded. When she spoke her voice echoed more loudly as before. "I can't keep walking."

When Alexia opened her mouth, Dane held up a hand, forestalling what looked to be the beginning of a diatribe. "You go on ahead, Alexia. I'll stay here with Tabatha. If we can, we'll catch up to you later. If not, we'll meet you back at your camp."

After glaring at Tabatha for a moment, Alexia simply turned and walked away. Almost instantly, she had been lost to sight, blocked from view by the wide tree trunks.

Iktomi pondered going after her, and leaving Dane and Tabatha unwatched for the time being. Watch two lesser threats, or keep an eye on the single larger danger? Ultimately, he opted to remain with the pair before him. Heath, Guy, and Ursula were, presumably, still hunting him. The more he moved through the woods, the greater the chances were of him leaving footprints or other evidence of his passing for them to discover. Besides, given Dane's earlier deception, he still couldn't be completely sure that he didn't pose just a large a threat as Alexia. He kept track of Alexia as long as he could, relying on the sounds of her feet in the dry leaves on the ground, and her scent.

"Let's get you settled in for a rest," Dane said to Tabatha. "Alexia knows the woods. She's quiet. She might be able to sneak up on Heath and the others. If they do manage to track the Forest God, maybe Alexia will be able to do something to intervene, and save its life. One person can move undetected more easily than three. We're better off staying behind right now."

"I never should've left camp," Tabatha complained.

Dane got her situated on a fallen log. He crouched down, gently lifting her right leg, rubbing her ankle lightly. "You could've stayed in Alexia's camp. You'd have been safe there."

She shook her head. "I mean my camp. I shouldn't have wandered so far to potty."

"Oh." Dane's face reddened. "You have to be careful in the woods—especially at night. I must say, though, the guy you came out here for is very lucky."

Frowning, she asked, "How so?"

"No woman has ever gone to such lengths to be with me, or try and impress me before," he told her. "Things might not have worked out as you and he had hoped, but he's very lucky to have such a beautiful woman care so much about him."

She ducked her head, smiling coyly. "You really think so?"

"I do, yes."

Tabatha patted the log next to her. Dane accepted the silent invitation, settling in.

"So," she asked, "you know why I'm out here. What about you? I mean, I know you're out here looking for those creatures, like Alexia. But you two aren't, like, together. Are you?"

"No," he answered, grinning. "She and I aren't together. We're not together personally, or professionally."

"She's a grouch."

Dane chuckled. "She is at times, yes. That's because she takes her work seriously. She knows that the Forest Gods are real. Like me, Alexia wants to bring proof of that to the world. We want to do that in order to get protection for them."

"Why do you called them Forest Gods?"

"Because I believe that's what they are."

"Can you, like, explain that to me?"

Dane shifted his position, angling to face her squarely. "A lot of people—myself among them—believe that sasquatch are actually beings from another plane of reality."

"Another plane? You think they, like, fly or something?" Her normally smooth forehead wrinkled in puzzlement.

Dane grinned. "No. I say 'plane' as in dimensional plane. Another level of reality."

"Oh. I see."

He continued, saying, "We believe that these beings have some sort of abilities that most people would consider to be supernatural. We think that they have the power to travel from their world—their plane of existence—to ours, and back again at will. This explains so much about them, that it seems obvious."

"What does it explain?"

"One very common question people ask is why haven't physical remains of these beings been found," Dane said. "If they're from another world, that would explain it. They don't live here; they're not from Earth. They only pop in to visit for some reason."

"You don't know why?"

He shook his head. "No one does. We haven't yet found a way to truly communicate with them. But if they only come here for brief visits, that explains why they're not seen often, and why none of their dead are found. It also explains trails of their footprints that have been left in soft mud, yet just vanish before the end of the mud. People have said it's as if sasquatch can just disappear into thin air. If one happened to be strolling along, leaving a nice line of footprints, and then return to its home dimension, we'd expect that to be the result—tracks that simply end before the mud."

"Wow."

"Yes, wow," he agreed. "People who have tracked Forest Gods through the woods have simply lost all sign of the creature's presence. It's as if the being they were following just vanished."

"And you think they did?"

"Yes. Me, and a lot of other people," he told her. "You'll find a huge number of stories regarding sasquatch in Native American lore. A lot of those tell us the same thing that so many of us believe today—that sasquatch are some form of being, possibly spirits, from another world. The Forest Gods are to be revered, maybe even worshipped. People shouldn't be running around with guns, trying to murder them!"

Tabatha nodded, her eyes appearing slightly glazed.

Dane took her hand gently. "I'm so sorry. You're in pain, I'm rambling on."

"It's all right. I asked. Remember?"

"Still..."

She held his hand back, watching him. "You've never really had a woman to go out of her way to spend time with you?"

"No. Never."

She leaned in fractionally. "Maybe," she said, her voice just above a whisper, "you've never met the right woman yet."

Captivated, eyes widening, Dane inclined his head

toward her. "Maybe not."

****

Heath slammed his rifle to the ground in frustration. "It's gone," he growled. "We've lost it."

Guy and Ursula stepped further away from him. "Maybe if we fan out again..." Guy suggested.

"No." Heath scowled at the trees ahead of them. "We haven't seen a fresh track for hours. We haven't smelled the thing's scent for well over an hour. It's gone. It slipped into hiding somewhere, and we missed it."

Toylona couldn't understand their words, but their frustration came through clearly. She rejoiced, knowing that anything which worked against the humans could only be of help to her people.

Heath turned, kicking a pinecone hard with the toe of the strange covering he wore on his foot. The punted seed container arced through the air before ricocheting off a tree trunk. It bounced and rattled away, out of sight.

"Dane said he had been playing his guitar when the thing approached him," Ursula said. "Maybe you need to try something like that."

Whirling to face her, Heath snorted in disgust. "I'm not some little hippy. I don't sit in the woods, play music, and hope that some sappy, good-natured teddy bear of a creature walks up to say hello! These things are hunters; so am I!"

Ursula backed away, shock written on her features. Guy, his face twisted in anger, strode up to Heath.

"You do not speak to my wife like that!" he bellowed at the larger, younger male.

Giving a disdainful noise in response, something between a laugh and a grunt, Heath pushed by him. "Come on. Let's go back to camp."

"I don't think we should follow you anymore," Guy said.

"We have to," Ursula told him. "We can trace our way back to Alexia's camp, but what good will that do us? We'll be right back where we were before Heath came along."

Heath stopped, turning back to the older couple. "Alexia's camp," he muttered, grinning. "That's a good idea."

Ursula frowned up at him. "Why?"

"I had planned to take us back to my camp. But there would only be the three of us there. If we go back to Alexia's camp, there'll be the three of us, her, that ditz that I found in the woods, and maybe Dane, too. Even if he isn't there, his camp isn't far from Alexia's, I don't think."

"Safety in numbers?" Guy asked.

The look Heath shot him told even Toylona just how dumb he thought he was. "No. More eyes in numbers. We know there's at least one sasquatch out here. We know it visited Dane in Alexia's camp earlier today. Maybe, between us, we can find a way to lure it back in. Maybe we can see what we're up against. The smaller the creature, the better the chances are that what we're after is a young, inexperienced one. It would be less dangerous, but able to hide in places where a fully-grown adult wouldn't. On the other hand, an adult, being better skilled at avoiding humans, not to mention stronger, would pose more of a threat anyone hunting it."

Guy and Ursula traded a nervous look.

Heath beckoned to them as he set off. "Getting a glimpse of this thing might help us change up our game plan for finding it. Come on."

****

Dane sat so close to Tabatha that the sides of their knees pressed together.

"I never knew so many people, like, believed bigfoot is real," she told him.

"Between the number of people who have seen them, and the number of people who realize that there's too much evidence for them not to be real, somewhere around thirty percent of people in the United States accept their existence."

"Wow!" she chirped. "Had you seen one before today?"

"I have, yes. I've spent a lot of time looking for them. I've never had a good, clear sighting, but have gotten glimpses of them a few times."

"Wow." Tabatha pondered for a few moments before asking, "What other, like, evidence is there besides the footprints, videos, and things like that? Anything?"

"There's an overwhelming amount of it," he explained. "The things you mentioned, plus photos, audio records, hair samples. DNA studies have been made from some of those. There's even a cast of most of the body of one of the Forest Gods."

Her eyes grew even wider. "How did that happen?"

"Researchers poured water onto a patch of dirt, turning it into mud," he told her. "They put fruit in the middle of it at night, as bait. They hoped one of the creatures would step in the mud while getting to the fruit."

"And leave footprints?"

"Right. But it did them one better." Dane grinned. "The next morning they found an impression that looked like the creature had sat in the mud, and then leaned over, reaching for the fruit. They made a plaster cast of the impression. The cast is of nearly one whole side of the body of the Forest God who made the imprint."

"Wow. Where did this happen?"

"In Skookum Meadows area of the Grifford Pinchot National Forest in southern Washington state."

She stared at him in awe. "I'd never heard of that before. When was it found?"

"In September of the year two-thousand."

"Have you ever found anything like that?"

He shook his head briefly. "I've found a few tracks, yes. But never anything on that scale. I've found a few rock cairns, too."

Tabatha frowned, the expression almost a pout. Iktomi easily detected the increase of her pheromones in the air. Dane leaned a bit closer to her in response, his own scent altering slightly, growing more receptive to her. Iktomi thought of Toylona, missing her. Hopefully she had long since made it back to their offspring, and gotten them stashed away somewhere safe from human intrusion.

"What are rock cairns?" Tabatha asked.

"I'll show you."

A new smell caught Iktomi's attention. He turned his head slightly. Alexia. She was returning to Dane and Tabatha.

Dane slid off the log, and began searching the forest floor, gathering up rocks no larger than his fist. He stacked the stones, creating a small clustered pile of them.

"That's a cairn," he told her once he had finished. "The Forest Gods seem to use them as some form of communication. Some people think them to be territorial markers for them."

The rustle of leaves made them look up. Alexia stepped between two trees. "I didn't know if you two would still be here, or if you'd have gone back to camp."

"We're still here," Tabatha answered. "Dane has been telling me about the..." She glanced at him.

"Forest Gods," he supplied.

Tabatha nodded. "Right. Dane's been telling me about the Forest Gods. He just showed me a rock cairn, too."

Alexia glanced from her, to Dane, and back. "Can you walk now?"

The corners of Tabatha's mouth quirked down. "Maybe."

She started to slide off the log. Dane hurried to her side, steadying her.

"Thank you," Tabatha whispered. She kissed him lightly on the cheek. "You're sweet."

His face turning red once more, Dane angled Tabatha back the way they had come from. To Alexia, he said, "I assume you want to go back to camp?"

"You assume right," she said, and started to walk.

Dane helped Tabatha limp along after her. "Did you catch up with the others?"

"No," Alexia reported. "I lost their trail. I'm not a great

tracker, and they veered off in another direction. I'm guessing Heath took them to his camp for more guns."

Dane frowned. "Go on."

Iktomi closed his eyes, hunkering down. He held still, not even breathing. The trio of humans went by, seemingly unaware that he hid only steps away, ensconced in low-hanging pine boughs.

"They backtracked to the sasquatch's trail, but overlapped their own," Alexia went on. "It was a confusing mess. By the time I got it sorted out, they were probably well ahead of me. I lost the track on dry, stony ground for a while, too. It'll be dark before long. Heath has probably led them back to his own camp for the night."

"When we get back to yours," Dane said, "Tabatha needs more aspirin."

"All right," Alexia said. She picked her way around a tangled group of roots that had punched up through the ground. "We should eat soon, too. You want to stay in my camp for a meal?"

Dane blinked, surprised. "Okay. Sure. Thank you."

Alexia dropped back to walk beside Dane. She leaned in, placing her lips very close to his ear, and whispered, "Thank you. I don't know if I could tolerate being alone with her."

Dane's lips twisted unhappily. Iktomi read anger in his body language and scent. Dane eased closer to Tabatha, holding her against him to help her walk.

CHAPTER 14

Toylona followed the trio back to Alexia's encampment. Upon their arrival, she saw no sign of the other humans, or of Iktomi. However, she smelled her mate's scent, and knew he had left the area not long before.

The smell of him made her want to forget about the humans, find Iktomi, and return to their young ones. From there, they could leave the entire region, finding someplace deep within the heavy, old forests where humans never explored. Such a place would be akin to paradise, given how prevalent human presence had become in the area her family currently called home.

But, what of the others of their people in the area? Iktomi had been right. They couldn't think only of themselves. Their offspring were safe for the moment. She would return to them soon to check on them. For now, she felt it better to keep watch over the three humans. They posed a danger. Iktomi had, apparently, gone off to follow the others. He couldn't be everywhere at once. Even if he could, the three before her were hunting him. She didn't want him anywhere near them.

Baring her teeth, she struggled to suppress her rage at the thought of them stalking her mate. If only they didn't have their guns! If only they would split up! Even armed, she felt confident that she could pick them off one at a time. Unarmed, she may well try to dispatch all three at once. But together, and armed? She refused to allow her anger at them to push her into so stupid an action.

For the time being, she decided, she would keep

watching, and forcing herself to wait.

"The others seem to be gone," Heath told Guy and Ursula. "Make yourself at home. When they get back from wherever they are, we'll work out a plan of action for the night."

He set down his weapon, and settled into the single seat. Ursula claimed a spot on the ground. Guy paced the area, staying near them. He kept his gun in hand.

"Put the rifle down," Heath told him.

"It's getting dark," Guy said. He peered up at the sky.

Heath followed his gaze. The blue had deepened, edging toward purple with the onset of twilight. "So? Put down the rifle. You're nervous. You're going to hurt someone."

"Yes, I'm nervous," Guy retorted. "We're out here with a monster roaming the woods around us!"

"There's nothing to worry about."

Guy spun to face him. "That thing came to this camp this afternoon! Dane saw it!"

Heath sighed. He opened his mouth to reply when Alexia's voice barked at him.

"What are you doing in my camp?"

Toylona started. She had been so intent upon the three before her—and her anger at them—that she had failed to notice the approach of Alexia, Dane, and Tabatha. She looked around, seeking Iktomi, aware, now, of how strong his scent had grown.

He slipped up to her side, low to the ground. "Are our young ones all right?" he asked, his voice so quiet she scarcely heard him.

"I haven't yet made it back to them," she said, stroking his massive hand. "Before I made it up the mountain to them, I found Heath, Guy, and Ursula deeper in the woods. I realized they were hunting you."

He nodded. "I eluded them, and took up watching the others again."

"You should leave before they realize you're nearby," she warned. "If they know that, they'll hunt you again."

"Not just me," he replied, touching her face. She leaned her cheek against his palm. "They would come after any of us. Heath is a great danger to us. Ursula and Guy are very afraid, but seem braver when they are with Heath. He makes them more dangerous, too."

"We should both leave," she told him. "Get our young, and leave this area. Let the humans have it."

"We cannot. This is our home."

"We can make a new home! We can carve out a new territory elsewhere."

Iktomi held up a hand, silencing her. She fell quiet, and they turned their attention back to the humans.

"With six of us," Heath said, smiling at Alexia, "we'll be better able to draw the sasquatch in, I think."

"As if we'd help you?" Dane shot back.

"Get out of here," Alexia shouted.

Heath's smile faded slowly. "You're making a mistake. We can all share in the money and glory if we can bag one of these things."

"Get out!" Alexia bellowed, stalking toward him. "This is my camp, and I want you gone. Now!"

Dane left Tabatha standing on her own, and moved to Alexia's side. "I second that." His voice had taken on a low, menacing tone.

"Me, too!" Tabatha put in from her place a few feet away.

Heath glowered from one of them to the next, holding his ground.

Alexia stared up into his face, jabbing him in the chest with an index finger. "Leave. Now."

Smirking, he asked, "Or what?"

Not breaking the hostile eye contact, Alexia made a show of swinging her gun forward on her shoulder. She held is casually, keeping her finger well away from the piece that made it work.

"If you stay," she said mildly, despite the blazing rage evident in her eyes, "in the dark, in such a tense situation, there just might be an accident. Hunting accidents happen all the time. Don't they, Dane?"

"All the time," he agreed, remaining firmly at her side.

Heath trembled with rage. "You think you can threaten me—"

His words cut off, his teeth clacking shut painfully, when Alexia lifted the weapon slightly.

"Go," she repeated.

He held her glare for a moment before turning, and striding away.

"Guy? Ursula?" Alexia said. "You can stay here if you like. Heath is bad news; I won't force you to stay in his company. If you do stay here, you follow my orders. Understood?"

As Heath reached the tree line, Ursula called out to him, "Heath, do you want your guns back?"

"Keep them," he raged, seemingly unwilling to turn back and face Alexia again. He kept walking.

The other five stood, watching him leave. Toylona tracked Heath's progress via sound and smell, wanting to be sure that he left the area. Beside her, Iktomi watched the others. Once Toylona could be certain that Heath had truly left, she turned back to the rest of the humans.

"I should go after Heath," she told Iktomi quietly. "The rest are together for you to keep tabs on."

"Go if you wish," he replied. "Though I'd rather you go to our young ones to make sure they're safe. And I recognize your tone, and the look in your eyes. You want to hurt Heath."

"I do."

"Don't."

She frowned deeply, barring her teeth. "Why?"

"Thus far, we've done nothing to harm them," he answered. "Yet they still hunt us. What would they do if we hurt one of them?"

"The others don't seem to care for Heath," she reasoned.

Nodding, he replied, "True. But we don't know what

they speak of. We don't know how much of a threat these others pose to us. We shouldn't take that risk. Track Heath if you wish, but, please, don't harm him. Don't give the humans more reason to seek us out. Still, though, I would prefer if you checked on our young."

"And what will you do?"

"Keep watch on the rest of them," he told her. "If I can learn anything at all more about what they are doing, that knowledge might be of use to us."

Toylona touched his face, and began to withdraw from their hiding place. Then she asked, "What will you do if they split up again?"

"Dane's own encampment is nearby," Iktomi said. "If he returns to it, I can easily move back and forth to keep watch on them all."

Watching the group, Toylona saw the tenderness that had come over Dane and Tabatha. "If Dane returns to his own sleeping place, I suspect he will take Tabatha with him."

"Yes."

"And if any of them wander off into the deeper forest again?" she asked. "What will you do then?"

"The only thing I can do," he replied. "I'll track whichever one, or group, that I feel I should watch the closest."

"All right," she muttered, touching his cheek briefly, letting her fingertips slide gently down to his chin. "Be careful."

"You, too."

"I'm going to go see to our young," she informed him. "If I were to go after Heath, the temptation to kill him would be too great, I'm afraid."

"Thank you."

With a last, lingering parting touch, she turned, retreating. She hated leaving him alone so near to humans. He seemed much more comfortable with them than she did. She couldn't imagine spending as much time in such close proximity to them as he had over the past days. Hopefully they would leave soon, and things would return to normal.

****

Tabatha took the seat. Dane sat on the ground before her, rubbing her injured ankle. Alexia had taken up a place a little to one side of Dane. Guy paced several steps away from the others in one direction, before turning, retracing his steps. He seemed to take great care not to move more than a few long strides from the rest of the group. While Alexia had placed her gun on the ground at her side, Guy and Ursula maintained tight grips on their own weapons.

Iktomi's estimation of the threats the various humans posed adjusted a bit. Tabatha still ranked at the bottom of the list. Dane came in just above her, though Iktomi still found he could not be completely certain about the younger human male. Alexia remained, he was sure, far more dangerous that Dane. After seeing so much more of Guy and Ursula, Iktomi now felt they posed a greater threat than Alexia.

Heath, he felt positive, had been the largest threat. He hoped Toylona took his advice, and left the other human alone. Eliminating Heath would help them out in one way, but doing so could make things much worse for them in others. Iktomi did not want to run that risk—not only for his own family, but for all of his people.

Yawning, Dane groaned and stretched, pulling Iktomi's attention back to him. "It's getting late. I ought to be heading back to my own camp for the night," he said.

Tentatively, Tabatha reached out, lightly touching his shoulder. "It's crowded here in Alexia's camp. Heath might come back, too. Would it be okay if I went to your camp with you, Dane?"

He froze at her words. Alexia, Guy, and Ursula went quiet and still as they focused on him. Alexia's lips quirked up at the corners. Her eyes twinkled with teasing mirth.

Dane squirmed under the attention. He looked up at

Tabatha, held her gaze for a moment, and then gently took hold of her hand.

"I'd be honored to have you as my guest," he answered. He stood, and helped Tabatha to her feet. "Lean on me. I'll help you walk."

"Thank you." She slipped an arm over his shoulders, letting him take part of her slight weight.

"What about your boyfriend?" Ursula asked. "Or, whatever your relationship to that guy you came out here is? Don't you think he's worried about you? Should you be more concerned about getting back to him?"

Tabatha hobbled around to face the older female, and hung her head a bit. "I got so lost in the woods before Heath found me, that I had no idea which way to go to get back to our camp. After Heath carried me here, I'm even more lost. I brought my cell phone with me, but left it in camp when I went to go behind a tree. Not that I got reception out here, anyway."

"No, there's no cell reception out here," Alexia said. "That's why I left mine in my truck."

"I didn't bring mine this far, either," Dane put in.

"We need to find him, and let him know you're okay," Ursula told Tabatha.

"I know, but I can't find my way back," Tabatha answered.

Ursula shifted to face Alexia. "Could you lead us back to where we met up with Tabatha and Heath tomorrow? Maybe we could back-track Heath's trail to where he found Tabatha, and, from there, back to her camp."

"No," Guy interjected loudly. "We're not wasting our time. That's her problem," he went on gruffly, pointing at Tabatha. "We need to get out of these woods! We need to get to safety!" He rounded on Alexia. "Tomorrow, you need to do what you promised us you'd do today! You need to lead us out of here!"

Alexia's eyes narrowed in anger. "I was leading you out! Then we crossed paths with Tabatha and Heath, ended up back here, and then you and your wife ran off with Heath to try and gun down an innocent creature!"

"Innocent?" Guy bellowed.

Face coloring with fury, Alexia rose to her feet. Dane drew Tabatha further away as Alexia shouted at Guy.

"I've explained why it did what it did!"

Guy staggered a step closer to her, hands clenched. He reeked of terror. "You're taking us out of here right after sunrise in the morning!"

She stared at him, fuming, before saying, "Only because I want you two out of my camp, and out of my way so I can work. Even then, I'll only do it on one condition."

"What might that be?" Guy spat out.

Alexia pointed off in the direction the other hunter had gone. "That you never have anything to do with Heath Varlas again—ever."

"Agreed," Ursula chimed in before her mate could speak.

Guy glanced at her, before turning his attention back to Alexia. He nodded, still glaring at her.

"Come on," Dane whispered to Tabatha.

He led her out of Alexia's encampment, toward his own. Iktomi groaned quietly to himself. He needed to try and watch all five humans. Just as Toylona had feared, though, they were splitting up. Which ones should he stay with?

Alexia and Guy continued shouting. Their loud voices hammered at Iktomi's ears. He winced as they grew even more raucous.

Iktomi turned in the direction Tabatha and Dane had gone. The lingering scent of their pheromones enticed him to ease from his concealment, and follow them. Maybe Dane would play more music, too. Plus, Alexia's camp could be reached from Dane's quickly. He sagged with relief as the deafening voices of Guy and Alexia faded slightly with distance.

"Alexia hates Heath," Tabatha said.

"I know. Everyone who wants to protect the Forest Gods does," Dane replied.

"He seemed so nice when I first met him. When he found me in the woods, after I got hurt, he acted so different."

"That's what he does," Dane replied. "Heath wears the mask of a nice guy. Peek beneath that disguise, though, and you see what he's really like."

Tabatha shuddered. "I don't like him."

Dane helped settle her onto the seat. "What about you?" she asked. "Where will you sit? Do you have another chair?"

"I'll be fine on the ground. I didn't anticipate company on this trip, and only brought the one chair," he replied. "Less weight to hike in and out with, and I didn't think I'd need more than one."

"Take the chair, then."

He waved a hand at her. "You're hurt. You keep the chair. I'll be fine on the grass."

"Thank you. You're very sweet."

Dane tossed wood into the ring of stones around a shallow pit. After a fire had been lit, he helped Tabatha closer to it.

"Even during the summer it can get cold in these mountains at night," he told her. "During the autumn it can dip below freezing most nights. Snow isn't out of the question, either. Keep near the fire for warmth."

"Thank you."

"We didn't get to eat once we got back to Alexia's camp. I have some things in the tent."

She graced him with a beatific smile. "I'm fine, Dane. Thank you. But if you're hungry, please eat."

He shook his head. "After the confrontation with Heath, I've lost my appetite. I'll be right back."

He opened the entry flaps of the artificial cave, and ducked inside. When he came back out, he held the same instrument that he had played before. Iktomi leaned forward slightly, not wanting to ease out of his new hiding place amongst the trees, but wanting to be as close as possible for the music.

Dane settled in on the ground next to Tabatha. He fiddled with the instrument, not yet creating a melody with it. As he tinkered, the sky grew fully dark, and the illumination from the fire played over the glossy surface of the contraption Dane held. Iktomi found the dancing reflections mesmerizing.

Tabatha twisted in the chair, watching him. "Are you going to play?"

"Will it bother you?"

"Not at all. Have you ever, like, been with a band?"

"No. I've never even tried. I never wanted to play in a professional capacity. It's just a hobby."

"So what do you do for a living?"

Dane twisted one of the pieces high up on the handle that the tiny, thin vines seemed to be attached to. "I consult on educational films for children. Most of my work is on nature documentaries."

"That's so cool."

"What about you?"

"Nothing as impressive as what you do!" she answered. "I run my own business on-line."

"Doing what?"

"Selling designer make-up."

He responded with a faint humming noise. "Sounds...interesting."

"You think it's stupid."

"I didn't say that."

"You didn't need to."

Looking up at her, he said, "Everyone has to make a living. What you're doing is honest work. It might not be something I'd choose for myself, but it suits you. Right? You like what you do?"

"I do."

"There you go, then. Are you sure the music won't bother you?"

She shook her head without actually looking away from him. "I'm sure. I like music."

"What kind?"

"Heavy metal, mostly."

He grinned. "I don't play heavy metal. Can you handle some soft, gentle music?"

"Okay."

Dane started to strum the instrument without looking away from Tabatha. He played a short tune, light and lilting.

"That's amazing!" she praised once the final note had ceased to vibrate.

Iktomi already missed the sounds, and wished Dane would continue.

"Thanks," Dane told Tabatha.

"You ought to play in a band."

Dane shrugged. "No interest in that. I just come out to play for the Forest Gods."

"Is that why that one showed up at Alexia's camp today? You were playing then?"

"Yes. I mean, yes, I was playing at the time. I can only assume that's why the Forest God approached me."

"Weren't you, like, scared?"

"In awe, yes. Frightened, no."

"You're so brave."

He started up a second gentle rhythm. The only other noise came from the fire as it crackled away merrily. "I think you're the brave one, Tabatha. You came out here in what, to you, in a totally alien environment. You did it for someone you care about, just to be with them, and be supportive of them. I know you aren't comfortable out here. I know you're frightened. As I said before, whoever you came out camping with is a lucky guy."

Tabatha glanced away shyly. When she started to refocus on him, she did a double-take in the direction she had just been facing. Her nose wrinkled.

"Do you smell that?" she whispered.

Iktomi jerked backward, realizing that, in his desire to be nearer the source of the music, he had extended himself too far from his hiding place. Tabatha had caught a glimpse of him, he suspected, judging by the expression on her pale face. Quietly, he withdrew, putting a bit of distance between himself, and the humans.

He heard Dane inhale deeply, and the human nearly jittered with excitement. "Keep still," he whispered.

CHAPTER 15

Dane played a little louder, yet kept the tune gentle and easy.

"It stinks!" Tabatha complained. She covered her nose and mouth with one hand. "It smells like...rotten garbage. Or maybe spoiled milk. It reeks!"

"Show some respect, please," Dane asked, shooting a harsh look in her direction.

Continuing to play, he stood, and slowly turned in the direction she faced. Iktomi held still, hoping that the fading daylight, combined with his immobility would prevent Dane from spotting him. Bad enough that Tabatha had.

"Is it coming closer?" Tabatha whispered. She tensed, as if ready to leap up from her sitting position.

"Shhh," Dane's voice remained low.

He eased forward, lightly strumming the instrument. He seemed to be trying to force relaxation upon himself, but looked tense to Iktomi. Little by little Dane moved closer. Tabatha sat rigid on her seat, wide-eyed, staring at the human male.

Iktomi realized that Dane had no intention of stopping. Despite his gradual pace, he advanced steadily. If Iktomi remained in place, the human would be upon him before long.

"Dane..." Tabatha whispered.

The male ceased playing the music just long enough to wave a hand behind him. The female went quiet once more.

Dane took several more slow steps. Iktomi tensed, realizing that he had involuntarily lost control of his warning

117

musk in his unease. The smell permeated the air. Dane stopped, wincing. Behind him, Tabatha gagged openly.

Keeping as low to the ground as he could, Iktomi inched backward, away from the humans. Silently, he chastised himself for allowing them to become aware of his presence. He rose to a crouch only upon being sure that enough vegetation screened him from the prying eyes trying to spot him. On his feet, he increased the pace of his retreat, circling around the encampment to the opposite side. He needed to keep watch on the humans, which meant he couldn't leave. Yet he needed to make sure that he stayed firmly out of their sight.

Dane crept forward until he had nearly reached the place where Iktomi had hidden before. Stopping, the human looked carefully around. He let his fingers fall still upon the instrument he held. In the silence, Iktomi could hear the heartbeats of both humans drumming with anticipation.

After a few moments, Dane muttered, "It's gone," and turned back to Tabatha, frowning.

"You could've been hurt!" she admonished, reaching toward him from her seat.

"They aren't violent by nature," he replied. "It wouldn't have hurt me."

"It might if you'd have scared it! And you could've done that by trying to sneak up on it like you did!"

He shrugged. "It doesn't matter. It's gone." Brightening, he asked, "Did you see the glow of its eyes when it peeking around the tree at us?"

Shivering, she nodded. "I saw."

Dane crouched next to her. "It's amazing! That's the second time my music has drawn one to me today!"

"Do you think it'll come back again tonight?" she asked, wrapping her arms tightly around herself.

"I hope so!"

Tabatha shuddered. "I don't."

He lightly touched her arm. "There's nothing to be afraid of."

"So you keep telling me."

He stood, and put his hand back on her arm, and shaking his head in a manner that struck Iktomi as sad or melancholy. "I'm afraid the tent is going to make for cramped sleeping quarters," he said. "I hadn't planned on anyone else being here with me."

Leaning forward slightly, she asked, "Is that a problem for you?"

"No," he said quickly, clearing his throat. "No, not at all."

Tabatha grinned, her eyelashes fluttering slightly. "Good."

"Will it be for you?" he asked, not looking away from her.

The rising levels of their pheromones struck Iktomi hard. He found that he couldn't be sure as to which of the humans had become the more open to the other.

"Not at all," she said, smiling wider. "In fact..." She pushed herself up, wobbling a bit on her injury. "I think we should turn in now."

Dane stared at her for several seconds, wide-eyed, before muttering, "Okay."

Tabatha frowned. "First, I need to, um... Do you...um...have, like, a toilet here?"

"No, sorry. Only trees."

She huffed out an irritated breath. "This is one of the things I hate so much about being out here. My...um...time of the month is starting. I'd so much rather have proper facilities. Do you at least have any, like, toilet paper?"

"In the tent," he answered, ducking inside the shelter. "If I had brought my camper trailer you'd have something better. I'd planned to keep it simple on this trip, so I brought the tent." He slipped back outside, toting a light source which swayed from a handle, and a roll of something. "Take the lantern. Be sure to bury the paper after you've finished. All right?"

He showed her something on the side of the light

source, turning the illumination off, and back on. As he did, he looked around, a hopeful expression on his face.

Tabatha flinched, "I hope it's gone."

"I don't see it."

"I barely even smell it anymore."

Dane nodded. "Don't go far, though. All right?"

"Don't worry, I won't. I don't, like, want a repeat of what happened before. I don't want to get lost from a second camp! Especially not with a monster hanging around!"

"They aren't monsters."

She pointed to the side of the clearing opposite where Iktomi had been. Her finger indicated his new hiding place almost exactly. "I'll be right over there. I'm just going on the other side of that tree."

"All right," Dane said. "I'll stand right here until you get back. Okay? If you need me, just shout; I'll hear you. If you aren't back soon, I'll come over and check on you."

She pointed a stern finger at him. "Just be sure you, like, keep on this side of the tree if you do!" She narrowed her eyes.

Dane grinned. "I will. I promise."

"Okay, then," she muttered, smiling back, playful.

She turned from Dane, limping toward the spot where Iktomi hid. Suppressing a grunt of frustration, he quietly slid away to one side. He thought of moving partway around the camp, maybe even back to his original hiding place. However, he settled for easing only a few trees away, curious about what Tabatha planned to do with the light she held, and the roll of whatever Dane had passed to her. He didn't want to let such an opportunity for human observation be wasted.

Tabatha's limp seemed far less pronounced now than it had earlier. Iktomi wondered if she had injured herself as badly as she seemed to be letting on to the others. Had she really needed to be helped by first Heath, and then Dane? Or had it all been some sort of ploy on her part? Narrowing his eyes, he watched her slip behind the first tree at the edge of the clearing Dane had made his encampment in.

Before, he had viewed Tabatha as the least threatening of the humans he had recently encountered. That opinion had been based, in large part, on her injury. But what if the hurt ankle had only been a ruse? He had no way of knowing just what, if anything, that meant for he and his people. He found himself forced to reevaluate Tabatha, and whatever threat she might represent.

Tabatha waved back to Dane, who returned the gesture. She then hid herself fully from Dane's view, shielding herself with the bole of the tree. After setting down the light, and the roll, she fiddled with the strange coverings she wore over her body, hands at her waist. A few moments later, she pushed the lower coverings down her legs. Iktomi saw another, brief, flimsy layer beneath the outer ones. This skimpy layer was a bright pink, too, matching the outer coverings.

Wondering anew at the absurdities of humans, he watched as Tabatha bent her knees, squatting low to the ground. Just before the weak, unsteady urine stream started flowing, he realized what she had gone around the tree to do. But why go out of her way to avoid Dane? Did humans have some strange taboo surrounding urination? Iktomi shook his head.

Tabatha's urine, he found, was strongly scented by the same pheromones that screamed of her desire to mate with Dane, and also others that told any receptive male that her preferred time of the month had come upon her.

Iktomi inhaled, studying the fragrance. He had never smelled this in humans before. He didn't know of any of his people who had. He crept forward, watching her, sampling the scents again. They were somewhat different, and much weaker, than those generated by females of his kind. Still, there could be no mistake about what he smelled from Tabatha. Dane would easily be able to claim her as his own that night if he continued to wish it.

"Tabatha?" Dane called. "Are you all right?"

Iktomi froze, unsure if the male would move forward, or not.

"I'm fine!" she called back. "It's just, like, taking longer than I thought!"

"All right," he answered.

"I'm not used to, like, going in the woods," she replied. "It's awkward."

"Take your time, but be careful."

"Thanks!" she told him.

Dane fell silent. Tabatha remained squatting.

"Relax," Tabatha muttered. "Think of rainbows, unicorns, puppies, triple-fudge chocolate brownies, a good massage..."

After a few moments, Tabatha's urine stream grew stronger.

"I'm going to get a urinary tract infection from doing this in the woods," she groused in a whisper.

Iktomi again shook his head. Humans spoke to themselves even during urination? He crept forward a few more steps, fascinated.

Tabatha sighed, and tore of strip of thin, white material from the roll Dane had given her. She wiped herself with it, frowning. "I'm not getting dirt under my nails digging a hole for this." She dropped the wad on the ground, and stood.

Iktomi moved a bit closer, still watching her intently. She had began pulling coverings back into place when he stepped on the twig, more focused on the human female than his surroundings.

Both of them froze in place. Tabatha's eyes were unnaturally wide. Iktomi realized that she was looking directly at him. After a moment, her eyes rolled back in her head, and she slumped to the ground.

A thrill of fear coursed through Iktomi. Had he killed her? He hadn't even touched her! Were humans so fragile that they could be slain so easily? No; he could still hear her heartbeat. Why had she collapsed? What had he done to her? Could the injury to her ankle have been so grave as to be responsible for this?

"Tabatha?" Dane called out. "Are you sure you're all

right?"

Iktomi looked from Tabatha toward Dane's direction, and back. What should he do? Should he leave Tabatha alone, and retreat? But what if there were some way that he could help her? Should he? Or would it be best to just move to another spot to watch, and see what Dane did when he found her?

Dane.

The human male still posed questions. At first, Iktomi hadn't thought him threatening. But after the deception he had pulled on Alexia with the music, Iktomi didn't know what to make of him. Would Tabatha be safe with him? Before, she probably had been. But what about now? She had become unresponsive, looking and acting as if she had fallen asleep. What might Dane do to her in her current state?

Footsteps let him know that Dane had began a slow advance. "Tabatha?" he called out again, more loudly this time. "Answer me, please. Are you all right?"

Acting as much on instinct as on rational thought, Iktomi scooped Tabatha up into his arms. Her sleight weight made no difference to him at all. He strode away into the deeper woods, covering large patches of ground with every step.

"Tabatha?" Dane said loudly. "Answer me now, or I'm coming around the tree! If you don't want me to see, say so now!"

Iktomi lay Tabatha down gently on a patch of soft moss. He then crept back toward the encampment, curious as to what Dane's reaction to Tabatha's absence might be.

Dane stood where Tabatha had fallen, holding the light Tabatha had carried as high as he could, looking from side to side. "Tabatha! Where are you?" he shouted.

When no answer came, he knelt to examine the ground. After a brief time, he brushed his fingers over the grass, murmuring "No! No, no, no!"

Squinting, Iktomi could just make out a faint outline in the vegetation. His stomach sank upon realizing the marks had been left by his own feet when he had picked up Tabatha.

Dane began to follow the trail, heading closer to Iktomi, who quietly eased away, backtracking to Tabatha.

The human female still remained where he had left her. She also remained as limp and seemingly asleep as before. Not knowing what else to do, Iktomi picked her up again, and set off. They weren't too very far from a temporary shelter that he, Toylona, and their offspring used on occasion. Tabatha would be safe there until he could figure out what to do with her. Maybe Toylona would have an idea as to what had happened, and how to help the human.

He increased the rate of his steps, and lengthened his stride. He needed to get Tabatha to the shelter, and find Toylona as quickly as he could. And, if during that time, Tabatha roused herself, he would deal with that then.

CHAPTER 16

Toylona slipped easily through the woods, content in the knowledge that her young were safely ensconced in a cave high up on the mountainside. She retraced her previous path back down, thinking to rejoin Iktomi. Humans were hunting him, but he refused to leave the area. No matter how sound his reasoning might be, he continued putting himself in danger. She refused to stay away, and allow him to deal with that threat alone. And, despite the wishes of her mate, she still hadn't completely dismissed the idea of eliminating Heath. Making sure he no longer posed a threat to anyone made her bare her teeth in an involuntary grin.

The question of where to find Iktomi presented itself. Over the past few days, he had been following the humans hither and yon, all over the surrounding area. However, every path eventually seemed to circle back to the encampment of the human female Alexia. Even if Iktomi didn't prove to be there just now, she had little doubt that he would turn up there before long.

She crept up on Alexia's camp to find Alexia, Guy, and Ursula there. Keeping still, she focused on smells and sounds. She found no trace of Heath, Dane, or Tabatha. Nor any of Iktomi. Heath must not have returned—something which filled her with a mixture of emotions ranging from happiness to frustration. She assumed that Iktomi remained out keeping tabs on the other two humans. Alexia sat on the single seat, a construct made of wood, and fabric. The other two sat on the ground, huddled close to a fire that blazed away in the ring of large stones. The flames were bright against the nighttime darkness. The sight of it made Toylona wary.

"You've said you're out here because of recent sightings of those creatures," Ursula asked Alexia. "When did the last one take place?"

"Only about a month ago. That's the most recent that I'm aware of, anyway," Alexia answered. "A pair of hikers heard wood-knocking. About half an hour later, they saw a sasquatch watching them from behind a tree."

Guy rubbed his hands together for warmth. "Did it chase them?"

Alexia shook her head. "No, it just watched them. The hikers were far enough away from it that they didn't feel threatened. Evidently, the sasquatch felt the same. They stood there, and watched it look at them for a few seconds. Then the sasquatch ducked fully behind the tree. They didn't see it again after that."

"That's all?" Ursula asked.

"That's it. Most sightings are shorter than that one. Most encounters with these creatures are brief, and from a distance. In the vast majority of cases, as soon as the sasquatch realizes that it's been spotted, it walks—or runs—away."

"So they never attack humans?" Guy inquired.

"Rarely," Alexia corrected. "The most famous case of an attack happened at a place in Washington State that's known as Ape Canyon. It's right next to Mount Saint Helens, so the area changed a lot when that volcano erupted back in nineteen-eighty."

Ursula scooted infinitesimally closer to the fire. "When did the attack happen?"

"Nineteen-twenty-four," Alexia answered. "In July of that year. A group of men were there, prospecting. One of them told the others that he shot and killed a sasquatch, saying that the body had fallen over a cliff. Because of the man's convenient story as to why he couldn't produce the corpse of the creature he claimed to have gunned down, the other men laughed off his story."

"It was real, though?" Ursula asked.

Alexia tossed a couple of pieces of wood onto the fire. Bright sparks swirled up. When they settled, she continued.

"It seems so. That night, the men were assaulted. They were sharing a single cabin. A group of sasquatch attacked the building—throwing rocks at it, shrieking and screeching, sometimes even running up to shake the cabin. At least one sasquatch even climbed onto the roof," Alexia said. She kept her voice low. "They later stated that one of the sasquatch even managed to reach inside, after knocking out some chinking between logs, and grab the handle of an axe. The axe got caught, and someone took a shot at the creature's arm, so it dropped the axe and withdrew."

Guy leaned closer, tense. "How many of the prospectors were killed?"

"None," Alexia told him. "They had guns. They shot through windows, and holes in the chinking. Apparently, that kept them from being overrun. When the sun came up the next morning, the group of sasquatch left."

Ursula took her mate's hand. "I trust the men did, too?"

Alexia nodded. "Yes. They fled. They didn't even bother to take their equipment back with them. They abandoned everything, and just ran."

Guy tightened his grip on his Ursula's fingers. "I don't blame them."

Alexia watched them closely. "My point in telling you this story is to help you realize that sasquatch don't often attack humans unprovoked. In the Ape Canyon incident, a human killed a sasquatch. Because of that, other sasquatch retaliated. In most cases in which attacks have happened, it's because humans acted as the aggressors first."

"Most, but not all," Guy pointed out.

Alexia fiddled with a twig from the wood pile. "I've mentioned the sub-species that we tend to find in the southern part of the United States. They will sometimes attack vehicles." She held up a hand as her companions both opened their mouths at the same time. "Even then, look at it from the point of view of the creatures. Humans keep encroaching further into their territory, depleting resources that the creatures need to survive. Frankly, I'm surprised we don't see more attacks by them against humans."

Looking uneasy, Alexia went on. "I will admit, despite having told you so many times that sasquatch are harmless to humans..."

"What?" Guy asked, putting an arm around Ursula. "There's something you haven't told us. Right?"

Alexia nodded.

Guy grunted softly. "Something connected to the Ape Canyon story?"

"Not really."

Ursula scooted a bit closer to the fire. "What, then? Tell us."

After inhaling deeply, and letting the breath out slowly, Alexia said, "There is an account, from well over a century ago, of a pair of trappers going into territory Native Americans claimed belonged to sasquatch. They realized the Natives were right. After a few days the trappers decided to leave. They didn't feel safe there."

"What happened?" Ursula asked.

"On their final day there," Alexia said, "the trappers split up. One went to gather up the traps they had laid out. The other man remained to pack up camp. It was evening when the first man returned. He found the other man dead."

The other two humans shuddered. "A bigfoot killed him?" Ursula asked.

Alexia nodded. "The signs pointed to that. According to the man's story, which he filed after hiking out of the wilderness, his partner's neck had been broken, and the corpse had been rolled on by something very large."

"The way a dog will do?" Guy inquired.

Nodding, Alexia said, "That's what it seemed like to the survivor. But, that was a long, long time ago—back before America had even become the country we know today. Look at it from the point of view of the sasquatch. Two humans invading its home territory, stealing its resources. It's understandable why one would react as that one apparently did."

"I want out of here," Guy put in. "Now. There's more that you're not telling us, too. I can see it on your face. These things are a deadly threat. I know it. Ursula knows it. You know it. Heath knows it, too. That's why he's hunting them."

"Don't even get me started on Heath," Alexia replied.

"Guy's right," Ursula said. "There's something else you're keeping from us. What is it?"

Alexia sighed. "I didn't want to frighten you more."

"It isn't working," Ursula told her. "Tell us."

After another heavy sigh, Alexia said, "Some people believe that sasquatch hunt people. For food, I mean. Some Native American and Native Canadian tribes refer to sasquatch as cannibals. They claim sasquatch will feed on humans. To this day there are places where, because of that, men refuse to allow women or children outside unattended by at least one man. They're even more insistent upon that if there have been recent sightings of a sasquatch anywhere nearby. "

"What?" Guy shouted. "And all this time you've been telling us that these monsters are harmless?" He tightened his arm around his mate.

Holding up a hand, Alexia said, "People go missing every year in the wild. Hikers. Backpackers. Campers. People out for picnics, fishing, or walking wilderness trails. Even if those trails are clearly marked, and not truly unknown wild terrain, people will still wander off of the pathways to get lost. It happens all the time. Not all of them are found."

"But..." Ursula prompted.

"Sometimes," Alexia went on, "evidence has been found that something...happened to them. Once in a while bodies, or body parts, will be found."

Ursula shot a wide-eyed look at Guy, and snuggled against him. Guy held her even more tightly.

"Tell us," Guy said.

Poking at the fire with the long stick, sending a spray of

orange sparks swirling, Alexia said, "People have been found with their heads missing. Sometimes arms or legs. At times the body parts have shown signs of having been partially eaten. Sometimes when this has happened, the area has been littered with sasquatch tracks. Once, a man's body ended up being found with the head missing. The head was found shortly thereafter—a few dozen yards away. No tracks led from the rest of the corpse to the head. The impression was that the head had been thrown from the kill-site, and landed where it ended up being found. That alone ought to rule out the killer being a bear, or any other more mundane wildlife."

Ursula wretched a bit. Guy shivered.

"Has anyone ever done any testing on these partially-eaten body parts?" Guy asked. His voice remained low, holding a tremor. "Maybe DNA testing? If a bigfoot ate part of the body, it may have left saliva behind."

Stirring the fire a bit more with the stick, Alexia answered, "Not that I'm aware of. It's possible, though. I know the government knows a lot more about sasquatch than they let on to the general public."

"You've talked about that before. How do you know that?" Ursula asked.

"When kill-sites like I told you about before have been found," Alexia responded, "government workers, or the military, or sometimes both, have blocked off the area. They've been known to arrest and question and hunters, hikers, people fishing, or campers they find in the area. Though the people are normally told not to speak a word of what they've been asked or told afterward, some have. Reports have leaked out due to that. Some of these people have even gotten close enough to see the kill-sites, and add those details to their reports to sasquatch researchers. I've also spoken to people who do, or have, worked for the US Forestry Service, and other governmental organizations. Some of them have told me about their own sightings of sasquatch, and how standard government policy is not only to not talk about such occurrences, but also to encourage those witnesses to simply forget that they've seen anything."

"Wow," muttered Ursula.

Nodding, Alexia said, "What's more, I've been told by some of those same sources that the US Forestry Service keeps reports of sasquatch on file—for all of about a year or so, before they're destroyed. A couple of the employees who have spoken to me claim that the United States government is fully aware that sasquatch are roaming the woods. They don't want that knowledge out there with the general public, though."

"So you've said before," Ursula commented. "People have a right to know about the danger."

Alexia shrugged. "Some people in the government don't want the public to know they've been lied to. I mean, if the government admits one lie, it implies that they've lied about other things, too. It'll make people wonder what else we're not being told. And, if people knew for sure sasquatch were real, it would raise all sorts of issues regarding evolution, and religion. No one seems willing to open that can of worms. On top of those things, add what we talked about earlier regarding the logging corporations."

Guy nodded. "I'd be perfectly happy to be able to go back to not knowing about them. I'd like to be able to go on thinking that they're nothing more than stories, and that anyone who actually believes in them is stupid, or gullible."

"But you can't," Alexia said.

"No," he replied. "I can't."

Ursula shook her head slowly. "Neither can I."

Muffled shouts made Toylona hunker down lower. The noise came from the direction of Dane's encampment. A few moments later, the humans before her noticed the sounds, turning to look, too.

"What's he saying?" Ursula asked, standing up.

"I can't tell," Alexia said. "Something's wrong, though."

Guy got up, facing the same direction as the females. "He's moving this way."

"Dane?" Alexia called out. "What's wrong? What

happened? Are you and Tabatha okay?"

Dane rushed into sight through the trees at the edge of the encampment. Twigs, and bits of leaves and bark clung to his hair, and the coverings he wore on his body. His eyes were wide, and Toylona could easily smell the fear coming off him in heavy waves. He carried a light that swung from a thin handle.

"Alexia, I need help! Tabatha needs help! It took her!" Dane nearly screamed.

She glanced at Guy and Ursula, and then refocused on Dane. "What happened?"

"It took her!" Dane shouted. "It took Tabatha!"

Alexia shook him. "What took her?"

"A Forest God!"

Sagging, Alexia clung to Dane for support. "Are you really telling me that a sasquatch took Tabatha?" She took the light from him, holding it higher, staring at his face.

"Yes! She had to relieve herself before going to bed! She went behind a tree, and vanished!"

"How do you know it was a sasquatch?"

"We saw it a few minutes before! There are tracks leading away from where she was taken!"

Guy pressed forward. "You saw it again?"

Alexia pushed Guy back. She turned again to Dane. "Are you sure?"

"Yes! Shortly after we saw it, Tabatha went behind one of the trees nearest the edge of camp. When she didn't return, or answer me when I called out to her, I went over. She's gone. Her lantern was still there, but she's gone! There are prints on the ground. She was taken by a Forest God!"

Alexia, Guy, and Ursula stared at him, open-mouthed.

Dane looked at them, pleading. "You have to help me find her!"

Turning away from Dane, Alexia kicked dirt over the fire, snuffing it. "Ursula? Guy? Grab your guns!" She snatched up her own. After handing the light back to Dane, she rushed into the shelter. When she came back out, she carried a pair of lights similar to Dane's. She passed one to Ursula, and kept the other for herself.

Guy snatched the light from Ursula, holding it as high as he could. He peered around, shaking, and wide-eyed. "Wait!" he shouted. "You can't expect us to go running off into the woods, at night, chasing a monster!" He shook, and his eyes had gone wide. "Not for some girl we don't even know!"

"Guy!" admonished his mate. "She needs our help!"

He stared at Ursula. "It's too dangerous! We can't do this!"

Dane grabbed him by the front of the body coverings over his chest, jerking him so hard that Guy nearly came up off his feet. "Tabatha needs your help!" he raged.

Alexia pulled Guy free of Dane's grasp. "We're going to help her, Dane. We're leaving right now."

"Speak for yourself," Guy muttered.

Ursula scowled at him. "You're coming, too."

"Why?" he shot back.

"Because I'm going with Alexia and Dane to help that poor girl. If you don't come, too, I'll be out there without you. Do you want me to face this without you?"

"No."

"Also," she went on, "you'll be left here, alone, with that monster creeping around in the dark. Do you want that?"

"No."

"Then grab your gun, and come on!" Ursula yelled.

Abashed, Guy nodded, standing ready.

"Let's go," Alexia told Dane.

Dane turned away, hurrying out of her camp. The others followed. Between the four of them, they carried three lights and as many guns.

Toylona didn't know what had them so worked up, but the thought of what they might do with their weapons made her bristle. Forcibly, she smoothed her hair back down, hoping that Iktomi had gone somewhere well away from all of the excitement.

Baring her teeth, she thought again of Heath. The others

were acting more and more like him. Maybe all of the humans were more threatening than Iktomi thought. Maybe she should take it upon herself to make sure none of them posed a danger to any of her people. Iktomi wouldn't like it. But she could live with that as long as she kept him, and their young ones safe. If they split up, she just might make a move.

Debating on the best way to proceed if given that chance, she tailed the humans as they rushed off toward Dane's encampment. If she did opt to take action against them, it wouldn't be the first time one of their kind had resorted to such things against humans. Most didn't like to do so, but some saw the wisdom in it. More and more, Toylona did, too.

CHAPTER 17

Toylona watched Alexia push her way past Guy and Ursula, her light held high, and her gun gripped tightly. All four humans looked to be on high alert, seemingly trying to look everywhere at once. Dane crouched down, running his fingers over the grass.

"This is where she vanished," he told the others.

Alexia squatted, looking more closely at the ground. "You were right about the prints."

"Over there," Dane said, pointing, "is where I found the clearer tracks."

Tugging at Alexia, he led her to an enormous pine tree. He knelt, indicating the marks in the dirt.

"I've heard of abductions like this before," he lamented, "but didn't think they ever actually happened!"

"Wait," Guy said as he and his mate hurried over. "What? This is common?" He glared at Alexia.

"In British Columbia, Canada," Dane said, "in nineteen-twenty-four, a prospector claimed to have been abducted by them. He said he ended up being held captive by a family unit of these beings for six days before managing to get away."

Guy shuddered, and glowered at Alexia. "Nineteen-twenty-four? Isn't the same year that story you told my wife and I about Ape Canyon happened?"

"It is," she confirmed.

Ursula watched the darkness around them nervously. "The bigfoot were busy that year."

"They took that man," Guy said to Dane, "but didn't eat him?"

Dane shot a questioning look at Alexia, replying, "No. He said in his reports that it seemed as if they were keeping him as a pet." His shoulders began shaking. "Many Native American tribes—here in the lower forty-eight states, as well as up in Alaska—still refuse to allow women and children outside without a male escort. That's because of the number of such kidnappings that have been reported over the years." Tears welled, rolling down his cheeks, sparkling in the illumination from the lights. "I never thought those accounts were true! I thought they were just stories made up to frighten people. How could I have let her out of my sight? I knew the creature was nearby!"

Alexia put her free hand on his shoulder. When she spoke, she kept her tone soothing. "We'll get her back. She'll be okay."

"Talking isn't accomplishing anything!" Dane cried out. "We need to find Tabatha—now!'

Alexia laid a gentle hand on his chest. "There isn't much we can do right now. It's too dark. We'll have to start looking for her in the morning."

"No! We need to find her!"

"And we will," she told him. "It isn't going to do us any good to be stumbling around the woods in the dark, though. We'll lose the trail, get ourselves hurt, or both."

Guy uttered a hoarse grunt. "I still say we need to just get out of here."

Ursula slapped him on the shoulder in a hard warning blow. She turned to Dane. "We'll find her. Alexia is right, though. We'll be better off to wait until daylight."

"Come on," Alexia ordered. She turned, retracing their steps.

Dane rushed to her side. "Where are we going?"

"Back to my camp for some sleep. Once the sun is up, we'll come back here, pick up the trail, and find Tabatha."

"Why don't we stay in my camp?" Dane suggested.

"My tent has more room. I also brought more survival equipment out with me than you did."

"I'll stay in my own camp, then. You three go to yours. We'll meet up back here at sun-up."

Alexia shook her head. "No way, Dane. Soon as we're out of sight, you'll go charging off after Tabatha."

"Someone needs to!"

"Not in the dark," Ursula interjected, backing up Alexia.

Nodding to the older female, Alexia told Dane, "You're coming back with us. This way we'll know you're not running off in the dark. In the morning, we'll all come back here. Together, we'll pick up the trail."

Dane sighed before nodding slowly. He turned, plodding slowly back the way they had come. The others trailed after him. Each of them peered intently into the darkness beyond the reach of their lights.

Toylona kept low, moving slowly, determined not to allow the humans a single clue to warn them of her presence.

She continued debating her options. Should she attack the humans if they split up? But what had happened to Tabatha? She could smell the other female strongly around Dane's encampment. Yet there had been no further sign of her. Iktomi's scent had also been strong; he had been there recently. But where had he gone? After Tabatha? But the female had been injured. Seemingly, she could barely walk. Where had she managed to go?

Dane had also seemed very upset. Could that be due to Tabatha's absence? Were the two so closely linked? And if Dane cared so much for the female to cry when not with her, that cast a whole new light on her feelings toward that particular human. If humans could be so emotional, and feel so much, so strongly, how would she feel about attacking them? Especially Dane, who had been the one to display such feeling?

Once returned to Alexia's encampment, Toylona slipped into place behind a screening of dense vegetation. Settling in, she continued her vigil.

"Who's sharing my tent with me?" Alexia asked. "We can fit two, maybe three, in there."

Dane began pacing the camp, looking forlornly into the black woods. "I won't be able to sleep. I'll stay out here. Someone needs to keep watch for some sign of Tabatha. What if she gets away on her own?"

Guy joined Dane, walking back and forth with him. "I'll stay with him. We need to maintain a guard. That monster has already stolen one person. Who knows when it'll be back for more!"

Alexia sighed. "Ursula, the tent is all yours. I'll stay out here with these two. Someone needs to make sure they don't go running off."

Ursula shook her head. "No, Alexia. It's your tent. Get some sleep. I'll stay out here with the men. If they try to leave, I'll stop them. If I can't stop them alone, I'll shout for you."

Eyeing the older woman, Alexia asked, "Are you sure?"

Ursula nodded.

Alexia hesitated. When she yawned, she ducked her head. Without another word, she slipped into the shelter, sealing it behind her.

"It must've had a reason," Toylona heard Alexia mutter. "Probably not for food. Almost certainly not as a mate—though there are reports of that happening. Why did it take her?"

Guy and Ursula built a new fire with in the ring of stones, working by the illumination of the artificial lights. As they did so, they watched Dane closely. Once the flames were burning, they extinguished the hand-held lights.

Toylona yawned. Her trek up the mountain to ensure that her young were safe, followed by the trip back, and the time spent following the humans around had left her worn out. How had Iktomi managed to keep up with them for days? She lay down on some soft moss. She would do as her mate had done, and sleep near the humans. The moss would help keep her warm. Should any of the humans venture from the encampment, the noise they made would wake her. Humans didn't belong in the woods. Even when they tried to be stealthy they made almost as much noise as an enraged mother bear when she charged through the brush.

She woke to the sound of Dane's voice calling, "Alexia, the sun is up! Come on! Let's get going! Tabatha needs us!"

Faint weak rays of sunlight filtered though the limbs above her. Toylona rolled over, grunting softly. Her breath fogged the chilly morning air. Her stomach growled. She would need to forage for food while watching the humans. She hoped they opted to wander the woods, allowing her to do so easily.

Sounds of Alexia's stirring came from inside her shelter. Soon, the entry unsealed with the usual stuttered snoring noise. Alexia pushed her way through the flaps, rubbing her eyes.

"Come on!" Dane said, already striding away.

Guy began kicking dirt at the fire. Alexia waved a hand at him, shooing him back from the struggling flames.

"What we need," she said, squinting against the brightening light in the sky, "is breakfast."

"There's no time!" protested Dane.

"We're going to set out after a creature that is bigger, faster, and stronger than us. We'll be doing a lot of walking today, most likely. We need food."

Physically dragging Guy away from the fire, Alexia returned to her shelter. She emerged carrying various items, and set to work. After a brief time, Toylona realized she was preparing food. The smells coming from the flat-bottomed metal piece resting over the fire made her stomach rumble louder.

Dane sulked off to one side, dropping listlessly to the ground. Alexia ignored him, concentrating on her work.

Ursula traded a quick glance with her mate. She then moved toward Alexia with tiny, hesitant steps. "There's something Guy and I need to tell you."

Alexia paused, looking from the older female, to her husband. "What might that be?"

"We're leaving," Guy told her.

"What?" Dane shouted, leaping up. "You can't! There are only four of us! We need to find Tabatha! The more of us who are out looking for her—"

Guy cut across his words. "I don't care about that little bimbo! I care about myself, and my wife! We're getting out of here."

"I can't guide you out," Alexia said. "Finding Tabatha is more important."

Ursula nodded. "We thought you'd say that. We'll take our chances. Just point us in the right direction."

Dane grabbed Guy by the shoulders. "You can't do this!"

Guy shoved him away forcefully. "We can. We are. Deal with it." He turned to his wife. "After breakfast, we're gone. Understood? No more excuses."

Ursula nodded. "I fully agree. It's gotten far too dangerous out here."

Dane sagged.

Toylona bared her teeth at Guy. The display of aggression against Dane, after the younger male's display of emotion the night before, upset her. If she did chose to attack the humans, maybe she would take Guy and Heath, but leave Dane alone. Tabatha, too. She remained undecided in regards to Alexia and Ursula.

Alexia put a hand on Dane's arm. She frowned at the hunters. "I understand. You want to look out for yourselves. Before you go, though, just think of how badly you'll feel if Tabatha is never found. Or if she's found just a bit too late."

Dane's breath hitched.

Ursula hung her head, turning away.

Guy glared at Alexia. "We've made out position clear. We need to look out for ourselves."

"Uh-huh," Alexia said. "Let me make myself clear on something, too. I'm under no obligation to help you—be it feeding you, giving you directions, or anything else."

Guy squinted at her. "What do you mean?"

Alexia squared her shoulders, staring him down. "I mean you can get out of my camp. Right now."

"Without food?" Guy protested.

"That's right," she said, starting to scoop food from the metal thing over the fire. She put it on two round, flat things, and handed one to Dane. Hot food steamed in the cool morning air. "We need to start looking for Tabatha. We need the supplies to look after ourselves and her. You two are no longer part of this group, therefore no longer entitled to anything of mine."

Sputtering, Guy almost choked on his rage. His face turned a color midway between red and purple. "You can't just send us off with nothing, not even a direction to move in!"

"Dane," Alexia muttered, "get them out of here. If you need my rifle to help with that, feel free."

Eyes wide, Ursula tugged at her husband's arm. "Let's go. We'll be okay. If we're not, Alexia, just think how you'll feel!"

"I'll feel fine, knowing that I didn't abandon the person who has the least knowledge of how to survive outdoors. I'll feel fine, knowing that I didn't just write off the person who was kidnapped by some form of barely-known primate in the woods," she replied, without looking up from her meal. She ate by moving pieces of food to her mouth with an odd pronged piece of metal. Toylona cocked her head, wondering why Alexia didn't simply pick up her food with her fingers.

Guy and Ursula stared at her for a long moment before turning away.

Dane slipped into the fabric shelter. When he emerged, he held a long gun.

The pair of older humans glanced back as they stepped from the clearing. Both frowned and glared. Then they were gone, vanished amongst the trees.

Toylona briefly thought of going after them, but dismissed the idea. Dane had driven them off, further proving himself to her. Alexia seemed to have been a part of that, too, though she took no physical action. Again, Toylona wished she understood the strange speech of these odd creatures. Hopefully, Guy and Ursula were gone for good.

"Do you think they'll come back?" Dane asked.

Alexia nodded. "I think they'll either wait until we leave to come back, and raid my camp for supplies, or circle around to yours now."

"Let them take whatever they want of mine." His tone held only tension. "I just want Tabatha safe. Nothing else matters."

"Are you in love with her? You just met her, but..."

"No, I'm not."

"Then why are you so bent on finding her?"

He sighed. "She was in my camp. She depended on me to keep her safe. I let her down."

Alexia looked up from her food, focusing on him. "It's more to it than that. Tell me the truth."

Dane glanced away, then back. "I can't believe the Forest Gods would do this! I've heard the stories, but..." He wiped his eyes. "I can't believe they'd kidnap someone!"

"They're not the beings you thought they were," she said quietly. "That's upsetting to you. I get it."

Nodding, he told her, "When you first started setting up your trail cameras, I followed you. I've gone around since then, and wiped the memory cards."

She stared up at him, stiff with anger. "You did what? Why?"

"To protect the Forest Gods! If proof—or even decent photos or video—turns up, people would be crawling all over these forests. People like Guy and Ursula, and Heath, who only want to kill them. Heath wants to kill one to throw the body at the scientific community. Those other two are terrified of the Forest Gods, and want to kill them due to that. I just want to keep the Forest Gods safe! At least I did..."

"But one of these beings that you practically worship just kidnapped the woman you could be falling for."

"Yes!" he wailed.

Alexia gave him a brief hug. "We'll find her."

"How can you know that?"

She sighed. "I don't. I just really, really hope that we do." She drew Dane close against her, holding him.

Toylona watched, her estimation of Alexia rising as well. Clearly, something had upset Dane. Guy and Ursula had been driven off; they must've had something to do with Dane's current state. Alexia obviously wanted to offer comfort.

Then her brow furrowed. Dane had said the names of Guy, Ursula, and Heath. Despite previous appearances, were those three enemies of Alexia and Dane? And how did Tabatha fit in? Human social structure was still a total mystery to her. Maybe Dane, Tabatha, and Alexia needed to be protected from Heath, Ursula, and Guy. Pondering that idea, Toylona settled back again. She watched Alexia and Dane consume the warm food, trying to ignore her own empty belly.

CHAPTER 18

Iktomi stared down at Tabatha. She lay on her back, resting in the shelter he, Toylona and their offspring had built some time ago. Brown, dead woody vines had been used, woven into three walls, and a curved roof. The shelter reached to Iktomi's waist, requiring them to crawl inside of it. Given the thin, green vines creeping over it, the shelter had become nearly invisible from even a few steps away in the heavy growths of ferns that surrounded it.

He didn't know what else to do with the young female. At one point during the night, she had woken briefly, seen him, screamed, and went to sleep again. As yet, she had not woken a second time. Could this be normal for humans? Little as he knew about them, he still didn't think so.

Toylona might be able to help, but he had been unable to locate her. Twice, he had crossed her trail, another time he had picked up her scent. But he hadn't been able to locate her as yet, and hadn't felt comfortable devoting much time to doing so carrying Tabatha. He had no way of knowing if being carried might hurt her further. Given Toylona's time and knowledge caring for their young, she might know of a way to help the human. He only needed to find her.

Leaning back, Iktomi inhaled deeply, and let out a brief, high-pitched cry, calling for his mate. After a few moments, he loosed another, and then a third. Falling silent, he crouched low, listening for a reply. When none came, he stood tall, and repeated the summons.

Again, he heard nothing. Either Toylona had wandered out of earshot, or she didn't feel safe enough in her present location to reply.

He turned back to Tabatha, wondering if he should leave her to go seek out his mate. Before deciding, he heard leaves rustle, and crouched low. He closed his eyes to mere slits, and held his breath.

A scuffing sound came from deeper in the woods. He inhaled, grimacing upon detecting Heath's scent. The human still hunted him. Probably, he had been close enough to hear Iktomi's calls to Toylona. He had evidently followed the sounds toward Iktomi.

Heath posed a great danger. Though both Heath and Tabatha were human, Iktomi didn't feel safe leaving her with him. He rose slowly, slipping further away from the shelter where Tabatha lay. For the first time he hoped Tabatha wouldn't wake soon. If she did, she might lead Heath right to her.

Once Iktomi had positioned himself on the opposite side of Heath from the shelter, he let out another cry. A sharp intake of air told him that Heath had heard him. Footsteps moved slowly in his direction.

Iktomi moved further away, zigzagging, remembering Heath's gun. When the human called back, answering with a pale imitation of Iktomi's own vocalization, he nearly laughed. He moved further from Tabatha, responding to Heath's call. Heath answered again, following.

Humans! They made it too easy.

Iktomi half-walked, and half-slid down into a narrow, stony ravine. A thin, cold stream coursed through the middle of it. He took care to step over as much vegetation as he could. Let Heath wonder exactly where he had gone. The fewer signs of his passage that he allowed the human to find, the more driven Heath would probably be to locate him. Iktomi planned to draw him onward, well away from Tabatha, before shaking him off, and circling back to the female.

He followed the water upstream for a ways before leaving it to make his way up the steep side of the defile, returning to the thicker woods. Four more times Heath called out to him, mimicking the calls Iktomi had used prior to try communicating with Toylona. Each time Iktomi ignored him. Only when he heard the sounds of the human well off in the wrong direction did he cry out again.

Instantly, Heath changed course, the sounds of his passage in the forest getting closer once more. Iktomi took to the trees, moving from a heavy limb in one tree, to one in its neighbor. He covered a large tract of ground without ever setting foot upon the soil. He purposely allowed Heath to lag behind. He only wanted to tease his hunter, not risk being injured—or worse—by him. He took care not to completely lose the human, though, wanting to string him along.

"Tabatha is out here somewhere," a voice lamented. "I should've found her long before this!"

Iktomi paused, holding tight to the trunk of the tree, balanced perfectly on the broad limb. The voice sounded male, but not that of Dane, Guy, or Heath. Barring his teeth in frustration, he sniffed. The scent didn't match any of those three, either.

Another human! And he had spoken Tabatha's name.

Allowing himself a quiet groan, Iktomi angled toward the voice. He remained in the trees for as long as possible, reluctant to leave any footprints in the presence of this new threat. When he heard Heath getting closer, Iktomi pulled the largest pinecone in his reach down. He flung the seed pod far to one side—away from his current location, but away from Tabatha, too.

He held still, listening. Heath's footsteps paused as the thrown pinecone bounced off a tree, and fell to the forest floor. The noises Heath made told Iktomi that the human had turned away, going to investigate. Good; that left Iktomi free to worry about this newest arrival.

The new voice continued, saying, "I couldn't follow the trail in the dark. It isn't my fault. I shouted her for her. She should've stayed closer. She doesn't know the woods. She had no business going so far from camp."

Iktomi found the newcomer when the human walked by almost directly beneath the branch he stood perched on. This new lean male looked younger than Dane and Heath—far younger than Guy. As the others were, he had come to the forest clad in odd coverings on his body that reeked of unnatural odors, and had colored patterns that blended with the forest. Also, as the others all tended to do, this one spoke aloud to himself, as if to another.

"Wandering in the deep forest at night like that is crazy. Why did you wander off? No one can blame me for going back to camp, and waiting until morning to look for you again. It's not my fault you got yourself so lost that I still haven't been able to find you!"

Grinning, he watched the young male pass out of sight, and into heavier tree cover. He followed easily, drawn by the human's scents and the noise he made as he walked.

Pausing, the young inhaled deeply, and shouted, "Tabatha! Are you there? Can you hear me? Tabatha!"

Iktomi winced, his ears hurting from the volume of the outcry. The human might be unimpressive physically, but he could more than make up for it in vocalizations. Iktomi hoped that Heath had moved far enough away so as not to hear, and be drawn back in his direction.

The young human waited briefly, listening, before whispering, "Where are you? What if I can't find you? If I leave you out here, no one will ever forgive me—myself included. But I can't just stay out here looking for you forever."

He trudged onward. Iktomi followed, keeping to the closely-packed trees. He moved slowly, only just keeping the newcomer in sight. He didn't want the scrape of his foot on a branch, or a bit of falling bark, to alert the other of his presence above and behind him.

The sharp crack of a gunshot made Iktomi and his quarry pause. Iktomi wondered if Heath had been the one to use his weapon.

"Murdering hunters," the human grunted. "I'd love to

see someone design a gun that deer can use, and teach them how to use it. We'd see what you redneck Neanderthals think of your bloody 'sport' then."

The human moved on. Iktomi listened to the last fading echo of the shot, hoping that his mate and children were okay. If they weren't, no gun would stop him from having revenge upon the human who had hurt them. He trusted Toylona to keep herself, and their young, all safe. Still, things happened sometimes that were out of anyone's control.

When the newcomer had progressed far enough that even the sounds of his passing were hard to hear, Iktomi moved after him. He had said Tabatha's name several times. Iktomi suspected he and she were linked. This new human didn't carry a gun, so Iktomi doubted he posed much of a threat. Still, he knew so little about humans that he wanted to be sure. It wasn't just his own family that concerned him. Others of their people called the area home. Human intruders were a potential threat to them all. The more they could learn about the humans who had invaded the area, the better off they all would be.

****

Alexia and Dane made their way through a particularly dense patch of woods. Dane's expression remained so downtrodden that even Toylona had no problems understanding that the human remained deeply saddened.

"We're not going to find her," he muttered.

Alexia grimaced. "Quit saying that."

He waved a hand at the ground. "The Forest God has hidden his tracks! We've barely found a trace since he took Tabatha!"

"They're good at that, yes," she told him. "This one is doing the same—avoiding leaving tracks when it can."

Dane nodded. "Exactly. Without a path to follow, we'll never find her. You're a better tracker than I am, and you can barely find any sign of this creature!"

Sighing, Alexia forced out the words, "Much as I hate to admit it, we need Heath. He's one of the best trackers I know of, and he's in the area."

Toylona barred her teeth in a silent snarl upon hearing Heath's name.

Dane remained quiet for long moments before nodding, his eyes tearing up. "Let's go find Heath. Tabatha could be hurt. We need to find her as soon as we can."

"His camp is in that direction," Alexia told him, pointing. "At least that's the way he went when he left my camp."

She angled that way. Dane followed without a word.

Following, Toylona pondered what she had heard. They had talked of Heath; that much she knew. Why the abrupt change in their direction?

"I still can't figure out why the sasquatch would have taken Tabatha," Alexia said.

Dane shook his head. "I hope he doesn't hurt her."

"Me, too. You're positive the creature is male?"

"No," he replied. "This is like some horrible, low-budged B-movie! Sasquatch carrying off a vulnerable young woman? It's ridiculous!"

"According to Native American lore, it's happened before. Apparently it has again."

His expression grew longer. A tear tracked down his cheek. "I shouldn't have let her out of my sight."

Alexia gently laid her free hand on his shoulder, gripping her weapon with her other. "She'll be okay. We'll find Heath. Together, we'll find her."

"And the Forest God will likely die. Heath will shoot if he gets half a chance to do so."

"In all likelihood, yes. But, it's threatening humans. We need to protect ourselves. Even if the creature hasn't harmed Tabatha at all, you know Heath. He wants to drop the body at the feet of scientists. He's driven by that chance at getting his name into the history books."

Dane sniffled a bit. "If that happens, at least we might be able to use that confirmation to get protection for the rest of the species."

"Let's hope so," she answered.

They continued through the trees, Toylona trailing after them. The repeated usage of Heath's name had filled her with rage. Alexia and Dane might not be the threats she and Iktomi had first thought them to be. But Heath, she had become convinced, more than made up for it. She debated further on whether or not to kill him if given the chance.

CHAPTER 19

Iktomi followed the new human, still pondering what to do about him, when a familiar scent registered. The smell instantly put him on full alert. It belonged to Heath. Iktomi couldn't yet see him, but he knew Heath lurked somewhere nearby.

The newcomer continued on, Iktomi trailing after him, hidden by the scrub and trees. Heath's scent grew stronger. The realization that they were headed directly toward Heath made Iktomi pause, thinking.

Could there be a connection between Heath, and this new arrival? Were they working together? The new human said Tabatha's name several times, but that told him nothing. Maybe he and Toylona were wrong about the names. Maybe the things they had been calling the various humans weren't really what they called themselves. Regardless, the nearness of the new one in comparison to Heath made Iktomi very wary of him. He hung back, tracking more by sound, and smell than by sight.

"Hello?" the new human called out. "Anybody there?"

Iktomi heard a grunt from Heath, followed by the distinct stuttering snore that signified the opening of one of the humans' artificial shelters. After he had last seen him, Iktomi realized, Heath must have given up the chase, and circled back to his encampment.

"Who are you?" Heath asked.

"My name is Ray Marque," the newcomer answered. "I'm glad to have finally found someone."

"Ray, huh?" Heath replied. "Lost?"

Iktomi frowned. Despite not being fully sure, having something to call each human simplified things a little. Having already heard the word twice in the brief exchange between the two, he opted to call the newcomer Ray.

"Not me, no," Ray went on. "I came out to the woods with someone. She's lost. Her name is Tabatha. She's a blonde with blue eyes, and—"

"I know her," Heath broke in. Even to Iktomi's ears the disgust weighed heavily in his voice.

Ray exhaled slightly. "You do? You've met her?"

"Yes."

"Is she here? In your camp, I mean?"

"No," Heath answered. "Last I knew, she was with a woman named Alexia Hollander. They were in Alexia's camp. I can give you directions."

Iktomi sagged slightly. Every time he left Alexia, another trail took him right back there. And now her name had just come up again. Is that were Heath and Ray were going to go? The human female's name had been spoken. He settled down to watch, and wait to see what they would do.

****

Alexia led Dane through the woods. "We don't know where Heath is camped for sure. All we know is the direction he went in when he left my camp. Since I can't follow the trail well enough, we can either spend the time trying to find Heath—who probably will be able to follow it—or try tracking the creature ourselves, and probably not find it."

"Or Tabatha," Dane lamented. "Either way, we're losing time."

Alexia climbed over a moss-covered log, waiting for Dane on the other side. "This way, I think, we'll lose less time."

"Only if we can find Heath's camp quickly."

"True."

Toylona bared her teeth. Heath, again. Even with the most aggressive member of the group off elsewhere, his name came up over and again. They had driven him off. Why keep mentioning him? Did they expect him to return? Had he done something to stir them from the encampment that she had simply been unaware of?

Dane strode half a dozen steps before pausing. He turned back. "Maybe one of us ought to find Heath, while the other goes back to my camp to start at least trying to track the Forest God."

Pulling him back around, Alexia told him, "No. I'm not a great tracker. You're much worse at it than I am. If I go back, odds are I won't be able to find Tabatha on my own. And you'd have to find Heath's camp on by yourself. Can you do that?"

He sighed. "Maybe. I don't know."

"Also," she continued, "you've already tried following the sasquatch. You couldn't. So, if you turn back, you'd just be wasting your time. That might also mean that we'd need to locate you as well as Tabatha. We'll stay together."

Nodding reluctantly, Dane plodded onward. "Tabatha!" he bellowed, hands cupped around his mouth.

"What are you doing?" Alexia asked.

"We don't know where the Forest God took her," Dane told her. "Or if she might have gotten away. She could be wandering in the woods, lost. Calling for her can't hurt."

"It might."

"How?"

Alexia indicated the woodlands around them. "You said it yourself—we have no idea where it took her. The sasquatch could be nearby. Your shouting might alert it to our presence. If that happens, it might hunker down with Tabatha, keeping her hidden. If that happens, we'll be even harder-pressed to find her."

Dane shook his head. "The tracks led off in a different direction from my camp."

"So? What's to say the sasquatch didn't loop around, and

come this way at some point? You know as well as I do how adept they are at avoiding people."

"I still don't think calling out for her can hurt," he retorted. "Tabatha!" he shouted again.

Sighing, Alexia continued on. Dane followed, looking around eagerly. From time to time he called out Tabatha's name again. Each time he did so, his companion flinched, and shot him harsh looks through eyes narrowed to small slits.

****

Iktomi winced, crouching so low that he nearly sat on the ground, when he heard the outcry.

"Tabatha!"

Dane's voice, he realized, and not too far off. The call repeated a few more times before Ray and Heath reacted to it. Each of them turned toward the sound.

Ray bounced on his toes. "Someone else is looking for her?"

"Dane," Heath grunted, his voice low.

"Who is Dane?"

Heath turned away. "Some crack-pot. Ignore him."

"How does he know Tabatha?"

Sighing, Heath replied, "I found your little girlfriend in the woods. She'd hurt her ankle."

Ray spun to face the older male, fists clenched tightly at his sides. "What happened to her?"

Heath shrugged. "She doesn't know the woods. She was lost. She panicked. She'd tripped, and fallen. Don't worry; she didn't get hurt badly. I think she made it sound a lot worse than it was just for the attention and sympathy."

"What does this have to do with her, and this Dane guy?" Ray stepped closer to Heath.

The older, larger male sneered down at him. "I carried

her out. Along the way we met some other people. Dane was one of them. Last I saw of her, they were with her. If Dane is shouting for her like that, I'm guessing she's wandered off again, and gotten lost. Go if you want. I don't have time for this. I'm busy."

Ray stared at Heath for a long moment before turned away. He trotted off in the direction of Dane's calls.

Iktomi hesitated, unsure whether he should remain to keep Heath in sight, or follow Ray. Too many humans had come into the area. It had gotten to be overwhelming. Given that Heath had been hunting him, he thought it might be best to move away from him. Yet Ray didn't seem threatening at all. Iktomi opted to let Ray go in favor of keeping watch on the worse threat.

****

Toylona heard the sounds of the approaching human, and slipped behind a tree. The thin, outreaching lower branches, with their dense clusters of long, thin needles, provided an ample canopy for her to duck beneath, and remain hidden. She held her breath, and narrowed her eyes, waiting. After a few moments, the pair she had been following stopped.

Alexia held up a hand, whispering, "I heard something."

"What?" Dane mouthed back.

Alexia shrugged. "I'm not sure."

Dane slipped by her, as if to press onward. "You probably heard an animal."

"Did you hear it, too?"

"No."

"It didn't sound like an animal call."

"We're in the woods," he said, his voice rising to normal levels. "There are all kinds of sounds out here. Let's go. We're wasting time that we ought to be devoting to finding Tabatha."

A twig snapped. Alexia pointed in the direction of the

noise. Quietly, she said, "That's what I heard before. That time it was closer and louder. Something it out there, and headed this way."

Dane returned to her side. Alexia fingered her gun. She looked quickly at Dane.

"I wish you had a rifle of your own. What we're hearing is probably just a squirrel digging for acorns. What if it's something dangerous—coyote, badger, mountain lion, bobcat, or bear? You need to be prepared, Dane."

He shook his head. "I've gotten along fine in the woods for years without carrying a weapon."

Nodding, Alexia said, "We all do—right up until that one time when we need a gun, and don't have it."

A new voice called out, "Is anyone there? Hello?"

Barring her teeth in a silent snarl, Toylona pressed closer to the tree. Another human! This one male, judging from the timbre of the voice.

"Over here," Alexia replied "I'm armed."

Toylona silently congratulated herself on her reasoning as yet another human male stepped into view. He looked younger than Dane. She judged him to be not much more than a child. He wore the same type of coverings on his body as the other humans who had invaded her family's territory. Such things made the humans a bit harder to spot, but did nothing at all to cover their scents, or the sounds they made.

The new male focused on Dane, saying, "Were you the guy I heard calling for Tabatha?"

Evidently surprised by the question, Dane blinked. "Yes. That was me."

The younger male stepped forward, excited. "Have you found her?"

"No, I'm sorry." Dane met the newcomer halfway. "You're the one she came out camping with?"

"Yes, that's me. My name is Ray Marque. I've been looking for Tabatha ever since she vanished from our camp the other night."

Dane reached a hand toward the younger male, who

156

clutched it in one of his own. "Ray. Good to meet you. I'm Dane Wessler."

The newcomer turned to Alexia, saying, "And you are?"

Alexia slung her gun back over her shoulder. She, too, partook in the odd hand-grasping with the young male, and said, "I'm Alexia Hollander. Nice to meet you, Ray."

Taking in the exchanges, Toylona zeroed in on the word "Ray". Could that be the name of the new male? She decided to think of him as that.

Ray looked around, obviously nervous.

"What is it?" Dane asked.

"You seem frightened," Alexia added.

"I am." Ray swallowed hard.

"Why?" She moved slowly closer to him.

He swallowed harder. "Earlier, I found...signs, let's say...of something else out here. Not someone—something." He looked from Alexia to Dane and back, wide-eyed.

Dane shared a quick look with Alexia before urging, "What did you find?"

Ray swallowed again, peering at the trees around them. "You probably won't believe me."

"We probably will," Alexia pressed. "What did you find?"

"Prints," Ray finally said. "Footprints. Big ones."

Dane leaned forward. "Where?"

"I don't know. Just outside of someone's camp."

Frowning, Dane asked, "What did the camp look like?"

"I don't know; it looked like a camp. It had a small tent, ashes from a fire. A chair was sitting close to where the fire had been." He paused, thinking. "The tracks stopped behind a tree at the edge of the camp."

"Sounds like my camp," Dane replied. "Behind that tree is where I last saw Tabatha."

"And?"

Dane hesitated before turning away.

Alexia inched closer to Ray. "That's when and where we lost Tabatha."

"Lost her? What do you mean?" Ray's voice held a hard

edge.

"She was...taken," Alexia added.

"Taken?" Ray watched her for a moment. He opened his mouth, as if to say more. Then he froze, staring wide-eyed at the other two humans. "Are you telling me that..."

Alexia reached for his shoulder. "You saw the footprints yourself. I'm sorry. Dane and I tried to follow the trail. Neither of us are good enough trackers to do that, though. We're looking for someone else who we know is out here; someone who's a far more skilled tracker than the both of us put together. It's our hope that he can find the creature who took Tabatha."

Ray stared at her for several seconds. "Find the creature, you say. What about Tabatha? Did it hurt her?"

"Probably not," Dane answered, turning back. "We don't know why the Forest God took her, but they aren't violent beings."

"Also," Alexia put in, "we didn't find evidence whatsoever to point toward Tabatha having been injured by it. Far as we know, her only injury is still her twisted ankle."

Nodding, Ray said, "I heard about her ankle from some other guy I met out here. He found her when she had gotten hurt."

"Heath?" Alexia asked. Her hand flinched toward her gun.

Ray looked around. "Yeah. I was actually at his camp, talking to him, when I heard Dane shouting for Tabatha."

Alexia and Dane shared a look. "Heath is close, then." she said.

"Where is Heath's camp?" Dane asked. "Can you take us there, Ray?"

"Sure," the younger male replied. "It's this way."

He set off back the way he had come. The others followed him.

Toylona growled low in her throat. Heath again! Did Ray also have some connection with him? What was it about Heath that every new human she encountered seemed to make mention of him?

As she slipped from her concealment to stay on the trail of the human trio, she again pondered the wisdom of simply eliminating Heath if given the chance.

CHAPTER 20

"Heath! Are you here?"

Iktomi ducked, wide-eyed at the shout. He had been so intent on watching Heath dismantle his gun, and fiddle with the parts, that he hadn't been paying close enough attention to his surroundings.

Keeping low, he tested the air, and listened intently. Three other humans were closing in fast. He knew their scents—Alexia, Dane, and Ray. Now that he paid attention, the trio made enough noise for a herd of panicked deer.

Another scent caught his attention. Toylona was nearby! He slipped back from Heath's encampment, circling around. He let out a very soft, short call every once in a while. When she slipped out of the trees, he caught her in a tight embrace.

"What are you doing here?" he asked her.

She nuzzled him. "Helping you keep watch on these humans. And before you ask, our young ones are safe. They're far up the mountain; don't worry about them." She drew back, snarling now. "As for you, why are you here?"

"Doing the same as you."

She tipped her head toward Heath. "No. Why are you near him? He hunts you!"

"I know. I followed a new human here."

"Ray?"

He stared at her. "You know him?"

She nodded, saying, "I followed him, Alexia, and Dane here. They keep calling for Tabatha. Well, Dane does. I get the impression that they've lost track of her."

Casting a look at the ground, he replied, "They did. I

took her."

Toylona gave him a hard shake. "You did what?"

"Something happened to her! I didn't know what else to do! I had been watching her and Dane. I got too close. Tabatha saw me. She fell, and seemed to be sleeping."

"Dead?"

"No."

Shaking him again, Toylona asked, "Why did you take her?"

"I thought that whatever happened to her must have been my fault. I wanted to help her. I didn't know what Dane might do to her since she couldn't look after herself."

"Where is she?"

I put her in the shelter we built a couple of summers ago near here."

Toylona sagged. "You should've just left her. We should leave her, and all of these humans. We should go up the mountain, collect our young, and leave this area. There are too many humans here! You've already been seen, and more than once."

"I know."

"So let's go!"

He shook his head. "Not yet. I'm curious about them. And they won't stay for long. Humans never do. This isn't their environment."

"It's been days, now, since Alexia showed up. The others have been arriving one by one. How many more will it take for you to listen to reason?"

"They'll leave soon."

"How do you know that?"

He sighed. "I don't. But that's the usual pattern. Humans come out here, stay for part of a day, or maybe a few days. Then they leave. This group will leave soon."

Toylona sagged a bit, still holding his arms. "I hope so. They're dangerous."

"I agree. And Heath is especially so, I think."

Her grip on him tightened. "Then why be so close to

him?"

"Because he strikes me as the most dangerous! I want to watch him. I want to know where he goes, and what he does!" he explained. "Would you rather he wander our territory without us having the slightest idea of where he is at any given time?"

She stepped back from him. "No. You're right. If we're going to remain here, we need to know. What can I do to help?"

He motioned toward the encampment, where the other three humans were just then approaching Heath. "Help me keep watch; just as you've been doing."

She nodded, saying nothing more.

"Thank you for this," he added. "There are too many for me to watch all the time."

Together, they hunkered down, peering through the low tree limbs and boles to see what would happen. Toylona's lips peeled back from her teeth. She growled low in her throat. Her eyes focused intently on Heath.

Alexia passed her gun to Dane before stepping forward. "We need your help."

"What now?" Heath grunted. "I thought you didn't want me around."

"We don't," Dane cut in. "But, as she said, we need you on this."

Fixing Ray with his gaze, Heath asked, "On what? Getting his girlfriend back?"

"She isn't my girlfriend; not yet," Ray said. "But, yes." He indicated Dane and Alexia. "They say you track really well. We need that to find Tabatha. Will you help us? Please?"

"You are aware that helping you to find the girl means helping you to find the sasquatch that took her," Heath asked them. "Right?"

"Sadly, yes," Alexia replied.

"You're also aware that if we find it, I'll take down the sasquatch the first chance I get. Right?"

Alexia's jaw tightened. Dane's hands clenched into fists.

Ray stared at Heath, his eyes and mouth wide open.

"We can't do this without you," Dane lamented. Tears welled at the corners of his eyes. "Even if it means endangering one of the Forest Gods, we have to rescue Tabatha. If I'm right about them, your rifle won't do anything to him even if you do take a shot."

Heath took a few moments to stare at each of them in turn. Finally, he nodded. "All right. Let me grab a rifle that I haven't disassembled for cleaning, and we'll be on our way."

Toylona leaned in closer to Iktomi. "None of them like Heath. I saw Alexia and Dane drive him away from Alexia's shelter before. Why have they come to him?"

"I don't know."

"They're getting ready to go somewhere else. Look."

He nodded. "They do this a lot. They never seem to stay in one place for very long."

"What should I do?" she asked.

"If they stay together, so will we," he told her. "If they split up, we can, too."

"All right. I hope they stay together. I've missed you."

He embraced her. "I've missed you, too. and our young ones."

When the four humans set out, Iktomi and Toylona crept after them. They lagged back, speaking in quiet tones so as not to be heard.

"I still think we need to eliminate Heath," Toylona told him.

"You're only saying that because he has hunted me," he replied.

"In part," his mate admitted. "But he strikes me as the most dangerous of the group. Even the other humans seem very put off by him."

"True."

"If his own kind doesn't like him, what does that say about him?"

Iktomi sighed. "We don't understand what they're saying. We can't even be sure if we're referring to them by their names. We're only guessing. We really don't know why they're here, or what their goals are."

"All the more reason to gather up our young, and leave."

"And then what?" he asked. "Look for new territory? Compete with any who are already there, and possibly be driven out by them? Learn a whole new landscape in a new area? Winter will be upon us soon. Do you really want to be wandering in the ice, cold, and snow?"

"No."

"Neither do I. Nor will our young. The humans, dim-witted as they are, as out of touch with the land as they seem, must still know that the cold season is on the way. They won't be here for long. Hardly any come here during that time of year." He put a hand on her shoulder. "Everything will be okay. Just be patient. And don't harm any of the humans. If we do that, more are sure to come here looking for us. By not harming any of them, we're doing a lot to ensure that they leave, and don't return."

Her expression turned skeptical. "Inaction is the best action?"

"Yes; I think so."

Shaking her head, she told him, "We need to agree to disagree on that point."

Ahead of them, just barely within sight, Ray walked beside Heath, in front of Alexia, and Dane. Eying the gun carried by the Heath, Ray asked, "Did you fire that last night?"

"I did. Why?"

"Just curious."

Venom dripped from Alexia's tone when she asked, "What did you kill?"

"Nothing," Heath replied, not bothering to turn to face her. "I left my camp, and did some whoops in the deep woods. Something responded. I followed it. Eventually, I thought I saw a tall, dark silhouette move between two trees. I shot at it, but don't think I hit it. I couldn't find any blood, anyway."

"You saw something, and just opened fire on it? What if it had been a person?" Dane spat the words out, furious.

Heath shrugged. "If what I saw was human, they were pretty stupid. You don't go walking in the woods, peeking from behind trees, during hunting season. Especially not at night. Anyway, I don't think it was a human."

"You're disgusting!" Dane shot back.

Again, Heath shrugged. "Wait until I drop a body in front of the scientific community. Wait until my name is all over the news, and in the history books, as the man who proved that sasquatch are real. We'll see who's disgusting then."

They walked in silence after that, until arriving at the edge of Dane's encampment. Iktomi pointed out a spot to Toylona. "That is where I took Tabatha from. You're right; they're searching for her. I think they went to Heath to help them find her."

She nodded. "I think you're right. If they only went to Heath because they had no other choice, it might explain why none of them seemed happy to be with him again."

"Heath must be a good hunter," Iktomi reasoned. "Better than the rest of them."

"He hunted you," she answered. "I like him even less now."

They settled into a hiding place to watch, and listen. Heath crouched down, examining the ground closely. The others stood nearby, alternating between watching Heath, and peering into the gloom of the deeper forest.

"The trail goes that way," Dane said, pointing.

"So I see," Heath muttered. "But you guys brought me in because I'm a better tracker than you are. Let me look around."

Dane went quiet, drifting over to stand by Ray. Alexia moved to stand with them, scowling at the other member of their group.

Seemingly oblivious, Heath examined the ground. "So many footprints! Why did you three tramp around the area so much? If I can't pick up a trail..." His words tapered off as he wandered a short distance away. "It went this way," he added.

Snorting, Dane stared at the hunter. "I told you that a few minutes ago."

Without replying, Heath set out. The others were forced to follow, or be left behind. Iktomi and Toylona followed discretely.

"Why did the sasquatch grab the girl?" Heath asked a couple of minutes later. "If I lose the trail, having an idea as to why it took her might give me a clue to where to go to pick up the trail again."

Alexia shrugged. "Who knows? We've thrown around some ideas, but none of them feel right."

"I might have an idea," Dane replied. "Tabatha told me that it's her 'time of the month', as she put it. I can't help but wonder if the Forest God took her because it smelled that when Tabatha went to relive herself."

Ray stared at him. "You seriously think some big monkey took Tabatha because of her period?"

"He could be right," Alexia said. "That might be at least part of why it grabbed her."

"The Forest Gods are primarily a gentle race," Dane added. "Tabatha's ankle had also been injured. Maybe the creature carried her off to try and help her. Maybe we'll learn the truth when he find Tabatha. Right now, though, we have no idea what was going through the Forest God's mind when he took her."

Toylona nudged Iktomi. "They keep talking about Tabatha. I'm sure they're looking for her. Maybe you should return her to them."

He inclined his head. "Probably. It was foolish of me to take her, thinking I might help her. I don't know enough about humans. By taking her I may have done far more harm than good."

"Go get her. Return her."

"If she's awake, I will. I don't trust the others much, and Heath any at all," he replied. "I won't return her to them if she is still in that strange sleeping state."

"All right. Go check on her at least."

He touched her shoulder. "Please remain with the others. Watch them. If they split up, use your best judgment. I'll find you later."

"Be careful," she answered, nuzzling him.

"You, also," he told her, embracing her briefly before turning away.

He moved silently through the woods until he presumed to be far enough from the humans for them not to hear him. Then he increased his pace, not caring about broken twigs, leaves crunched underfoot, or the splashes as he crossed waterways.

CHAPTER 21

Tabatha groaned softly, reaching to feel her head. She rolled onto one side, moaning.

"Ray," she muttered, "you wouldn't believe the dream I had. I don't think I ought to, like, be in the woods any—"

She opened her eyes wide, freezing in place. Slowly, she moved her head, looking around the interior of the shelter.

Iktomi crouched low, remaining still. Even knowing as little as he did about humans, he could see that Tabatha was terrified. He didn't want any abrupt movements on his part to upset her further.

Tabatha cringed. "It, like, wasn't a dream..." Tears welled in her eyes. "The monster is real! Where is it?"

She continued looking around. Eventually, she looked toward her legs, gasping. Scrambling, she started drawing the weird, thin, small under layer back up her thighs. As she did, her head twisted this way and that. She peered around with an intent stare, breathing heavily.

Once the under layer had been put back in place, she pulled the outer layer up, covering her legs. She did something to the fabric at her waist, and rolled over onto her stomach. After holding still, and watching out the opening of the shelter for a brief time, she got up on her hands and knees, and crawled out.

Iktomi watched intently, glad to see the human female alive and well. He needed to get her back to the others now that she had woken, and could look after herself. However, he remained reluctant to move. She seemed fragile, even for a human. He didn't want to just step in front of her, startling her. Sneaking up on her would probably elicit an even worse response. How to proceed?

Tabatha stood, her legs shaky. At her sides, her hands trembled. "Ray?" she said, her voice quiet. "Alexia? Dane? Heath? Anyone?"

Iktomi scowled at Heath's name. Toylona hadn't been wrong; everything with these humans seemed to link back to the most aggressive of them.

"Anyone?" Tabatha repeated softly. "I need help. There's a monster. I'm afraid it'll hear me if I call out. Is anyone there? Can anyone hear me? Please? Anyone?"

Iktomi waited, pondering his course of action. Maybe it would be best to announce himself to her vocally before moving into her sight. If she knew he lurked nearby, maybe she wouldn't be caught off guard when he approached her. He stood, filling his lungs.

"Do not be afraid," he called to her. "I will not harm you; I promise."

Tabatha whirled in the direction of his voice, screaming. A moment later, she collapsed back to the ground, returned to the same state as before.

He stepped cautiously toward her, lamenting the fact that her reaction. While he knew she wouldn't be able to understand his language any better than he understood hers, he had hoped that his peaceful intent would have gotten through to her. Apparently it had not. Or did she have some other reason for lapsing back into her unresponsive state?

Not knowing what else to do, he scooped her up in his arms. He returned her to the shelter to rest. He hoped that, when next she awoke, she would remain awake, and he could get her back to her people.

****

Toylona heard Iktomi's call, and her heavy brow furrowed. Who had the outcry been meant for? The humans were getting uncomfortably close to the shelter where Iktomi had taken Tabatha. Why would Iktomi risk making such noise? She stopped as the four humans before her halted when Heath held up a hand.

The quartet waited, apparently listening. They, too, had heard Iktomi—even with their poor senses. Toylona bared her teeth. If they attacked her mate, she wouldn't hesitate. Heath would be her first target, but the others would follow.

Each of the humans looked unsteady. Ray, especially had quivering legs. All of them stared around with varying degrees of amazement.

Ray staggered back a step, bumping against Heath. The larger male gave the smaller one a shove, almost knocking him from his feet.

"That..." Ray began, and then trailed off. He took a series of quick, shallow breaths. "That"..." he started again. "That was..."

Dane put a hand on Ray's shoulder, steadying him. "Yes."

"They're real?" Ray asked, turning his terrified gaze toward Dane. "Seriously? They're really out here?"

"They are, yes," Dane replied.

"And that one is close," Heath whispered, hefting his gun. "The sound came from that way. Come on."

"Is it the one that took Tabatha?" Ray asked, walking very close to Dane.

Alexia said, "We'll find out soon."

"I can't," Ray told them, his voice barely loud enough to be heard. He stopped walking.

"We have to," Dane told him. "Tabatha needs us."

Ray remained rooted in place. "After what we just heard, how can any of you think of facing that creature! We need to get out of here!"

"Keep your voice down before it hears you, and bolts!" Heath whispered harshly.

Alexia waved a hand at Heath, who snorted, and continued onward without them. Alexia turned to Ray, saying, "What we just heard? That's nothing. They can get a whole lot louder than that."

Ray's eyes went wider. "You've heard them do that?"

"I have."

"Me, too," put in Dane. "She's right. What we just heard wasn't anything special."

"I don't want to hear it do more," Ray told them softly. He backed up a few steps. "I don't want to see one. I just want to get out of here!"

Heath turned back, glowering at Ray, aiming the front of his gun at him. "I told you to be quiet," he growled. "I meant it. If this thing gets away because of you—"

"Drop it," Alexia said, stalking toward Heath.

The large male shifted the weapon's aim to her. "I want this thing! I mean to have it! If it's the one that ran off with the girl, all of you should want it shot, too."

Dane stepped forward. "We're not like you, Heath. We want Tabatha back, but we don't want the Forest God harmed."

"Tough," Heath sneered. "Now all of you, keep silent."

Turning from them, he crept forward once more, headed in the direction from which Iktomi's call had come. Toylona narrowed her eyes, tensing. How long should she wait before pouncing on Heath? Alexia also carried a weapon. Would she defend Heath in the attack? Doubtless, she would defend herself when her own turn came.

****

Iktomi watched Tabatha stir once more. She roused much quicker this time. He hoped her malady had passed, and she would remain awake now. He wanted to return her to the other humans, and rejoin Toylona.

Tabatha crawled slowly out of the shelter, shaking, and wide-eyed. "Please don't still be out there," she whispered.

Iktomi leaned further to the side, peeking around the

tree he hid behind for a better view of the human female. His previous attempt at communicating with her had failed. Should he try again? She had fallen into the strange sleeping state upon hearing his voice. Had he caused it? Or had it been nothing more than coincidence?

"Ray, where are you?" she whispered. "Dane... Somebody..."

Not knowing what else to do, and unwilling to risk the sight of him frightening her worse, Iktomi called out to her again. Tabatha shrieked, wrapping her arms around herself. She sat, rocking back and forth, sobbing.

Iktomi shook his head. This hadn't been what he wanted. He only wanted to keep her safe, to protect her. She seemed frail and defenseless, even for a human. Her ankle had already been injured. Now, his attempts at communication only seemed to terrify her. He didn't know what else to do. If the sound of his voice did that to her, how would she react if she saw him approaching her again?

****

Toylona paused, listening. Pine needles scuffed as someone stepped on them. She growled low in her throat. Another human? Sniffing the air, she found that she recognized the scent—two of them, actually. Guy and Ursula were nearby, and approaching quickly.

The growl intensified. She couldn't risk an attack on the humans now. Even if only two of them were armed, that would still leave four others. If they all scattered, she'd probably be hard-pressed to chase them all down. And if Guy and Ursula had weapons with them, that would be four armed humans to take on at once. Angry as she might be with the presence of the invaders, she refused to allow her emotions to goad her into doing something so stupid. Unable to do anything else, she kept low, and watched.

The passage of Ursula and Guy through the woods caught the attention of the other humans a few moments later. They turned, Heath and Alexia raising their guns. When the older humans burst into view, running quickly as the forest would allow, they stopped so fast that their feet nearly skidded out from beneath them.

"Alexia!" Ursula shouted, staring at the other with wide eyes.

"Ursula? What are you doing here?" Alexia responded. "You two are still out here?"

"No thanks to you!" Guy raged, stalking closer to her.

Ursula put a hand on his arm. "We were trying to find the trail out. Then we started hearing the sasquatch. We ran, and..."

"You're lost again," Alexia said.

"Yes," Ursula answered.

Heath pushed in between the two women, confronting the hunters. "Did you see anything?"

Guy shook his head. "We only heard it."

"Us, too," Heath grunted. "Come on."

He set off again in the direction from which Iktomi's calls had come from.

Dane turned to the youngest of the males. "Ray, we need to stay with Heath. He's still our best bet at finding Tabatha."

Dane set off after Heath. Ray followed wordlessly, his brow furrowed with worry. Alexia focused on Guy and Ursula.

"Where are you two going? Will you just keep wandering the woods, lost, or come with us, and help rescue Tabatha?"

"We're done with you," Guy snarled.

Ursula shot him a harsh look. "Alexia, we need to get out of here."

"Help us," Alexia replied, "and I'll personally take you out of this forest once Tabatha is safe."

Guy's face reddened with rage. "That's what you promised to do when we first met you!"

Alexia gritted her teeth, her jaw tight. "That was before

this mess really started. Things changed. Help us now, and I'll still help you."

"No. We'll find our own way out. Come on, Ursula."

He turned, but his mate's grip on his shoulder stopped him.

"We'll help," Ursula told Alexia. "Not only in exchange for your help, but because it's the right thing to do."

"No, we—" Guy began.

"Yes, we will," Ursula broke in. "It's what we should've done before. Let's go."

Alexia turned away, following Heath, and the others. Ursula trailed after her, glancing back to give Guy a harsh look.

Sighing, tamping down his fury, Guy fell into step. Toylona slunk along after them, raging at the reemergence of the other two humans. She would keep after them, and await a better chance for acting against them.

Ahead of her, Alexia caught up with Dane and Ray. Heath had vanished. Toylona sniffed the air, searching for his scent. It lingered heavily, but she couldn't be sure which way he had gone. She looked around, searching for him visually, but no clues to his whereabouts presented themselves. He had to be nearby, but she couldn't determine just where.

"Where did Heath go?" Alexia asked.

Dane pointed ahead. "He's moving fast. He said he could cover more ground without us."

Alexia groaned. "So much for us working together. We put him on the trail so he can help find the girl, and he leaves us behind to go murder the sasquatch."

"It did take Tabatha," Ray told her.

A dirty look from Alexia silenced him. "Let's try to catch up to him. Maybe we can still stop him from doing something stupid."

Dane led, Ray following him closely. Alexia lagged a bit behind with Guy and Ursula, keeping close watch around them.

They hadn't gone far when Toylona picked up Iktomi's

scent. He had been there not long ago. She inhaled deeply. He hadn't gone far. Her heart beat faster at the thought of what Heath might discover since he had wandered from the rest of the group. She silently swore to kill all of these humans, or die trying, if Heath managed to harm Iktomi.

"Uck!" Ray shouted a short distance further on. "What is that smell!"

"One of them has been here—very recently," Dane said.

"That's so gross!" Ray protested. "How can anything smell that bad?"

"Shush," Alexia said. Holding a hand over her nose, she turned in a circle. About a quarter of the way through her turn, she abruptly pointed at something in the woods.

Toylona looked, but saw nothing.

Dane rushed to Alexia's side. "Did you see it?"

"I saw something," she told him. "I didn't get a clear enough view to be able to say what."

"How tall was it?" Dane asked, staring in the same direction in which she looked.

"Maybe five feet," she said. "It might have been a juvenile. Or an adult hunched down low."

"You really just saw one?" Ray asked. He quaked, looking around with wide eyes.

"Maybe," Alexia told him, turning away. "Like I said, I didn't get a good look." She marched on. "Come on. If we don't hurry, we'll never catch up to Heath."

CHAPTER 22

Iktomi continued watching Tabatha, unsure what to do next. The human female continued to huddle just outside the shelter of woven vines, shaking and whimpering.

Footsteps sounded nearby, alerting him to the presence of another of the humans. Iktomi sniffed, frowning. Heath. Wouldn't he ever give up? Iktomi crouched lower, hiding himself in the brush and low-hanging, heavily-needled limbs.

"You're close by," Heath muttered under his breath. "I can smell you. Where are you?"

Iktomi heard Heath sniffing. He consciously worked to keep the scent secretions beneath his arms under control. Heath crept nearer. Tabatha seemed unaware of him as yet, but for how much longer? Heath posed the largest threat of the group of humans. Should Iktomi allow Heath to reclaim her? Or should he drive off the aggressive male to keep him away from the female?

When Heath broke through the cover of the foliage, gun in hand, his expression set in a silent snarl, Iktomi made up his mind. He had taken Tabatha to keep her safe. At the time, he had questioned the wisdom of leaving her in her unresponsive state near Dane. Heath had proven himself far worse. He had no intention of allowing Heath to have Tabatha back, even though she had woken.

"Heath!" Tabatha shrieked, spinning toward him.

He froze, staring at her is shock. Tabatha scrambled to her feet, rushing toward him. When Iktomi rose from his concealment, she screamed, coming to a halt so quickly that her feet went out from beneath her. She landed in a sitting position, staring at him with extremely wide eyes. Heath stared back at him for a long moment before hefting his gun higher.

Iktomi screamed, the sound of challenge blasting out long and loud. His chest vibrated as he unleashed an underlay of infrasound. Heath's legs wobbled as he staggered backward. His mouth worked soundlessly until he tripped over a root protruding from the ground. He bawled as he toppled over, dropping his weapon.

The gun struck the ground, discharging. The sharp crack of its firing caused Iktomi to flinch, but he kept up the audible assault. Tabatha's own shrieking formed a high-pitched counterpoint to Iktomi's outcry.

Heath curled into a ball, wrapping his arms around his head. He shook with hard sobs, hiding his eyes. One hand flapped feebly in Iktomi's direction.

Cutting off the sound, Iktomi turned, scooping Tabatha up in his arms. She let out one final yell before going limp, once more returned to the sleeping state that so mystified Iktomi. Not taking time to ponder it this time, he strode away, leaving Heath cringing on the ground.

****

Toylona whirled toward the sound of her mate's bellow. Unthinking, she rose up, tense, ready to charge in to help defend him. Though she stood revealed, the humans had also turned toward the disturbance. She stood only a short distance behind them, completely unnoticed. Heath's scent grew strong. Toylona realized that he had gone in Iktomi's direction. Her teeth bared. If he had harmed her mate, she would tear the human to pieces!

Ray shook, barely keeping his balance. "That sound..."

"Yeah," Alexia muttered quietly.

"A gunshot, too," Dane added. "Did Heath just..." He trailed off, shaking his head.

Alexia put a hand on his shoulder. "We don't know. Let's go look."

"Are you insane?" Ray shouted. "That thing sounded enraged!"

"I agree with Ray!" Guy said.

Ursula nodded furiously. "Me, too!"

Dane pushed by them, taking point. "Come on; we have to hurry!"

Alexia matched his speed. "Running up on Heath—or anyone else—when he's shooting at something isn't a good idea."

Toylona fought down the urge to rush by the humans. If Iktomi needed her, she had to get to him. But she had heard nothing more. Surely it would take more than a single attack from one of the humans' weapons to render him incapable of sounding out again if he needed to. She forced herself to follow the humans, unwilling to let them see her if that could be avoided. As she crept after them, she took care to smooth her hair back down, making herself appear as small as possible in the event that they spotted her.

When the humans entered the clearing where the vine shelter had been built, Toylona remained at the edge, peering from around the trunk of a large tree. She watched as Dane knelt to examine something on the ground while the others looked around. She saw no sign of Iktomi. Heath had also gone, but his scent clung heavily to the area. She inhaled, detecting Tabatha's scent, too. Where had she gone? Given that Iktomi had also gone, she suspected that he had taken Tabatha elsewhere. Heath's absence made her wonder if he had followed Iktomi and Tabatha.

"What did you find?" Alexia asked Dane.

"A footprint."

"Sasquatch?"

He nodded, standing. "It's fresh, too."

Guy and Ursula moved slowly closer. "Can you tell what

happened here?" Ursula asked. "There's no one here. But given what we heard, something was."

"Right," Alexia replied. "They've left. They can't be far away, though."

Guy wandered a little to one side, staring intently at the trees. Toylona kept still, held her breath, and closed her eyes most of the way. Behind Guy, the others continued their examination of the ground.

Alexia crouched next to Dane, tracing her fingers over an area of grass. "We know a sasquatch has just been here. Heath was nearby, too. My guess is that he saw the creature, and went after it."

"We have a bullet casing!" Guy called out from a couple of feet away.

Alexia rose, and went to him. The older male pointed at the gleaming bit of metal on the ground. She picked it up, lifting it to her nose. "Fresh. I think this is probably from the shot we heard."

Crawling around the area, Dane muttered, "I don't see any blood." He stood, looking at Alexia, relief evident in his features. "Whatever Heath shot at, I think he missed."

"Dane?" a weak, feminine voice called out.

His head whipped around. "Tabatha?"

Toylona turned as well. She couldn't see the younger female from her current position, but recognized her voice. Tabatha remained hidden from view by ferns, and low tree branches. Oddly, her voice came from the path she had just followed the other humans along. How had Tabatha gotten behind them? She felt positive that she wouldn't have missed Tabatha's presence upon passing so close to her.

"Dane?" she said, louder.

Ray joined Dane. "Tabatha, where are you?"

"Ray?"

"Yes! Where are you?"

"Here!" Vegetation rustled a few yards away.

Ray dove in, as Alexia and the others followed. Toylona held her position, watching and waiting.

The two young males reached into the plants, leaning almost double. When they stood, they held Tabatha between them. She appeared unsteady, quivering, and weak-kneed. Her eyes were wide, staring around. Tears marred her face, which remained half-hidden behind a mess of tangled hair. She reeked of fear.

"Are you okay," Ray gushed. "What happened? Did it hurt you?"

"Get her out of here," Alexia ordered. "Take her back to my camp."

Tabatha held Ray back. "I'm okay. It didn't, like, hurt me. I fainted when I saw it. It, like, brought me here, I guess. I woke up, heard it, and fainted again. I tried to leave, and saw Heath. Where is he?"

"We don't know," Alexia replied.

Tabatha went on, saying, "Heath showed up. I wanted to get to him, but the monster got between us. I fainted again. When I, like, woke up again, the monster was carrying me. It put me down behind you guys, and then ran off."

Scratching her head, Alexia asked, "Wait a minute. The sasquatch kept you away from Heath, but brought you to us?"

"Uh-huh."

Alexia glanced quickly from Dane, to Ray, to Guy, to Ursula before focusing firmly on Dane. "This isn't making sense to me. The sasquatch took Tabatha from your camp. Right?"

"Right," Dane answered.

"Yet," Alexia continued, "after taking her from you, now it keeps her from Heath, and gives her back to you?"

Ray stood taller, holding tightly to Tabatha. "Back to us. Back to me."

Dane frowned, and eased a bit to one side, putting some space between himself, and Tabatha. "Maybe Ray is correct."

"A match-making sasquatch?" Alexia shook her head. "Unlikely. Unless, maybe, it had seen Tabatha and Ray together before they got separated."

"We hadn't seen it before," Ray told her.

"That doesn't matter," Dane said, turning to him. "The Forest Gods are masters of their environment. They know how to blend in. Most of the time they won't be seen unless they want to be. One could have been near your camp, and you'd never have known it."

Tabatha shivered, hugging Ray. He held her more tightly.

"I guess it's possible," Dane continued, "that it could've seen you two together, found Tabatha at my camp after you were separated, and she had gotten hurt, and then took her, only to return her to you here. Maybe he thought he was bringing her back where she belongs."

"He was," Ray said, giving Tabatha's side a light pat.

Tabatha frowned, looking from Ray to Dane. She said nothing.

Alexia watched Tabatha, Ray, and Dane for a couple of moments before saying, "Ray, take Tabatha back to my camp." She then turned to the oldest male. "Guy, any further sign of Heath?"

"No," he replied. "And there's no need to keep looking for him. We have the girl back."

At his side, Ursula nodded. "He's right. Alexia, get us out of here like you promised."

"We should still go after him," Dane protested. "What if he's chasing the Forest God?"

"What can we do to stop him," Alexia asked. "We very well might just get ourselves shot."

"Or," Guy put in, "we might be able to help him kill a monster."

Dane and Alexia turned to him in the same instant. "It's not a monster!" they said in unison.

"You couldn't prove it by us," Guy shot back. "If we find Heath, and he finds that creature, we're going to help him bring it down. What will it be, Alexia? Are you going to help us? Or do we find Heath, and help him kill a monster?"

"I need to make sure Tabatha and Ray make it to camp safely first," she said.

Guy snorted in disgust. "Ursula, come on. She's not going to help us." He hauled his mate after him, departing into the trees.

"Morons!" Dane shouted after them.

"For once we agree," Alexia said. "Ray, take Tabatha back to my camp. Dane, should we go with them, or follow Guy and Ursula to keep them from helping Heath do something stupid?"

CHAPTER 23

Iktomi ran. Behind him, the tumult of Heath's charge through the forest spurred him onward. The human had recovered from the fright Iktomi had given him at the vine shelter far more quickly than expected. Rage as strong as his fear now mingled in Heath's scent. Iktomi doubted the human would allow him to slip away as easily this time as before.

A sharp cracking noise split the air. Iktomi felt an intense burning sting lance along his upper right arm. He slapped at it with his left hand. When he looked, his palm was smeared with red wetness. A moment later numbing pain rolled up to his shoulder.

Throwing back his head, he loosed a bone-jarring howl of pain. Behind him, the sounds of pursuit ceased briefly. Then Heath started toward him once again. Iktomi ran on, each step pounding agony deeply into his injury.

Heath had used his gun on him, he knew. He had been told stories of how the humans' weapons affected those they were used on. He had never experienced it firsthand before now. He wished he could still say that.

Splashing across a wide stream, he hesitated. Should he keep going straight? Or would a turn to head upstream or downstream better throw Heath off his trail? Leaning against a large bole with his left hand, he pondered his choices quickly. Ultimately, he kept going straight. He needed to lure Heath as far from Toylona as possible, and the last he knew, she had been keeping watch on the other humans.

Behind him, the noises indicating Heath's progress grew

closer. Growling low in his throat, Iktomi scooped up a rock with his left hand. He waited, poised, until he saw the dark mass of Heath's hair peeking through a few low-hanging tree limbs.

He hurled the rock hard, intending, despite his warnings to his mate about harming the humans, that it smash Heath's skull. However, thrown with his off-hand, his aim was slightly less than ought to have been. The rock merely glanced off the side of the human's head.

Heath shouted, dropping his gun, and clutching the injury. Iktomi held his place, chest puffed up large, towering over the human. Heath dropped to his knees, staring at him, eyes wide, tears running freely down his cheeks, lips quivering.

Once the face-off had gone on for a brief time, Heath reached for his gun. Iktomi scooped up another rock, lobbing it at him. This one missed altogether, landing out of sight behind the human. Iktomi turned, racing away before Heath could use the weapon on him again.

"I'll kill you!" Heath screamed.

Iktomi heard a few scuffing sounds, and knew the human had gotten to his feet. Slightly dazed he might be, but Heath's rage and fear were driving him. The human had become a serious threat, a berserker driven by emotion. Iktomi doubted he'd have any choice, now, but to slay the human in self-defense. But could he manage it? His one attempt at doing so had failed, serving only to spur Heath to greater anger and drive. Could he, injured as he now was, close on the human, and end his life before Heath took his own with the gun?

****

Toylona paused behind Dane and Alexia as they almost ran full speed into Guy and Ursula. The older humans had stopped, and stood staring around. Terror poured from them in waves. Sounds of Iktomi's screams combined with another retort from a gun. Toylona tensed, wanting to tear apart the four humans in front of her, and then go after Heath. As she thought over her choices, she watched and listened.

"It's echoing," Guy muttered. "I can't tell where it's coming from."

"We'll stay right here," his mate told him. "We know the creature isn't here. If we move, we might run into it."

He turned to her. "What do we do if it does come this way?"

"Run."

"We're looking for Heath," Alexia said. "Have you seen him?"

"No, but we've heard him," Ursula replied.

Alexia grimaced. "Us, too."

The sounds tapered off.

Toylona strained her ears, listening for some audible sign of her mate. She heard nothing. She trusted him to be able to take care of himself. Gradually, she made herself relax. He would have been leading Heath far from her, and away from their offspring, too. The commotion he made would have been for no other purpose than to goad Heath into following him. He had not been speaking coherently, after all. He had simply been making nonsense animal sounds. Still, toward the end, his screeches and bellows had sounded pained. Had he been hurt in some way? Taking care not to be seen or heard, he began a slow circle around the humans. She needed to slip by them, and continue on after Iktomi. She had to be sure that he was okay.

"It's quiet now. Maybe Heath killed that thing," Guy said.

Shuddering, Dane said, "Let's hope not."

Ursula looked beyond Alexia and Dane. "Where are Ray and Tabatha?"

"Gone back toward my camp," replied Alexia. "At least that's where they were supposed to have gone. Tabatha is shaken up—understandably—and doesn't have any outdoor experience to begin with. I have my doubts about Ray in that department, too."

Guy waved his hands, cutting her off. "Whatever. Just get my wife and I out of here! You said you'd do that once the girl had been found. She has. Now honor your word, and show us the way out of these woods!"

Sighing, Alexia shook her head. "She's safe, yes. But the sasquatch isn't. We need to find Heath."

Eyes bulging, Guy snarled, "You'd rather help that monster than us?"

Alexia set off away from them at an angle. "It isn't a monster."

Toylona stopped moving, hoping her stillness would hide her from the young human female. Alexia passed not far from her, Dane walking quickly to return to her side. Guy and Ursula came along more slowly, reluctantly. They were continuing on in the same direction Toylona had intended to go. She waited until they had passed, and then trailed them again. As she walked, she remained alert for any sign of Iktomi.

Dane said, "Come on, you two. Help us find the sasquatch. If Alexia doesn't help you after that, I will."

"We've had more than enough of that thing already!" retorted Guy.

Grumbling, the older humans closed the gap between themselves and the younger pair, forming a more cohesive group. Toylona thought about going around them, and simply tracking her mate. She decided against it, though. If she did, she might move to quickly, and miss some slight trace of him, and lose his trail completely. This way, she could do a more thorough search for signs of him, and keep tabs on four of the humans, too.

****

Iktomi sat high up in the tree, rocks in hand, waiting.

Judging from the sounds of Heath's pursuit, the human would be coming into sight very soon. His right arm had become a mass on numbing pain from the elbow to the shoulder. Climbing the tree had been an extremely trying ordeal. The wound continued bleeding freely. However, so long as Heath followed, he could not safely spare the time and focus to tend to it. The human needed to be dealt with first. Afterward, he could see to the injury himself, or seek out Toylona, and ask for her help.

Heath crept into view. His eyes were squinted nearly closed, his entire pinched expression one of pain. He blinked rapidly several times.

Waiting for the human to get closer, Iktomi leaned forward slightly, hefting the rock in his left hand. If he missed, Heath would likely kill him before he could transfer the other rock from his right hand to his left, and hurl it. The knowledge made him hesitant. Maybe if he remained quiet and still, Heath would go on by, never knowing how close he had been.

No, he decided. If he let Heath go, the human would keep hunting him. That search could well lead him to Toylona, or even their offspring. For their sakes, he wouldn't risk the human getting away. He tensed his arm, preparing.

When Heath drew closer to the tree, Iktomi hurled the rock down at him with a snarl. The human started to look up, but the projectile struck him hard on top of the head before he could do so. The hunter dropped, unmoving, to the ground. His gun tumbled from his grasp.

"No!" Alexia screamed, rushing through the trees.

Startled by her abrupt presence, Iktomi drew himself higher into the tree. She must know he was there. But if he could get out of her sight in the branches, he might be able to cross to another tree, and slip away without being seen further, or put himself at more risk from the humans.

"Iktomi!"

He froze at the sound of his mate's voice. Below, Dane, Guy, and Ursula gathered around Heath with Alexia. Each of the four looked back the way they had come—back in the direction of Toylona's call.

"There's more than one!" Guy bellowed.

"Toylona?" Iktomi shouted back to her. "Go! Get out of here!"

"You're hurt!" she responded, still unseen. "I can smell the blood!"

"It's minor. We'll deal with it later. Now go! They have more guns. Keep yourself safe!"

Apparently ignoring the non-human conversation now, Alexia turned her attention back to Heath. After a moment she said, "He's alive. The rock just knocked him unconscious. We need to get him back to my camp."

Guy shook his head. "What we need is to get out of here! Don't try to tell us that those monsters don't attack people! We all just saw it!"

"The Forest God simply defended himself," Dane said, his voice low. "Heath pursued him, and shot at him."

The hunter glowered. "Get my wife and I out of these woods. Now!"

Toylona called out, "They're not paying as much attention! Get out of the tree! Get away from them!"

Iktomi replied, "I'll try. My arm—"

"Stay where you are," she commanded him. "I'll circle around the humans, and climb up another tree to help you."

"All right," he agreed.

Below, Heath remained still. The other humans, stinking of fear looked around at the sounds of his voice, and Toylona's.

Long moments after they had gone quiet, Ursula whispered, "I don't hear them now. Do you think they've left?"

"I hope so," Guy replied.

Dane refocused on Alexia. "We'll have to carry Heath. Do you think it's wise to move him?"

"I don't really want to," she whispered. "But what if the sasquatch come back? They've proved to be aggressive. Yes, that's because of Heath. But will they make a distinction between him and us? Besides, I have first aid supplies in my camp."

"Right," Dane agreed, standing. "Guy? Help me. We'll carry Heath back to Alexia's camp."

The older male crossed his arms. "I'll do nothing of the sort!"

"You will, too," his mate said, jabbing him in the ribs. "That man is hurt. Help Dane get him to camp. We'll probably be safer in a larger group, anyway."

Guy glared at her before turning his scowl to Dane and Alexia. Finally, he heaved a great sigh, and bent to help Dane lift Heath.

As the humans eased away, Toylona worked her way up the tree beside the one Iktomi sat in. "They're leaving," he told her.

"Good. Let them," she said, reaching for him.

He shook his head. "There's no need for me to move to another tree, and sneak away now."

She easily crossed to his tree. "Your arm!"

"I know."

"How bad is it?"

He peered down at the injury, unable to see much through the veil of long hair, dark, blood-matted on his arm. "Not bad, I don't think."

"You're losing a lot of blood," she informed him. "We need to get a poultice on it."

"Yes, please," he said. "Help me to climb down."

She went first, stopping every few limbs to help his follow her. He found it humiliating to need the help. He had climbed up on his own. But during the brief time since, his arm had stiffened. Now, it had become all but useless.

"What do we do about the humans?" he asked once they were safely on the ground.

"Kill them," she snarled.

"Heath is already dead, I think."

"Good. If the others stay, we need to do the same to

them."

"With Heath dead, maybe the others will leave soon," he told her.

"They had better," she grunted. "Come on. We need to find herbs, and mud so I can care for your arm."

CHAPTER 24

Iktomi nodded to her. "Please. But we need to keep watch over the humans still."

She stared at him, outraged. "You're not serious?"

"Now, more than ever."

"Why? After the one you killed—"

He made his way deeper into the forest, on a heading that would take him back to Alexia's encampment in a roundabout way. Toylona walked at his side.

"Why?" she repeated. "Leave them alone! Or kill them! Personally, I prefer the latter; especially now!"

"No. We'll continue watching." He held up a hand, forestalling the argument he knew she would make. "For now, at least. Heath is dead, I think. I didn't see him move at all after the blow to his head. Maybe that will be a lesson the others will learn."

"Or it could goad them into more hostility against us!" she raged.

"If it does, we will act accordingly," he assured her, continuing on. "Heath seemed to be the most violent of them. He's gone. Maybe the others will simply leave. In the meantime, we need to know that they aren't gathering more evidence of our presence. The more they take back to show other humans, the more likely we are to have others here, searching for us. They've already found far too much— footprints, hair, they've seen us, and Heath forced me to kill him. I fear his death alone will bring humans in droves."

"Then kill the rest of them!" she urged. "If none of them return, they can't send others here in their place!"

He glanced at her, saying, "If none return, others will come here looking for them. We'll be in the same place we are now. We'll be trying to hide from a group of humans wandering around our home territory. Do you want that?"

"No."

"Nor do I."

She sighed, nodding. "So we keep watching this group, do what we can to ensure that they find nothing else, and leave."

"Right."

"Then we can go back to our lives."

"Yes."

Plucking up a cluster of small leaves growing near the base of a tree, she said, "We still need to tend to your arm."

"Please."

She tucked the leaves into her mouth, chewing quickly, grimacing at the taste. He would be grateful when she had applied the needed medicines to the injury. It still bled, though not as badly. Pain throbbed from his wrist to his neck with each beat of his heart.

As they went along, she collected five other types of herbs, adding them to the growing wad she worked between her teeth. Finally, she stopped him beside a narrow stream.

Toylona knelt, scooping a handful of sticky mud from the edge of the water. She worked it in both hands, wringing as much of the moisture from it as she could. Finally, she spat the mixture of well-chewed leaves from her mouth into her hands. She kneaded them into the mud.

"Ugh," she grunted. "I need something to get rid of that taste. You're lucky this is going on your arm, and not into your mouth."

When she deemed it ready, she stood, pressing the finished poultice over his wound. She held it in place for long moments before slowly lowering her hand. Iktomi looked, seeing the long, dark hair that covered his shoulder entangled with the mud and herbs, helping to anchor it in place.

"There," Toylona said. "That will help keep the wound

from festering. It'll heal more quickly, too."

"Thank you."

She embraced him, nuzzling his neck gently. "We'll replace it with fresh each day until you've healed."

"Again, thank you."

Pulling away from him, she cast her gaze around before grinning. She trotted over to a low bush, and picked several berries from its small branches. After eating three helpings of them, she turned back to him.

"Much better," she commented. "Sweet, to cover the bitterness of the herbs."

He smiled at her, happy just to be with her. She smiled back. For the moment, he nearly forgot the pain lancing through his arm. Finally, he turned away. "We should move on. We need to find the humans. They're probably back at Alexia's camp. They always seem to return there."

Her smile faded. "Must we?"

"We've been over this," he said, and started walking.

She followed. "I know, I know. I'm so tired of humans, though."

"Me, too."

They came upon the encampment slowly and quietly, taking care to remain low, and hidden behind tree trunks, and tall ferns. Ray and Tabatha looked to be the only two humans there at the moment. Iktomi listened closely, inhaling deeply as he did so. He heard nothing to indicate that the others had yet returned. Their scents lingered from past visits, but were not strong enough for them to be there just then.

Tabatha sat on the lone seat. Ray crouched beside her, his hand on her wrist. Tabatha shook slightly, and her head whipped around at the slightest sound—a bird chirping, the breeze sighing through the trees, a squirrel chattering.

"You shouldn't have come out here," Ray told her. "The woods are no place for you. I ought to have seen that sooner."

"I wanted to impress you," she replied, her voice quiet.

Ray nodded. "And I'm flattered. Some people just aren't

suited for the woods, though."

She leaned over, snuggling against him. Ray held her back. The pose looked awkward to Iktomi, given their respective positions. "I just wanted you to like me," Tabatha whispered to Ray.

Holding her tighter, he whispered, "I do like you."

A raven cawed somewhere nearby. Tabatha sat bolt upright, gasping.

"It's only a bird," Ray soothed.

She slowly shifted her focus back to him. "Aren't you afraid?"

"After seeing a bigfoot? I was terrified when we were watching it, yes. Now? Now I'm only a little nervous."

She shook her head. "How can you be so calm?"

Shrugging, Ray said, "When I found out that it had taken you, I was very scared. It didn't hurt you, though. Did it?"

"No."

"See? I keep thinking about what Dane and Alexia have said about these things," he went on. "They don't think bigfoot are dangerous. Dane even sees them as some type of gods."

The scents of Alexia, Dane, Guy, Ursula, and Heath caught Iktomi's attention. Beside him, Toylona craned her head, giving a silent snarl. Iktomi placed a calming hand on her arm. The others were passing by far enough away that he doubted they would see them as long as they remained still. Ray and Tabatha didn't seem aware of the returning presence of the others.

"It kidnapped me, though," Tabatha protested.

"It did, yes. But you were hurt. Maybe it wanted to help you. Dane also has a theory that it grabbed you because of the scent of your urine because it's that time of the month for you." Ray shrugged again. "Maybe it was only curious about you. There's no way of knowing. What matters is that we got you back safely, and that it didn't hurt you."

"It hurt Heath."

"Heath chased it, and shot at it, too."

"Right," Alexia chimed in as she led the others into camp.

Tabatha started, gasping. Ray patted her leg, turning to watch the others.

Guy and Dane carried Heath between them. He hung limp, blood trickling from a wound on his temple. Alexia walked in front of them, while Ursula brought up the rear. Both females held guns at the ready.

"Set him down near the fire ring," Alexia told the males. "I'll grab the first aid kit. We'll get him cleaned up."

"Are we safe?" Tabatha asked. "Will that monster come back here?"

"We're safe," Dane told her. "And it isn't a monster."

Tabatha shuddered. "I think it is."

Alexia slipped into her artificial cave. When she emerged, she held a gleaming white box that smelled oily. A bright red marking adorned one side of it. She moved to Heath, opened the box, and removed a thin package. She tore one end open, releasing a sharp, pungent scent that caused Iktomi to flinch. Toylona backed away a few steps, distancing herself from the smell.

They watched Alexia pull a damp, white piece of material from the open pouch. She used it to wipe at Heath's bleeding injury.

"Humans have odd customs for dealing with their dead," Toylona whispered.

Iktomi nodded, agreeing silently.

Alexia took more strange items from the white box, doing various things to Heath's head that Iktomi couldn't fathom. At his side, Toylona bristled.

"He's alive!" she snarled quietly.

"Who?" Iktomi asked. "Heath?"

"Yes!" She began to stand up.

He pulled her back down. "We can't let them know we're here. Even if you're right, and Heath is alive—"

"He is!"

"—they will probably attack us on sight now. And how

do you know he's still alive?"

Toylona pointed. "The things Alexia is doing tell me that. I don't understand the items she's using, but I think this is the human version of the poultice I put on your arm. She's helping Heath! We thought she didn't even like him, but she's helping him! He hurt you! I want him dead!"

She began to rise. Again, he restrained her, saying, "No. This is a good thing."

"How?" she snarled.

He glanced toward the humans to see if they had noticed. Heath remained unresponsive. The rest of the group was fixated on him.

"It's good," he answered her, "because if Heath still lives, there's no need for other humans to come out here to try and avenge him. He seems to be badly hurt. Maybe this will frighten them all away."

She wrenched free of his grip, staring at him. "I want him dead."

"No. It's better that he's alive."

"I disagree."

He nodded. "I know you do. But I never really wanted to harm any of them to begin with—not even Heath. I did what I did to protect myself. That situation has passed; it's over. We don't need to be aggressive toward them right now."

She held his gaze for a time before finally turning away. "I'm going to go up the mountain, and check on our offspring."

"I'm sure they're well. But thank you for checking," he replied. "I'll be along as soon as the humans have left our territory."

"If you don't rejoin us soon, I'll come and find you," she said. "I don't want you left alone for long."

He nodded, thanking her without words.

She turned away, retreating into thicker woods.

In the camp, Alexia continued her work on Heath. The others watched, intent. After a few minutes, Toylona loosed a long scream of utter frustration from deep in the forest.

All of the humans, aside from Heath, looked up sharply at the outcry. Tabatha began sobbing. Ray stroked her head, making soft noises to her.

"I think we need to get out of here," Tabatha said between sobs.

"Us, too," Guy put in.

When the echoes of Toylona's scream tapered off, Dane hung his head. "Heath angered the Forest God."

"Give me a gun," Heath said, stirring slightly, his voice weak. "Let me kill it."

"No," Dane and Alexia replied in unison instantly.

Iktomi stared at Heath, a mix of thoughts and emotions roiling within him. Part of him couldn't help but be proud of Toylona for figuring out the strange ritual that Alexia had been performing. Part of him was happy that Heath lived for the same reasons he had quoted to Toylona. At the same time, a living Heath would be able to recover, and continue pursuing him. And that hunt could well endanger Toylona, or their young ones, too. Were he dead, Heath would no longer pose a threat to any of them.

Propping himself up on one shoulder, Heath said, "We need to protect ourselves." His face scrunched up in a pained expression. He touched his head. "You bandaged me? How bad is it?"

"You need to rest," Alexia told him. "There were at least two sasquatch—one in the tree, and another nearby in the woods."

"The one in the tree is the one that threw the rocks at me."

"We saw," she replied. "When the creatures left, Dane and Guy carried you back to my camp. I didn't want to move you, but we couldn't stay there. I think having us to show up frightened the sasquatch away. They weren't afraid of one human, but a larger group seemed to drive them off. We didn't know if they'd return, or not. So we came back here."

Heath groaned as he shifted position. "Here isn't any safer."

Tabatha whimpered.

Alexia barely spared her a glance before saying to Heath, "We have a campfire here. Reports in the past have suggested that they're cautious of fire."

"Right," Heath muttered. "And others have suggested they're curious of it. Regardless, do you think a little campfire is going to keep one away if it wants us? Even if it won't approach the camp because of the fire, what's to stop it from just hiding in the trees, and bombarding us with rocks? A good hit or two to the head, and any one of us would drop dead without the creature having to even get near us."

Tabatha's sobs grew harder. She hugged Ray tight. Ray and Dane shot a long, dirty looks at Heath. Guy and Ursula looked around, reeking of fear. Alexia only nodded.

"So give me a gun," Heath said. He struggled to stand.

"Lie down," Alexia told him. "You were knocked out by a blow to the head. You're bleeding."

"You put a bandage on it."

Alexia shook her head. "A bit of tape and gauze won't help if you have a skull fracture, you idiot! Or brain damage. Or internal bleeding."

Ray stepped forward. "It's angry because you tried to kill one of them. If we show them we don't mean any further harm, they might leave us alone." He turned to Alexia and Dane. "Right?"

"I hope so," Alexia told him.

Dane nodded. "I think so."

"No," Guy barked, joining in. "That thing has been after my wife and I ever since we first ran across it! It kidnapped that girl, too!" He pointed angrily at Tabatha. "We have to kill it. This is a survival situation. It's that monster, or us!"

Ursula stepped to her mate's side. "I have to agree with him."

"Why?" shot back Dane. "Because you're married to him?"

"No," Ursula countered, "because I think he's right. We can't take a chance that we can reason with an animal."

Dane folded his arms. "It isn't an animal! And we can't just gun down an intelligent being!"

"Tabatha?" Ray said quietly. "We're three for trying to kill it, and three for trying to avoid killing it. What do you think we should do?" He shifted his gaze to the others. "Three and three. Tabatha hasn't voted yet. I say we do whatever she wants. She's the tie-breaker." He looked back at Tabatha. "What will it be? What do you want us to do? Try and kill it, or not?"

CHAPTER 25

The rest of the group stared at Tabatha. Even Iktomi picked up on the tension among them. Tabatha glanced from one of her companions to the next. She shook her head slowly.

"Come on," Ray said. "It's up to you. You're the tie-breaker."

She stared at him for a moment. Finally, she whispered, "Don't kill it if you don't need to."

Some of the others gasped. Some of them frowned, turning away.

"It needs to die," Guy muttered.

"I disagree," Tabatha replied.

"That thing kidnapped you," Guy told her loudly, closing with the young woman. She leapt up from her seat, backing away, eyes wide, but he pressed on. "How can you not want that thing dead after what it did to you?"

Ray stepped between the two of them, shoving Guy backward. "Leave her alone!"

"Ray," Tabatha said quietly. She stepped around him, facing Guy. "It took me from Dane's camp, yes. It didn't hurt me, though. Whatever reason it had for taking me, it didn't hurt me. I was terrified—I still am. But the creature didn't harm me. I don't want it hurt, either, if that can be avoided."

"Good girl," Dane praised.

Guy rounded on him. "You're all stupid! That thing is a monster. It needs to be killed!"

Spinning away from them, he grabbed Heath's arm, helping him to his feet.

"My wife and I are with you," Guy said.

Ursula quietly moved to his side, a silent show of support.

"No!" Ray shouted. "We had a vote! We agreed—"

Guy waved a hand in the air, cutting off whatever Ray planned to say. "No, we didn't agree. You did."

From somewhere in the woods, a scream from Toylona, louder and longer than before, echoed. Heath winced, holding his head.

"Maybe..." he said.

Ursula moved to his side, supporting him as he wobbled. "Maybe what?"

Heath glanced from the other hunters to Alexia, Dane, Tabatha, and Ray. "Maybe we ought to stay together as one group."

Ray turned from them, leading Tabatha with him. Alexia began tossing broken tree limbs into the ring of stones, building a fire.

"A little help?" she asked.

Dane hesitated, combing his gaze over the trees around them.

"Remember Ape Canyon?" Alexia prodded.

Shuddering, Dane turned to help prepare the fire. As he worked, she glared at Heath, Guy, and Ursula. "If we stay together, we adopt a firm no-kill policy. That's non-negotiable."

Alexia nodded toward Dane before looking to the others. "We only kill one—or try to—in self defense. Got that?"

"Agreed," Ursula said.

Guy's jaw dropped. He took a step away from his mate, staring at her in open astonishment. "We're not agreeing to that!"

"Yes," she replied firmly, "we are."

"Why would you want that?" Heath asked. "That creature kidnapped Tabatha after aggressive acts toward you and your husband!"

Ursula shrugged. "We know there are at least two of them nearby. How are we to know which one did what? And, as Alexia has pointed out, what happened with Guy and myself was likely our own fault. And, as Tabatha pointed out, the creature that took her from Dane's camp didn't harm her. It could have, but it didn't."

Guy snorted. "I can't believe I'm hearing this!"

Ursula moved closer to him, closing the space he had opened. "You, Heath, and myself could set out on our own. Would you rather be in a group of three with that thing out there? Or in a group of six?"

He frowned, remaining quiet.

She nodded. "That's what I thought. And Alexia and Dane know a whole lot more about these creatures than we do. Which means we'll be best served to listen to them. If they say no shooting unless it's a matter of life or death, then I'm okay going along with that. You should be, too."

Guy stared at her for a time before nodding marginally. He then drifted away from her again, moving closer to Heath.

Ursula stepped to Alexia, Dane, Ray, and Tabatha. "I'll abide by your rule for now. I'll see to it that Guy does as well."

"Thank you," Dane replied.

Shrugging, Ursula said, "I can't speak for Heath, though. You'll want to keep an eye on him."

"Always," Alexia answered, standing from the fire they had built. "If we're lucky, the flames will keep the sasquatch away from us for the night, and the question of whether or not to open up on it won't even be an issue."

"And if they don't?" Ursula questioned.

Alexia took a deep breath, and slowly let it out. "If the fire doesn't keep it away, then we may be in for a very interesting night."

Iktomi continued watching as the humans settled in for the night. They kept the fire burning bright and high. From time to time, one of Toylona's aggravated screams would echo from higher up on the mountain, voicing her frustration over not being able to carry out the attack that she wanted. Each time she cried out, the humans would look around, shaking and wide-eyed, before huddling closer to the fire.

"It's nowhere near us," Dane said after one of Toylona's tirades. "It sounds like it's a good two or three miles away."

Heath warmed his hands over the fire, saying, "Uh-huh. And how long would it take a sasquatch to cover two or three miles?"

"How long?" Tabatha asked, focusing on him.

"Not long," Heath snapped.

Cringing away from him, Tabatha snuggled more tightly against Ray. Dane glanced their way, frowned, and looked away, staring off into the dark forest.

Iktomi kept low, and still, his eyes nearly closed so as not to reflect the illumination of their fire should one of the humans look his way.

"Before," Tabatha said to Alexia, "you and Dane both mentioned someplace called Ape Canyon. What happened there?"

Dane half-turned to look at her. "Nothing you want to know about just now."

Tabatha glanced from him to Alexia, and back. "Why?"

"Trust him," Heath said. He touched the side of his head, wincing. "If we make it out of here, I'll tell you that account myself."

"What was it?" she pressed.

"Later," Heath grunted.

"A group of men were attacked by some of those monsters," Guy said.

Eyes wide, Tabatha turned to him. "Really?"

Dane moaned softly in exasperation. "You shouldn't have told her."

Guy stared back, saying, "She has every right to know what's going on. She's as much at risk as any of us. Maybe more, given that the monster has already grabbed her once."

"They aren't monsters," Alexia retorted, her voice tight.

"Thinking back on what you told us of Ape Canyon,"

Guy argued, "and seeing the mess we're in now, I have to say they are."

"What happened in Ape Canyon? Why were the men attacked?" Tabatha asked.

"The Forest Gods there were defending themselves—and possibly trying to avenge a fallen member of their family," Dane said.

Alexia sighed. "Fine, Tabatha. Since Guy had to start this, I'll finish it."

As she talked, another of Toylona's screams drifted down the mountain. Iktomi turned carefully, looking up the incline, thinking to maybe catch a glimpse of her silhouetted against the moon and stars. He saw nothing. She cried out again, louder than before. The sound of a tree trunk breaking followed.

"It's getting closer," Heath interrupted Alexia. He leaned closer to the fire, while touching his head where the rock had struck him.

Dane nodded. "It's dark. They're mostly nocturnal. It makes sense that anything it planned to do it did at night."

Heath abruptly stood, snatching up one of the guns. Snarling, Dane leapt to his feet, standing nose-to-nose with the more mature male, hands fisted at his sides.

"We all agreed, Heath!" Dane bellowed. "No killing unless it's unavoidable!"

Heath shook his head slowly, not removing his gaze from Dane. "You're as bad as he is!" He pointed at Ray, saying, "You, he, and the women all agree. Guy didn't; his wife spoke for him. And I certainly didn't! If I get a shot at that thing, I'm taking it! That's what I came out here to do to begin with, before getting drawn into all of this nonsense with the rest of you. Now, we have an angry creature out there, that seems to be headed this way. That creature is bigger and stronger than any of us." He touched his head once more, adding, "It's already proven its hostility. Far as I'm concerned, we're already in a pure survival situation. Give me half a chance at taking that thing down, and I'll do it!"

Dane drew back an arm in what Iktomi felt sure was an attack posture. Before the smaller human could strike, however, Alexia jumped up, grabbing him. She eased him away from Heath, forcing him to turn around. With Heath out of his line of sight, and with Alexia's soothing touches and voice, Dane seemed to be calming.

"Don't let him get to you," she told him gently. "He's a jerk. You know that. I know that. Everyone who meets him know that. Don't let him provoke you. It'll be okay."

"We can't let him just kill one of the Forest Gods!" Dane almost wailed.

Alexia nodded, saying, "We won't. There isn't one here right now. Heath is just talking to blow off steam. He's scared. We all are, but he's already been hurt by this thing. I know why it lashed out at him, but I still understand his fear of it."

Toylona screamed again, further down the mountainside. Heath jumped, startled, and lifted the gun. He aimed in the direction of Toylona's outburst. Iktomi snarled, leaping to his feet. He bellowed a wordless challenge at the human, his entire body quaking as he unleashed a blast of infrasound to underscore the sheer volume of his verbal assault.

Heath started to whirl toward him, gun still up. Iktomi, furious though he may have been, still recognized the danger. He ducked behind the bole of a tree, hoping it would protect him should Heath use the gun on him again. However, halfway through his turn, Heath's legs gave out. He dropped to the ground, the weapon spilling from his grasp.

The other humans sat still, gaping wide-eyed in Iktomi's direction, holding their collective breath. He had no idea if they had spotted him, or not. He didn't care. Heath had made a threatening action toward Toylona; Iktomi refused to allow that to go unanswered. Scowling, he inhaled deeply, readying himself to unleash another infrasound hammer at Heath—or any of the others if the need arose.

Toylona called out, not wordlessly this time, but in an intelligible manner. "What happened?" she shouted down the mountain to him. "Are you all right?"

"Yes," he called back. "One of the humans aimed a weapon in your direction when they heard you last. Be careful!"

Iktomi peered around the tree to see Heath scrambling back to join the other humans. All of them shook. Tabatha whimpered piteously as she clung to Ray and Dane at the same time.

"Both of them are here!" Heath shrieked. His voice had turned far higher than Iktomi had previously heard it. "Two of them!"

"One of them is very close," Alexia said. She pointed almost directly at Iktomi. "It sounds like it might be right on the other side of those trees."

Heath pulled himself behind the others, crouching low, cowering. His scent spoke eloquently of his terror. Every few moments, he let out a soft whine.

"The Forest Gods are typically shy," Dane said. "Heath acted is blatant aggression toward one earlier today. Now they're retaliating. This isn't their fault. This is the price we pay for intruding on their territory. It's the price we pay for Heath's actions."

"This isn't my fault!" Heath bellowed, reaching for Dane.

Ray swatted his hand away, apparently ignoring the burning look of outrage Heath fixed him with. "We don't need to fight each other. Much as I hate saying it, Heath may be right about this having become a survival situation."

Alexia stepped to Dane's side, placing a calming hand on his shoulder. "Ray is right. We need to stick together. We have at least two angry sasquatch out there. This is going to be an interesting night."

CHAPTER 26

Iktomi watched as Dane hung his head. "You're right. And, assuming we make it through tonight, would you be willing to sit down with me sometime for a long talk about sasquatch? I'd like to hear more about your opinions regarding them."

Alexia blinked, surprised. "All right."

"Thank you. Today's events are making me question my own thoughts about them—in part, at least."

Higher up on the mountainside, Toylona shouted, "Are they holding their positions, Iktomi?"

"Yes!" he bellowed back, putting enough power into his reply to ensure that she heard him over the distance separating them.

"Good!" she replied, and then screamed out a rallying cry for others to join them.

Iktomi shook his head. "What is she doing?" he mumbled. "This isn't what we need."

In the human encampment, Heath's eyes grew even larger. "They're both still there! Hear them?"

Other voices called back to Toylona. The answers mostly came from near the top of the mountain. A couple came from below them, in the thicker, heavier forest.

Heath started so abruptly that he nearly toppled over. "There are more of them!"

Tabatha cowered against Ray. "How many?"

Heath shook his head. "I can't tell. There are too many overlapping calls. I'm going to guess at least six of them, but there may well be more."

"Six?" Guy gulped.

"At least," Heath pointed out.

Dane stared at him, hands shaking. "We'll be okay." His voice quavered slightly. "They won't harm us. We're grouped together, and we have a fire. They aren't likely to even approach us."

Touching his head, Heath said, "They don't have to. They can stand back in the darkness, and lob rocks at us. We might not even see them, but they could still kill us easily if they decide to."

Whimpering, Tabatha clung to Ray. He rubbed her back, obviously attempting to sooth her. Alexia, Guy, and Ursula kept shifting their gazes around, searching the dark beyond their camp.

Iktomi made sure to hold still, keeping his eyes almost closed for fear of the humans spotting them reflecting in the illumination of their fire.

Heath staggered to his feet, closing his eyes for a few seconds, grimacing, and touching his head. When he opened his eyes, he glowered at the darkness, lifting his gun.

Dane stood, snatching the weapon from the older male's grip. He held it behind him, backing up as Heath stalked toward him.

"Give it back!" Heath demanded.

Dane answered, "If you can calm down. The way you look, I'd say you're as apt to shoot one of us by accident as anything else."

Heath held his gaze for a moment before sagging. He nodded. "You're right. I knew they were real, but..."

"You can never prepare yourself for something like this," Dane said gently.

"Right. What about you?" Heath asked. "You think these animals are some sort of gods. Why aren't you afraid of them?"

Shrugging, Dane replied, "I'm terrified right now. Still, maybe deep down I still don't think they mean to hurt us. Or maybe I'm so terrified that my brain is sort of short-circuiting, and I'm not even feeling the full amount fear at the moment."

After staring at him for a brief time, Heath slowly sat back down. Dane waited several more seconds before returning the gun to him. Heath clutched the weapon, hugging it tightly, as he looked first one way, and then another, and another into the night beyond the camp.

Iktomi remained quiet and still, listening as Toylona called out directions to the human encampment. She interspersed those with requests that the humans be driven out. Iktomi shuddered. His mate's fear of what the humans' presence meant, and might mean in the future, had evidently overwhelmed her. She had set events in motion that he wouldn't be able to stop. Too many others were replying, and converging on the humans. He could hear their return calls growing closer and closer. Strong musk, designed to mark out territories, and warn off enemies thickened in the air. The message being sent seemed perfectly clear to him, yet the humans remained in place, waiting, and cowering.

A large rock arced out of the darkness on the other side of the camp. It tumbled to a halt near the artificial shelter Alexia had erected upon her arrival. The humans let out gasps, turning quickly to watch the projectile roll to a stop.

Iktomi hoped the warning would send them running. If they broke and ran, making it clear that they were leaving, Toylona's retaliation against them might stop. However, he saw that his hopes were made in vain. The humans only hunkered down further, holding their places.

More stones, some small, others larger, began to pelt the encampment. Iktomi sighed. What could he do? He didn't want the humans harmed. Now that he had failed so thoroughly, and they were so aware of the presence of his people, what could he do to drive them away, yet spare them harm? Injuring them would only serve to bring them back, or others in their place, to seek out his people. Killing them would ensure that more humans arrived to find this group.

"Everyone, down!" Alexia bellowed as more rocks fell

among the humans.

"See?" shouted Heath, curling himself into a tight ball on the ground. "See? They can stone us to death without even getting close enough for us to catch a glimpse of them!"

The attack continued until Alexia lifted her weapon, firing two shots into the air. Guy and Ursula followed suit.

Iktomi winced at the sharp cracks of noise their guns made. The sounds echoed off the side of the mountain. But the assault upon the humans ended. Iktomi heard one voice screaming defiance at the humans in the aftermath of their weapons use. He didn't recognize the voice. Not knowing the individual, he had no way of knowing if the vocal expression of anger would be enough to sate them, or if something more would come.

After the last of the rocks fell, Alexia climbed to her feet, screaming wordlessly at their unseen assailants. She shot off round after round into the darkness until her weapon clicked empty.

Other voices joined the first in screaming back at the humans. Iktomi thought about calling out to them, telling them to stand down. He would need to move well back from the humans' encampment before doing so, however. Their heightened nerves and aggression would likely lead them to turn their weapons in his direction the instant he revealed his continued presence so near to them.

As he debated a course of action, silence fell. The final echoes of his peoples' outrage went quiet. He felt sure that wouldn't last for long.

The other humans slowly got to their feet, standing with Alexia.

"We might have bought ourselves some time," Alexia commented. "There's no telling how much, though."

She began a slow patrol around the edges of the camp, weapon in hand. Heath, Guy, and Ursula walked with her. Soon they settled into a rhythm, with each of them wandering back and forth over a quarter of the circle.

Dane, Ray, and Tabatha huddled together next to the

fire. Both of them started at the slightest sound. From time to time, Tabatha let out a soft whimper.

"Keep the fire burning as high as you can," Alexia told Ray. "The last thing we need right now is for it to burn down."

He tossed two pieces of fuel into the flames. "What happens if we run out of wood?"

Guy shuddered. "If that happens, I think we're in big trouble."

Glaring at him, Alexia said, "Not necessarily. Even if the creatures were to try direct physical confrontation, there are seven of us here. Four of us are armed. Sasquatch are cautious. They've seen people use guns before." Her stare shifted to Heath.

He put his hands in the air, gripping his rifle loosely. "A body is the only thing that will make mainstream science accept the reality of the species."

"We're beyond that motivation now," Alexia replied. "All we can do now is deal with the consequences of your actions."

"My actions?" Heath spat back. "I'm not the only one out here!"

Dane looked up from his place at the fire. "True. But you're the only one who tried to murder one of those beings. You're with us. In their minds, apparently, we're all guilty."

"Thank you so much for that," Ray joined in.

Heath turned a withering look on the younger man. Before he could retaliate, a branch cracked in the darkness not far beyond the edge of the camp.

Iktomi looked in the direction of the noise. He had been so intent on the humans, and trying to think of a way to chase them away without further harming them, that he had been unaware of the approach of anyone else.

Spinning, Heath fired off three quick shots. High-pitched shrieking undulated through the air. The sound was picked up from several other sources. Iktomi bit down on his own enraged outcry. He wanted to help the humans to get away.

Yet they continued to prove themselves a threat which needed to be dealt with harshly! Maybe Toylona had been right all along. Maybe her way of dealing with the humans would be the best course of action.

"No!" Alexia screamed, rushing at Heath. "You idiot! That's what got us into this mess to begin with! Stand down!"

When Heath looked ready to protest, Dane and Ray slowly approached him. Heath grimaced before sagging. He lowered his weapon, and moved toward the fire.

"I need to warm up, anyway," he groused.

Alexia sighed, and nodded thanks to Ray and Dane. Around them, the screams continued.

A rock arced through the air, tumbling to the ground a few feet beside the fire. Tabatha leapt up, screaming. Ray rushed to her side. Dane stood, seemed to reconsider, and then sank back into a crouch by the flames.

A sharp cracking sound came from the woods behind the camp, followed by a series of thundering crashes. Everyone turned in that direction.

"Was that what I think it was?" Alexia asked to the rest of the group in general.

"A tree being broken in half?" Dane suggested.

Alexia nodded. "Classic sasquatch scare tactics."

"'I'm strong enough to tear down a tree with my bare hands. Get out of my territory'," Heath put in.

"I've heard stories of sasquatch actually uprooting whole trees. They turn them over, and jam the treetops into the ground, leaving the roots sticking up into the air," Alexia told the others. "What Heath just said is what those displays seem to be meant as, too. They seem to like using damage to trees as territorial displays."

"We're going to die out here," Tabatha moaned.

Alexia faced the younger woman. "No. We aren't."

Tabatha pointed in the direction from which the sound of the breaking tree had come. "If they can snap a pine in half, what will they do to us?"

"Nothing," Dane interjected. "They're just trying to

frighten us away."

"Then why don't we give them what they want, and leave?" Tabatha shrieked.

Heath stared at her. "At night? Not knowing the territory? And with a whole troop of giant apes out there in the darkness who are very angry with us? You're joking, right?"

Alexia took a few moments to check on the others.

Guy and Ursula held each others' hands tightly. Each of them gripped a gun in their other hand. Their knuckles were tight from the pressure of their grasps.

Heath looked pale. He trembled, knees slightly bent, his weapon aimed into the darkness beyond camp.

Dane crouched at the fire, calmly feeding bits of wood into the flames. Their pile of fuel dwindled rapidly, Iktomi noticed, following Alexia's gaze.

Ray and Tabatha clung to one another. Tabatha sobbed openly, while Ray muttered to her.

Toylona called out again, from lower down the mountainside than before. "Our young ones are in danger from the humans! Get rid of them! Protect your mates! Protect your offspring! Protect yourselves! Drive the humans out! Kill them! It doesn't matter! Just get rid of them!"

The cries of the others started anew. Sticks, pinecones, and rocks of varying sizes fell into the humans' camp once more.

Tabatha shrieked.

"If they were actually trying to hit us," Dane said, "I'm sure they would have."

"You don't know that," Heath replied. Sweat had broken out on his brow, despite the chill of the night. His finger twitched on his weapon, and his knees wobbled, almost knocking together.

"Heath, we need you to calm down," Alexia said.

The sounds of another tree being ripped down, this time from even closer, caused Heath to drop into a crouch. He stared around, eyes wide.

"Heath," Alexia whispered, her voice soothing.

Another rock thudded down in the middle of camp.

The hunter leapt to his feet, gun in hand. He whirled around, fired two shots in the direction of the most recent tree-fall, and raced off the opposite way.

"Heath!" Alexia bellowed.

He didn't stop running, vanishing almost instantly into the dark forest.

"Where does he think he's going?" Dane asked. "It's safer here in camp."

"He's too terrified to think straight," Ursula told them.

Ray shook his head sadly. "He's good as dead."

"And he took one of the guns with him," Guy complained. "We're down to three now, and it'll be hours before sunrise. We might be dead, now, too, thanks to him."

Dane stood, stretching. "He's running away. That's what the sasquatch want—us to leave. They might leave Heath alone. They might redouble their efforts to try and drive out the rest of us."

Tabatha stared after Heath. "Someone has to go get him."

"Didn't you just hear what Dane said?" Ray asked her. "Heath might be safer than us, now."

CHAPTER 27

Toylona rushed down the decline of the mountainside, half running, and half sliding. Loose bits of stones and other debris tumbled ahead of her, clacking and bouncing down the steep pathway she followed.

Before long, she grew close enough to the humans' encampment to see them clustered around the fire.

Wait.

One of them had vanished. Who?

She hurried closer, paying more attention to the humans than to the ground she sped over. She spotted Alexia, Ray, Tabatha, Dane, Guy, and Ursula. But she couldn't see Heath anywhere.

Uttering a scream of frustrated rage, she tried to increase her speed. Where had Heath gone? The other humans were all turned to face one side of the camp. She took that a sign, and went on her way. She skirted the encampment, rounding it on the side opposite where she scented Iktomi to be. She didn't want to risk him trying to stop her. She refused to allow it. Such a thing would only slow her down, allowing Heath to put more distance between them. The human had been a threat since arriving—just like the rest of them. Unlike the others, however, Heath had injured Iktomi. Her mate might not want her to take the reprisal she had planned, but he would get over it. Her ire would allow no other course of action.

Before long, she picked up the strong smell of Heath's terror. The darkness, roots, rocks, uneven ground, and tangles of low-hanging tree branches forced him to move slowly. She, however, simply trod upon, or leapt over, rough patches of ground, allowing her familiarity with such terrain to couple with her natural ability. Any limbs that hung in her way were dealt with easily by smashing them aside. Most of them snapped off, dropping noisily to the ground.

The noises drove Heath to greater panic, and he squealed high-pitched sounds of protests as he struggled to escape.

Toylona roared at him, underlying the vocal sound with a strong infrasound blast. Heath's screams rose in pitch and volume. Around them, others of Toylona's people called out, offering support. A few of them lobbed rocks or pinecones in Heath's direction.

Just as Toylona came within view of him, Heath ducked a rock that narrowly missed his head. His feet slipped out from beneath him, and he sat down hard. Teeth jarring from the impact, he grunted, and dropped his gun.

"Get away from me!" he bellowed. "Leave me alone!"

Toylona stopped, watching him. Heath stared up at her, mouth open wide. He screamed out a long, sustained outcry as she stepped closer.

****

Iktomi smelled Toylona's scent as she rushed by on the other side of the humans. He heard the commotion, and the screaming—from Toylona, and a few others of their people, and from Heath. He thought about slipping away, about trying to intervene and stop Toylona. In the end, he remained in place, listening, while he watched the other humans. Heath had hurt him. The injury still stung badly, despite the poultice Toylona had applied to it. Whatever ultimately happened to Heath, he had brought in upon himself. Iktomi found he no longer cared as much. He only hoped Toylona would be careful in her pursuit of Heath, and not give the human a chance to harm her, too.

In the camp, Alexia kept her gun aimed into the night, facing the direction Heath had run. A steady stream of wordless angry outcries, screams, breaking limbs, and crashing brush echoed in the night from that way.

Tabatha clutched Dane. "I still think we need to go find Heath. We can't just leave him out there!"

Alexia barely spared the young woman a glance. "No one else is leaving this camp—for the safety of everyone here."

"Right," Guy snapped.

Ursula nodded. "I agree."

"So do I," Dane said.

Ray hugged Tabatha. "Me, too."

Heavy footsteps thumped a quarter of the way around the encampment's perimeter. Iktomi turned, inhaling deeply. He didn't recognize the individual's scent. The newcomer must be one of those who responded to Toylona's calls.

Guy hefted his weapon. Alexia pushed it right back down.

"No," she said with a shake of her head. "If one of them comes into camp...maybe. But we're not going to shoot wildly into the darkness. Heath is out there."

Dane stepped up to them. "Even barring the chance of hitting Heath, you could well upset the Forest Gods even more. Heath shot one, and look where we are now! What happens if one of us shoots another one? Do that, and we'd really be in trouble."

Guy shoved his face closer to Dane's. "We're in trouble now!"

Calmly, Dane stepped backward. "All they're doing is trying to frighten us."

"It's working!" Ursula cut in.

"Come sunrise," Dane said mildly, "we'll leave. Until then, we don't want to do anything that might further antagonize them."

Alexia stood firmly at Dane's side. "He's right. Keep your rifles with you. Be ready to use them if the need arises. But do not open fire blindly without a target. Don't shoot unless there's no other choice."

Guy's attention turned to follow the series of heavy footfalls moving by the camp. "What if someone does shoot before you think there's a need? What are you going to do?"

"Take your gun, and toss you out of camp," she told him pointedly. "You can explain to the sasquatch in person why you shot it, or a friend, or a family member."

Ursula's voice shook. "You wouldn't!"

"Try me," Alexia answered, staring the older female down.

A flurry of twigs landed among them. Alexia and Dane didn't flinch. The others cringed. Guy and Ursula raked the edge of the camp with their guns. Alexia glared daggers at them until they relaxed enough to lower their aim.

"The Forest Gods are normally peaceful, and gentle," Dane told the group. His attention focused primarily on Guy. "They're intelligent beings. They know Heath is the one who attacked one of their number. They've seen him be part of our group."

"Heath isn't even here now!" Guy bellowed. "he ran off, and left us!"

Nodding, Dane replied, "I think the Forest Gods are aware of that fact, too. Notice how they've changed since Heath left? They're moving around more now, but they're making less noise. They're pitching fewer rocks at us, and just tossing mostly sticks now."

Alexia's gaze played over the rest of the group. "Dane is right. The sasquatch want us gone, but they don't seem as violently opposed to the rest of us as they were to Heath."

Tabatha, still holding tightly to Ray, watched the darkness at the edge of camp. "Do you think they, like, killed him out there?"

"Probably not," Alexia answered. "But we can't be certain. That's part of the reason for what I said before about no one shooting one unless they have no other choice. These things are defending their territory—their home. If we give them even more reason to be angry with us, they may cross that line, and start killing. I don't know how many of them are out there, but it sounds like a lot. Do we really want to risk chancing that we can shoot down all of them if they rush us en masse? And do so before any of them manage to kill any of us?"

One by one the others shook their heads slowly as Alexia turned her hard stare on them. Finally, she nodded slowly.

"Right," she continued. "Neither do I. So let's not give them any more reason to be hostile with us than they have already. We're all in agreement?"

Again, she focused on the others one at a time. In turn, each of them nodded. Alexia did so with them.

∗∗∗∗

Toylona stood still, staring down at Heath, savoring the moment. The human stared at her, wide-eyed, for a time. Slowly, he pulled himself backward, dragging himself over the uneven roots and rocks on the ground. When his back fetched up against the trunk of a large tree, he reached back, using the bole to help himself to his feet.

She towered over him, advancing a couple of steps. He whimpered piteously, and she smelled the sharp tang of urine as the front of the coverings Heath wore became wet.

He turned, clutching desperately at the lower limbs. Feet scrambling on the bark, he pulled himself into the tree, wiggling his way awkwardly up until he reached a fork in the trunk. His new position put him just out of Toylona's reach should she leap up at him.

She held her ground, watching him, wondering how to kill him. Should she be quick about it? Once she had hold of him, she could tear his head from his neck with little effort. Or, with less effort, snap his neck in the same manner that her people often used to kill deer and other prey when they hunted. Maybe, she mused, she would hold him by his legs, and slam him against the trunk of a tree over and over and over until he had been reduced to an unrecognizable mush.

But he had injured Iktomi. He should be made to suffer, rather than allowed to die quickly. Her fingers flexed as she thought of the pleasure it would bring her to pull Heath's arms and legs from his body. Such a thing would create a bloody mess, but she could easily wash herself clean in a river or lake. Coyotes and other scavengers would make a meal of anything of Heath she left behind.

On the other hand, some of their people had been known to treat humans as prey. Should he tote Heath back to a shelter, so that Iktomi, herself, and their offspring could feast upon him?

That thought gave her great pleasure. She admired the symmetry. Heath had injured Iktomi. It would be fitting if Iktomi consumed Heath's flesh, providing himself with the energy he needed to heal from that wound. Toylona bared her teeth at the human, decided.

Heath, possibly sensing her intent, let out another shriek. He attempted to climb higher in the tree, but a branch broke under his weight, dumping him back in the fork. He landed awkwardly, twisted around, and tried to climb once more.

Toylona blasted him with another round of infrasound, and he went limp. The only thing saving him from tumbling to the ground was a limb that snagged his clothing, holding him in the tree.

She hit him with more infrasound, and he slipped backward, dropping from the fork. He slammed hard to the ground, his breath leaving him in a rush. Showing off her teeth, hoping the human's eyesight allowed him to see them in the dark, she stalked toward him.

Heath cringed, gasping, struggling to pull himself away from her. When she finally stood over him, he gave up trying to escape, and simply curled into a tight ball, sobbing.

She again debated killing him then and there, and taking his carcass back to the shelter. But, as she reached for him, planning to squeeze his neck until he died, she rethought her plan. Iktomi had been most wronged by this human. It would be most fitting if Iktomi were the one to kill him.

Rather than slay the quivering human outright, Toylona scooped him up, tossing him over her shoulder as she would a dead pig, or deer.

"Thank you, everyone!" she called out to the others of her people that she still heard, and smelled in the surrounding forest. "Iktomi thanks you, too. There are other humans around, so be careful. The most dangerous of them has been dealt with, though."

As replies came back, she set off toward the nearest shelter built by herself and Iktomi. Over her shoulder, Heath jounced slightly with each step she took. He had ceased struggling, though. Toylona wondered if he had been hurt when he fell, or if he had simply become resigned to his fate. Either way, she would be ready if he tried to escape. She suspected the human would survive long enough even with both arms and legs broken for Iktomi to reach the shelter, and make the kill. If snapping his limbs didn't stop him from trying to get away, she could always break his spine. Even their normal woodlands prey could live for a short time with a broken back. Surely a human could, too.

CHAPTER 28

Iktomi maintained his position throughout the night. When his stomach insisted that he fill it, he backed away from the humans a bit to forage. Careful to keep them in sight, he broke open a rotted log, sifting through the crumbling detritus for grubs and termites. A few succulent shoots and grasses were there, too, fed by the wood's decay, and as yet untouched by the cooler weather proceeding the season of snow. After eating, he crept nearer to the humans to watch them more closely.

They remained tense, hyper-alert due to the sounds made by the others of his people in the forest. Those others continued pelting the humans' encampment with pinecones, twigs, and small stones at random intervals. Shouts suggesting that the humans leave punctuated the light bombardments. Iktomi knew the humans couldn't understand what was being said to them, though.

Each time someone called out, or threw something into their midst, the humans started. Guns would be aimed into the darkness. Luckily, they never actually tried to harm anyone else with those weapons. Given as stirred up as Toylona had gotten them, he seriously doubted any of the humans would live to see daylight if that happened. Iktomi found himself unsure whether or not he should even attempt to stop such a thing from happening if the humans acted more threateningly than they already had.

Maybe Toylona had been right all along. Maybe he should have taken stronger action from the start. Maybe he should have chased Alexia from the area soon as they became aware of her presence. He would have had to have done the same to Dane, and all the others, too. But it might have been worth it. Had he acted differently then, the dangerous situation now might not have been set up. He might not have been injured.

The rain of objects, and the shouts from his people tapered off slowly as the sky began to lighten. Those aroused to action by Toylona's ire were slipping back into the deeper woods. They would bed down, probably after eating, and rest. Any who returned to the site of the humans' camp that night would be even angrier if the humans proved dumb enough to ignore the obvious warnings, and threats of this night. If the humans stayed the day, Iktomi doubted that all of them would survive to see the following morning. Maybe none of them would.

Clutching Tabatha, Ray asked, "Is it safe to leave now?"

"We'll wait a bit longer," said Alexia. "Let them get clear of this area first."

Guy raked the trees with his weapon. "Are they really leaving?"

Dane warmed his hands at the fire. "At least one will probably stay close. It'll be on guard, watching to see if we leave. If we do, it'll let the others know. If we don't leave, it'll let them know that, too. Then, tonight, the rest of them will probably be back. If that happens, tonight will make last night look peaceful in comparison."

Ursula inched closer to her husband. "We'll be gone."

"Yes, we will," Alexia promised. "We need to start preparing for that right now." She turned away, walking toward her shelter. "Dane? We'll pack up here, and then head over to your camp. We'll get your things packed up quick as we can, and then hike to where my truck is parked."

Shaking his head, Dane replied, "Pack up what you're taking out. Then let's go."

"What about your stuff?"

"Leave it."

Alexia frowned. "Even your guitar?"

He nodded. "Let the Forest Gods do with it what they will. I have another guitar at home. And the sooner we're out of here, the happier the Forest Gods will be. We can't risk anything delaying us, and keeping us here tonight. We need to get out of here ASAP."

Alexia inclined her head toward the others. "The happier they'll all be, too."

She crossed to her shelter, and started the process of putting things into her fabric-and-metal pack.

Iktomi relaxed a bit. If the humans left quietly, things should return to normal soon. Should he ever again encounter a human in his home territory, though, he would act differently. He would no longer allow them to linger as he had this group.

Dane joined Alexia. "Let the others stand guard. I'll help you pack.

Tabatha watched them work. Every few seconds, she cast a fearful look at the trees beyond the camp. "I still think we ought to, like, find Heath before we go."

"No," Alexia said, very tone flat. "We're not staying here any longer than we absolutely need to. The sasquatch don't want us here—they've made that amply clear. We're leaving. If Heath is still out there, he'll have to take care of himself."

Guy pointed at Alexia, saying, "I couldn't agree more. Heath is the reason the bigfoot are so stirred up. Let him deal with them on his own."

Dane turned a glare on the older male. "You and your wife did your fair share to help him!"

Alexia laid a hand on Dane's arm. "It's too late for that now. Let's just pack up, and get out of here. Even when we leave, we have a bit of a hike to reach my truck. I want us out of these woods by sunset. Especially since most of the group will need to ride in the open truck bed."

Ursula and Guy both turned wide eyes toward her. "Whoever is in the truck bed will just be a target for rocks, or whatever else those things might choose to throw," Ursula said.

Alexia nodded. "That's part of why I want to be clear of the woods by dark. But that won't happen if we don't keep moving."

"Stop talking, and get packed, then!" Guy barked at her.

Alexia narrowed her eyes at him, and returned to her task.

Iktomi watched them work diligently as the sky brightened into true daytime. He didn't understand most of what he saw them doing, but knew each action, regardless of his comprehension, moved the humans that much closer to being gone. Finally, the last remnants of the Alexia's artificial cave had been stowed, and the fire doused with water. Steam still rose from cooling embers as Alexia turned to the rest of the group, pointing into the woods partway around the site from where Iktomi lurked.

"All right, everyone. Let's get going," she said.

Guy glanced around uneasily. "It's about time!"

Dane picked up a textured gray box that reeked of the same oily scent of as many of the odd human devices. Iktomi had seen some of Alexia's things packed inside the box earlier. "We're leaving now," Dane told Guy.

Iktomi hung back, following from a safe distance. He used downward-angled branches, tall ferns, and shadows to conceal himself. The humans were leaving. One of the last things he wanted was for one of them to detect his presence, and risk them staying longer because of the encounter.

On the other hand, after the events of the past night, spotting him nearby may well send them running and screaming from the woods. He barred his teeth in a silent grin at the thought.

As the humans trekked through the forest, Dane continuously looked left and right, eyes toward the ground. Alexia did the same, only less frequently. The others, especially the ones carrying guns, let their alert gazes roam over the trees to either side of them.

"I keep looking for them, too," Alexia said. "Them, their tracks, or some other sign of them."

Face flushing, Dane told her, "I don't think they'll hurt us."

"Not now. We're leaving."

Dane shifted his grip on the box's handle. "I wonder what happened to Heath."

Alexia snorted. "Whatever it was, he brought it on himself. We tried to keep him from hunting them. He wouldn't listen. We tried to keep him in camp. He wouldn't listen then, either."

"I know. But the idea of them harming someone..."

"If they hurt him," Alexia soothed, "it was in self defense. We both know that."

Dane nodded sadly. "One had already hurt him. That rock..."

"I know," she answered quietly. "Even after that he wouldn't stop. If they took more drastic action after he left camp, it's his own fault. We did everything we could. We did more, I think, than most people would've."

Nodding again, Dane whispered, "I know. But I've always had a set image of these beings in my mind. I've never believed them to be anything other than peaceful and gentle."

"Any animal, sentient or otherwise, will act to defend itself, or its territory," Alexia told him.

****

Toylona stood outside the shelter, Heath still slung from her shoulder. He had barely stirred since she had picked him up. This site would work well. She would keep Heath here until Iktomi found her. Then one of them would guard the human, while the other went for their offspring. Once the entire family had been gathered, Iktomi could kill Heath in whatever manner he chose, and they would eat. Heath had hunted them—Iktomi especially. Now, the roles had been reversed. The difference was that her people were the better hunters.

She lowered her arm, dumping the human to the ground. He landed hard, his breath being knocked from him in a loud whoosh. Groaning, Heath tried to roll over. Ultimately, he simply flopped back in place, panting.

Toylona grinned down at him. While she waited for Iktomi, she would enjoy watching Heath squirm. Maybe she should snap one of his arms or legs now, and let him suffer until Iktomi killed him? The added punishment would be well served.

No, she told herself. It should be Iktomi who decided what to do with the human. For now, she would make herself be content with simply ensuring that he did not try to escape.

Heath lay in place, gasping, trying to regain his breath. When his breathing finally slowed to something close to normal, he forced himself to look up at her.

"If you plan on killing me, do it," he said. "If you don't, I'll kill you instead."

Toylona cocked her head to the side. Despite his terror, he spoke to her? She had no idea what his words meant in his language. She assumed he meant to make some sort of plea for her to spare his life. She only glared down at him, baring her teeth in a silent threat.

Heath scrambled backward a couple of feet. She followed slowly, not intending to allow him the faintest chance of escape. His back drew up against a tree. Bracing himself, he got his feet beneath him, standing. He shook as he gazed up at her.

Toylona growled low in her throat. Her hands flexed at her sides. After long moments of staring back, Heath lunged at her.

Shrieking with rage, she grabbed him by the shoulder, her huge hand covering most of his upper arm, and tossed him aside. Again, Heath landed hard, his breath knocked from him. Toylona strode over, towering above him. She growled louder than before.

Heath, she realized had ceased moving. Had she killed

him? She hadn't thrown him very hard. Then again, humans were far smaller and weaker than her own people. Could she have inadvertently slain him?

No, she realized after a brief time of watching him. She could still hear him breathe. She still heard the beating of his heart. He lived, but had apparently slipped into that same odd sleeping state that Iktomi had told her about in relation to Tabatha.

Toylona hovered beside him, unwilling to step back and allow the human a chance at somehow using that distance to try to get away. She waited, but Heath made no move.

Frowning, she leaned in closer. His chest continued to rise and fall with slow, steady motions. His heart beat, although the rate had slowed. For a moment that concerned her. Then she likened it to the heart rate of a calm rabbit to the heart rate of a rabbit being pursued. It made sense that Heath's heart had slowed to what she assumed to be a more normal rhythm now that he had dropped into his weird sleeping state.

She continued staring down at him, pondering the odd penchant that humans seemed to possess for falling into such a sleep. Were they like opossums? Did they simply pretend to be dead as a defense? It didn't make sense. She could easily tell that he hadn't died. Or could this state be meant to fool other humans into thinking that the threatened individual had died?

That made more sense, she decided. Humans had poor eyesight, and almost no senses of smell, or hearing. Such a thing might be a blatant ruse when used against her own people, but another human would likely be easily taken in by it.

She prodded him in the side with her foot. He didn't move. Maybe this wasn't a ploy. Maybe humans really did drop into a sound sleep when threatened. How, she wondered, amazed, could such a thing be to their advantage? It made no sense! Such a thing would only be to the detriment of the human, and to the advantage of whatever threatened.

She nudged him harder, and let out a startled gasp when Heath grabbed her ankle, and rolled. Caught off guard, she lost her balance, tumbling to the ground. She howled at him in rage, as he used the roll for momentum to regain his feet.

As she tried to get to her own, Heath kicked a leg from beneath her. A moment later, a length of wood slammed down on her back. Toylona grunted harshly, and Heath hit her again, and again until she dropped, dazed.

Heath let the tree limb he had clubbed her with tumble to the ground next to her. He then kicked her in the neck before stomping on her leg.

"Iktomi!" she bellowed. "Help me! Help!"

Heath turned to run.

Toylona roared, working a nearly inaudible layer of infrasound into the vocal attack. Heath stumbled, almost falling. He caught his balance just before hitting the ground. Toylona climbed to her feet as Heath raced away, ducking and weaving around and under low-hanging tree branches.

She started to run after him, but her head and back hurt from his attacks with the makeshift club. Her leg ached where he had stomped on it. She continued after him, but moving far more slowly than typical.

Not knowing what good it would do, she unleashed another infrasound roar after him. The only reply was noises made by Heath as he retreated further and further from her. Snarling, she ran after him.

CHAPTER 29

Twigs broke in front of them. Tabatha and Ursula screamed. Guy and Ray looked tense, as if both were on the verge of flight. Alexia swung her gun around from her shoulder, taking aim.

Iktomi hunkered down, freezing in place. Someone crashed through the brush, unseen. He inhaled deeply, frowning as he caught Heath's scent. His frown deepened, and he fought down a displeased growl when he caught Toylona's smell mingled with Heath's.

Heath staggered up to them, panting harshly. His eyes, wide and wild, darted quickly. One arm hung limp at his side. The coverings he wore over his body were filthy and torn, hanging in rags.

Quickly, Alexia lifted the barrel of the gun to the air. "I nearly shot you!"

"Get me out of here!" Heath begged, stumbling toward her.

"What happened to you?" she asked.

"We can't stay here!" Heath shouted.

Before anyone could say more, the terrified, disheveled hunter veered away. Alexia and the others had to follow, or lose sight of him.

"What happened to you?" Alexia demanded, catching up to him.

"One of them caught me," Heath gasped, not stopping. "It knocked me out of a tree. I think it broke my arm! I didn't even feel it at first. I fought the thing, and managed to get away. But it's after me!"

Dane frowned, stepping in front of Heath, forcing the older male to stop. "Wait! You fought one of the Forest Gods?"

"I caught it off guard," Heath panted, clutching his injured arm. "I hurt it enough to slow it down. I think, anyway. If I hadn't, I'm sure it would've already caught me. But we need to get out of here. Now!"

Heath tried stepping around Dane, but the younger male stopped him. "Go tearing through the woods, wounded, and you'll only end up dead."

Eyes bulging, Heath screamed, "We'll die if we stay here!"

"It was probably the one you shot at before," Dane said. "You're lucky. Sasquatch have been known to slam hunting dogs, and deer against trees to kill them. You're lucky that didn't happen to you."

Ray put in, "Think what might've happened to you if you'd actually managed to kill one of them."

"Just get me out of these woods!" Heath shouted, shambling onward.

The others moved to keep pace with him. Iktomi followed, wondering why Toylona's scent clung so strongly to Heath. Why had she been with him? Heath had obviously been injured. Had Toylona done that to him?

He turned, scenting her, and hearing her approach through the trees. He put up a hand to stop her, and gasped when he saw her limping.

"What happened?" he demanded, rushing to her side.

"Heath did," she retorted.

Crouching to feel her leg, checking for a break, Iktomi said, "Your leg is only bruised. Heath just rejoined the others. I smelled you on him. He attacked you?"

"Yes."

"How?"

She hesitated, looking at the ground.

"What did you do to him?" he pressed.

Still not looking at him, she quietly said, "I captured

him."

He stood, cupping her chin to lift her face so that their gazes met. "Why did you do that?"

"I had planned to hold him until you returned. I wanted you to kill him."

He shook his head. "When I threw the rocks at him before, it was because he was actively hunting me at the time."

"He hurt you!" she shouted.

"Keep your voice down. The humans will hear."

"I don't care! He hurt you! He needs to be punished! I took him, planning for you to kill him. Once he died, we, and our offspring, could make a meal of him."

"No!" Iktomi snarled. "We will not do that!"

"Others have."

Nodding, he said, "Others have, yes. A few. But I don't agree with that practice. Humans aren't dumb prey. They're intelligent in their own way. We don't eat them. We don't slay them except for self defense. Which your attack on Heath wasn't!"

Toylona twisted her head, freeing her chin from his grasp. Her gaze returned to the ground. "I got so angry at him—at all of them—when Heath hurt you."

"I understand. I probably would have reacted the exact same way had it been you, or one of our offspring, instead of me."

She looked back up at him, smiling faintly. "So what do we do now?"

Waving a hand in the direction the humans had gone, he answered, "Watch them. Make sure they leave. Once they're gone, we go collect our young, and find something to eat."

"Life as usual?"

"Of course."

"They know we're here," she reminded him. "They've seen both of us, and probably some of the others that answered my call last night."

"I know. And because of that they'll probably be back.

Some of them, anyway. They might even bring others with them. Or they might send others in their place."

She nodded, asking, "What will we do then?"

Shrugging, he started walking after the humans. He took care not to step on dropped twigs, or dry leaves. He didn't want the human knowing they were there again if he could avoid it. In answer to her question, he said, "When humans, be it these again, or others, come back, we'll do whatever we think is best at the time. For now, we let these go. You aren't badly hurt. And Heath's actions against you were pure self defense. My own injury is minor, and will soon heal."

Moving to his side, Toylona only grunted softly.

Quietly as they could, they crept close enough to the retreating humans to see them again. Heath led the group, walking quickly. His breath came in short, harsh gasps of pain with each step. Ray and Tabatha followed him. Guy and Ursula walked behind them, sweeping the forest around them with their weapons. Alexia and Dane brought up the rear.

The humans were working their way slowly down a ridge, following a trail left by the repeated passing of many deer. Overhead, the sun glowed brilliantly in the cloudless blue sky. Off in the distance, sunlight glinted off the metal of an elongated, boxy thing in an area where the trees thinned. The odd contraption sat beside one of the artificial pathways that humans often created. The humans seemed to be headed toward it.

"Do you plan to come back out here," Dane asked Alexia.

She nodded, turning her attention to the woodlands around them. "I want to come back here, yes," she answered him. "But I'll give them a while to settle down. My guess is that they won't welcome human intrusion for some time."

"Will you do me a favor? Two, actually."

Alexia frowned, suspicious. "What might those favors be?"

"First," Dane told her, "when you come back here, let me know. Secondly..."

"What is it?"

He took a deep breath. "Secondly, will you please let me come with you?"

She hesitated before asking, "Why? I'm not looking for a research partner."

"I know. It's just that..." He walked several steps before saying, "We've been through a lot in the past couple of days. I've learned some things."

"We all have."

Dane cast a quick look back at the rest of the group. "Regardless of what sasquatch are—interdimensional deities, or terrestrial beings—they need protection. I think we stand a better chance of managing that if we work together."

Alexia's eyebrows lifted as she turned to look fully at Dane. "You think we'd make a good team?"

"Yes."

After giving it a few moments of consideration, she replied, "We'll talk about it."

"And...there's another reason why I, um..."

Dane stopped, and set down the box he toted. Reaching out, he touched Alexia's cheek. She started to draw away, but then hesitated, waiting. He leaned forward, kissing her softly.

Iktomi nudged Toylona gently, grinning. Though she fought it, she smiled, too, as they watched the humans.

Alexia grinned, ducking her head. "We can talk about that, too."

Ray glanced back, grinned, and took up the box Dane had been carrying. "Don't take too long, man. If Heath is right, there could be an angry bigfoot coming after us."

Dane nodded to him, hanging back as the others moved on. Alexia waited with him. Once the others were ahead of them a short way, Alexia took hold of Dane's hand. Together, they followed the rest of the group.

Iktomi stepped from cover, getting a clearer view of the departing humans. Toylona moved to remain at his side.

As Alexia and Dane carefully picked their way down the gentle slope, Alexia turned to look back. Her gaze froze on

Iktomi and Toylona. She stopped moving, standing still.

"Dane..." she whispered.

Toylona stepped toward cover once more. Iktomi took her hand, keeping her in view of the humans as Dane turned to look at them, going still upon spotting them.

"Keep quiet," Iktomi warned his mate. "Make no threatening moves. Remember, they're leaving. But let them get a look at us. They're frightened. Seeing us here might scare them enough to keep them away."

At his side, Toylona grumbled a soft agreement.

Alexia and Dane stared at them for a time, neither human daring to move. Finally, Alexia said, "They're just watching; making sure we're heeding their warning."

"We need to go," Dane replied. "Now. After what the Forest Gods have already done, let's not give them reason to be any more upset with us."

"Right. Let's go," she said quietly.

Tightening her grip on his hand, she led him after the others along the path.

Iktomi and Toylona held their ground, waiting. Alexia and Dane didn't seem to alert the others to their presence. None of the other humans looked back. The group just made its steady way toward the long, boxy shape glimmering the sun.

The items they carried were stowed in the empty, hollow back of the device. Ray, Tabatha, Heath, Guy, and Ursula climbed into the back, also. Alexia and Dane opened panels on either side of the device near the front, got in, and closed the panels after them. Almost instantly the thing they had entered gave an unpleasant surge of noise and smell, and rolled forward, picking up speed as it moved along the black, unnaturally smooth pathway.

Once the humans were gone, Iktomi turned back to Toylona. "We're safe."

"For now," she replied. "Others will come. Maybe some of these will return."

He took her hand, and started back toward where she

had left their offspring. "Yes, but as I told you before, we'll deal with that when it happens. For now, let us simply enjoy our family, and our lives. That's all any of us can do."

SCOTT'S SASQUATCH EXPERIENCES

The book you've just read is very important, and special to me. Varying amounts of myself go into each project I work on. That's true, I think, for any author. This project, however, takes that to a whole new level for me. While this novel has been a work of fiction, the reason I wanted to work on it is a very real, and personal one. Those fans and readers who know me personally probably already know why. For those of you who don't, please read on.

I grew up in central Ohio. Despite all of the evidence, and sightings of sasquatch that have come from that state, a lot of people still react to the topic with something like, "Sasquatch? In Ohio? You're crazy!"

Rest assured, they're there. I've seen at least one of them. During one encounter, there had to have been at least two of them present, although they weren't seen, but only heard that time.

Desirée Lee—my gorgeous, wonderful wife/best friend/co-author—has not had a completely certain sighting of a sasquatch as of this writing. She tells about that in her own words, in later pages. As I often tell her when the subject comes up, part of me hopes she is able to see one at some point. Paradoxically, another part of me hopes she never does. Seeing one changes you. After such a sighting, you're never the same. The encounter haunts you.

As I write this account now, about 17 years have gone by since I left Ohio. I moved to Florida in the summer of 1998, and lived there for 14 years. During that time, I met Desirée, and now live in northern California. We're three miles from the Oregon state border. So, when we say "northern California" we truly mean it!

Still, despite being so far from the location of the events I'm about to relate, and for so long, not a day goes by when I don't think back on these happenings. To this day, I still have occasional nightmares involving sasquatch, too. That isn't because the one I encountered was overly hostile. None of us were physically harmed by the sasquatch.

Honestly, I don't know why seeing, and experiencing what I did affects me so strongly to this day. These things happened when I was a child, and later, a teenager. By the time this book is released, I'll be 40-years-old. That's how deeply seeing one of these beings can affect a person. Again, part of me hopes for Desirée to see one someday, and part of me hopes she never does.

When I was all of 5-years-old, my parents and I—I'm an only child—moved into a house in Marysville, Ohio. An old railroad bed ran by a couple hundred yards or so behind our house. A narrow alley, and a neighbor's lawn separated our backyard from the rail line. I don't remember ever seeing a train on those particular tracks. Shortly after we moved in, the tracks were removed, leaving only an abandoned railroad bed. Beyond that was cow pasture, the town water tower, and woods.

A small group of friends, and myself claimed a section of the abandoned railroad bed as our territory. Everyone in the area knew to look for us there first. It became our hangout spot.

At the beginning of each spring, tall weeds would quickly grow up along the elevated railroad bed, and, even more so, in the lower area behind it. We would embark on an annual task of carving out a winding pathway through these weeds each year. At the end of the path, we'd hack down weeds in a larger circular area. We always made sure that the path itself curved back and forth, so as not to provide a straight line of sight from the entrance to the clearing where we hung out. Spaced here and there along the path, we'd thin out weeds and grasses to create a few hidden "emergency exits"—just in case. Raccoon, opossums, and some other local wildlife frequented the area. We wanted to be sure we could get free of the path easily at any time such a need arose.

We had no idea at all just what sort of "wildlife" we'd end up dealing with, though!

The sasquatch turned up while we were still young. I don't remember how old we all were at the time, but we weren't even in our teens yet. Evidently the sasquatch found the path and clearing to be comfortable, and easy to traverse. It seemed to like it there as well as we did.

At first, we didn't know anything had changed. We would have uneasy feelings of being watched. We started finding the occasional place where something large had pushed its way through the weeds. From time to time we'd notice a very strong skunk-like odor in the area, or oddly large droppings. Still, we were children. We dismissed the signs, and went about our business.

After these things had gone on for a while, one member of the group claimed to have seen a large, hairy creature walking on two legs by the railroad bed one night. The rest of us refused to take him seriously, despite his nonstop insistence on what he had seen.

Not too long after, another member of the group made a similar claim. The old railroad bed ran directly by her grandparents' home. She spent her childhood being raised as much—if not more—by her grandparents than her parents. Because of that, she lived almost fulltime at their house. Her bedroom window looked out toward the railroad bed. Having a second such report of a tall, hairy creature walking around the area made the rest of us take the claims more seriously.

Yet, the girl, being so terrified of what she had seen, convinced herself that she had dreamed of the creature, and nothing more. At the same time, she didn't want to be near the railroad bed at night anymore. She preferred to be safely indoors, and steadfastly refused to look out her bedroom windows at night after that.

Still, we were children. The old railroad bed had become our place. We had no plans to give it up. Only two members of the group had spotted the creature. They had no idea what to call it. We began referring to it as the Troll.

A few years went by. The "Troll" continued to make itself known in the same ways as before. We noticed a pattern over time. In the spring, when the weeds would grow up, it would return to the railroad bed. We would find signs of it throughout the rest of the spring, all summer, and into the autumn. When cold weather set in, and the weeds wilted, dying off—minimizing cover—the "Troll" would move on. We wouldn't have any indication of its return until the following spring. Things were peaceful between us, and it.

Eventually, that changed.

Over the years since, as I've talked about these events, it's been suggested to me that, maybe, the sasquatch had been a juvenile, and basically grew up with us. Once it reached adulthood, its outlook and mannerisms changed. It's also been suggested that the creature had been an adult from the time it moved into the area, and simply tolerated my friends, and I in territory it had staked out for itself because we were so young. I don't know which, if either, is the case. Regardless, something in the sasquatch's outlook toward us evidently changed.

Sasquatch have often been noted to be drawn to children. A lot of researchers presume this is because children are small, and unthreatening. Sasquatch also seem to be highly intelligent, and very curious. They've been known to simply watch humans, as if observing, and learning. What better way to learn about humans than to keep surveillance on a bunch of unthreatening young ones? But, we grew up. Maybe as we got older, and physically larger, the sasquatch began seeing us as a threat to it. I don't know, and probably never will.

The "Troll" slowly grew more aggressive toward us. More and more, we would have the feeling that something lurked nearby, watching us. We normally pinpointed these feelings, thinking that our watcher lay in the woods on the other side of a narrow area of cow pasture. Sometime, though, we were positive that our hidden watcher was somewhere very close, sharing space at the railroad bed with us. More and more we also had the feeling that whatever was watching us was very angry with us. Once in a while we'd hear a low growl from nearby.

During that time, something kept targeting the trash of the neighbors directly next-door to where I lived. The people refused to eat leftovers. So, any food not eaten during a given meal simply ended up pitched in the garbage—an easy meal for whatever might claim it. Their trashcans were kept right by the alley behind our houses. That put them within sight of the railroad bed, making them an easy target for anything coming from that area. And something kept tearing into their trash at night.

It became such a problem that a stomach-high, red brick wall was built to contain their trashcans. A slatted wooden gate, with a slide latch, allowed the garage collectors easy access to the cans. The neighbors thought it was raccoons, or something similar, that continuously raided their trash. They began using the handle-lock style of cans, too, in addition to the wall-and-gate enclosure.

Whatever kept feeding from their trash would open the slide latch, unlock the trashcan handles, often placing the removed lid atop the wall, and sometimes even go so far as to lift a bag of trash out of a can before ripping into it. To this day, I'm stunned at the persistent belief they had that whatever did all of this had been raccoon! This was in the days before technology allowed for motion-sensor trail cameras, or other such things. Far as I know, the culprit of these nighttime trash raids never got spotted.

As these things happened, and my friends and I grew older, and learned more, we finally realized what we had going on. We realized that our "Troll" was really a sasquatch. Stupidly, we shrugged it off. We had a sasquatch pretty much in our backyards. That being the case with us, it had to be a common occurrence. Right? There wasn't anything special about us.

After all the time that had passed, my first actual sasquatch sighting happened during my teens. I was outside, hanging out with the female friend who mostly lived with her grandparents.

We were in her grandparents' yard, walking up the short, gentle hill to the abandoned railroad bed. She froze, and put her arm across my chest, stopping me. I looked at her. She was staring, open-mouthed and wide-eyed, pointing straight ahead. Through a narrow gap in the weeds, I saw what looked like the peaked head and shoulders of a large humanoid figure with dark hair. It was either sitting, or crouched, holding perfectly still. We were seeing its profile. We backed slowly down the hill until it was out of sight, then turned, and ran inside her grandparents' home.

Had she not stopped me, I'd have walked right into the creature's lap. To this day, I often wonder just how many more steps the sasquatch would have allowed us to take before making itself known to us. Whatever the answer, the number had to have been very low, as we were only a few steps from it when she spotted it through the weeds directly in front of us. Thinking back on that afternoon still gives me chills!

After that sighting, the female friend in question refused to ever go back to the railroad bed at all. She wouldn't return even as part of a group. After that day, she could no longer tell herself that she had simply dreamed the creature she had spotted walking along the railroad bed at night so long before. She had to face the fact that this being was real, and it was there—living almost directly in her grandparents' backyard.

The following day, we told another friend. He wanted to see the spot where the creature had been. It was broad daylight, so I took him there, albeit reluctantly. The only sign we saw of it was a large patch of flattened grasses where it had been sitting, or lying down.

Somewhere during these events, he and I also found what we referred to as the "vine cave", which I now believe to have been a nest, or shelter made by the sasquatch. From our point of view, it simply popped into existence literally overnight in the large, open area we'd carved. He and I actually crawled into it a few times, but always felt very uncomfortable in it, and always left quickly.

This structure had been built in the clearing we had made that year, tightly woven with woody vines of varying thicknesses. The weaving formed three rounded walls, and a low, curved ceiling that was nearly domed. An opening had been left in place of most of the fourth side. The opening faced the spot where the path my friends and I had hacked through the weeds that year entered the clearing. The entire structure had been designed to be low enough to the ground so as to be hidden from view outside the clearing by the tall weeds growing around it.

Not long after the discovery of the "vine cave", a couple of rival teens destroyed it, thinking we'd built it. I think that may have well caused an increase in encounters with the sasquatch, and its attempts to chase us away that happened afterward. Even though we hadn't been the ones to ruin the shelter it had constructed, it may have blamed us. Or, since we persisted in hanging out at the railroad bed, we might have simply been presenting the sasquatch with easy targets. Regardless, the aggression stepped up after the destruction of the "vine cave".

My second and third sightings were spaced out over the next few years. Each time I saw it was in broad daylight—as had been my first sighting.

When the second sighting I had of it took place, I was in our driveway, pulling weeds that were growing up through the gravel. Movement at the railroad bed caught my attention. I looked up there to see a tall, humanoid being with a conical head, and long arms walking along the hill, moving to my right. It was covered in dark hair. I've always suspected it was the same creature I saw on my first sighting, but don't know for sure. I watched it walk for a few seconds until being blocked from view by a neighbor's storage shed. Then I turned, and ran into the house. I didn't go back up to the railroad bed for weeks.

My third sighting was from a far greater distance. On the other side of the railroad bed was a fenced-in area of cow pasture, and the local water tower. Beyond that was woods, and a trailer court.

I was in our upstairs back bedroom one afternoon, again, during broad daylight. I saw what I first took to be a rolled-up rug turned up on one end by a trashcan back in the trailer court. I could just barely see it, due to the distance. I looked away, then looked back. What I was seeing seemed shorter, as if it had sagged, or crouched. I kept looking away, then looking back, wanting to see if it moved. I couldn't tell if it was moving or not. Finally, I looked away for about ten minutes. When I looked back, whatever it had been was gone. My guess is that it had been the sasquatch raiding trashcans.

Aside from the direct sightings of the creature(s), we had other evidence as well.

Another friend of mine lived in a house just beyond the far side of the trailer court. A wooden privacy fence divided his backyard from the trailer court. He once told me that he and his family would sometimes smell a heavy, musky scent at night. They would sometimes hear what sounded like heavy footfalls outside their house at night, too. He said his mother even claimed to have heard a loud heartbeat on occasion as their nocturnal visitor prowled outside.

Once, in my teens, after the destruction of the "vine cave", I was at the railroad bed alone. Something that sounded very large was in the weeds and brush ahead of me, thrashing at the weeds, making a lot of noise. I thought at first it was the same friend who had wanted to go check out the site of my first direct sighting of the sasquatch. About the same moment I realized that whatever was ahead of me was too large to be him, a rock about the size of my fist was thrown at me, just narrowly missing hitting me in the head. I ran, and refused to go back to the railroad bed for weeks after.

It only occurred to me years later that I may have provoked the attack, warning, or whatever is had been meant as, simply because of what I had been doing at the time. Along with the weeds, a sapling maple tree had grown up in the area where we were hacking the path through that year. We curved it differently each year, trying never to follow the same path twice in a row. So, this sapling had been growing for a few years. It had gotten to be four-feet-tall, or so. Still small, it didn't require an axe, or anything of that nature to get it out of the way of that year's "construction project". I had grabbed a piece of a tree limb, and commenced using it as a club to "chop" down the sapling.

Wood-knocking is commonly thought to be used as a method of communication among sasquatch. It has also been documented with great ape species. Working to take down that sapling, I was wood-knocking—over and over and over—and doing so to the point of tearing down the sapling. Which was, of course, the whole point of my actions just then.

Next time I was at the railroad bed alone I was in the same place, and the same weed-thrashing occurred again. Luckily, no rock was thrown that time. Then again, I hadn't been wood-knocking that time, either.

Another time that same friend who wanted to see the spot of my first sighting and I were at the railroad bed by ourselves. There had to have been at the very least two of the creatures with us—one on either side of us. Nothing was thrown at us, but the same weed-thrashing noises started up to each side of us. Oddly, this time, nothing moved that we could see. Both of us clearly heard the sounds, but couldn't see a thing moving. Still, after holding our ground for only a few moments, we both ran.

Sasquatch are known to be mimics. They have been seen and heard making calls which sound like birds, and coyotes. Sometimes they will shift from one to the other in the same call. They've also been observed making mumbling sounds. These mumbles, especially when heard from a bit of a distance, sound like humans talking. The effect is what sounds like people talking—close enough to hear the drone of their voices, but far enough away to prevent the listener from hearing distinct words. Think of it as sort of an audible disguise.

We wondered afterward if that wasn't what we had heard that day. Could at least two sasquatch have been there, producing vocal sound effects that sounded like the weeds being moved around violently? However they created the sounds, the noises did what they were evidently meant to do, and chase us off!

This same friend also decided to step up our own claims on the railroad bed after we found a rock cairn built on our path one day. The cairn was little, consisting of only a few small rocks and stones. My friend spouted his usual line of, "No (expletive deleted) monkey is going to chase me away!" and promptly kicked the cairn, scattered the stones.

We gathered up stones, and built a new, larger, cairn in place of the one we'd found. We left, and went back the next day to find our own cairn scattered, and new, larger, one in its place. We immediately kicked it apart, and built a new one, larger still, in place of the one we'd found.

This went on for days. Each day we'd find that the cairn we'd built the day before had been wrecked, and new, larger, one would be in its place. Each day we would scatter the new one, and build our own, larger yet, in place of the most recent one we'd found.

Secretly, I thought he was going back to the railroad bed later, and building the new ones we'd "find" the next day. He thought the same of me.

Finally, after this had gone on long enough that the cairns were getting to be a bit larger than shoebox size, my friend decided to go one better, and scent mark the cairn we'd just built. He told me what he was going to do, and promptly unzipped his pants, and urinated on our newest rock cairn. Afterward, we left, and went to his house. We hung out on his front porch for two or three hours, talking, then decided to go check on the new, scent-marked, cairn.

The smell hit us when we were still yards from the cairn—not even yet on the path. We knew what we'd find, and it scared both of us. As we'd been together for the entire intervening time, each knew that the other had not gone back to the railroad bed to do anything. The scent was an overpowering musk so strong it made us sick. Think skunk concentrate. We held our breath, ran in, saw what we knew we'd find—a new cairn that was noticeably larger than the one we'd built a few hours prior—and ran back out into clear air to breathe. The stench that the sasquatch left to scent-mark its new cairn lingered for days, but that ended the rock cairn war. The sasquatch won that time!

We also once found what looked to be shallow, crude pit toilets. We saw what looked to be finger marks in the mud, and suspected they'd been dug out with very large bare hands. Several of the toilets contained what looked to be human fecal matter, only far larger.

Further from home, at a local park, my parents and I were walking wooded trails one summer afternoon. One of the trails passed by a small lake. I detoured from the path to go down near the water. On the bank, inches from the water, was a pile of fresh, soft, wet mud. It looked to have just been scooped from the edge of the lake. Murky silt from its removal had not yet settled all the way back down in the water. Sizable grooves, looking to me like marks left by large fingers combing through it, marred the mud, spreading it out a bit.

I pointed it out to my parents. Dad left the path to join me by the water. When he saw the mud, he did the same thing I had already started doing—scanning the tree line around us, looking for whoever, or whatever, had scooped the mud from the lake. It appeared to have been done just prior to us coming upon it.

I tried to get Mom to leave the path for a look at the mud, too. She said she only wanted to continue on quickly because of the mosquitoes. Dad agreed with her, and hurried us on our way. Mom hadn't seen the mud firsthand. Dad and I didn't fully relax after having seen it until we were out of the forest, and back in the park's asphalt-covered driveways and parking lot.

To this day, I strongly suspect that a sasquatch had been living in the park, or at least passing through. I think we disturbed it with our walk, and did so mere moments after it plopped that mud down on the lake's shore.

I have no proof or evidence to back up any of the events related here. When all of this went on, my friends and I were children, and later on, teenagers. Stupidly, we never once thought to try and gather evidence of anything we saw, heard, or otherwise experienced. Since we were growing up with all of this going on, we didn't know we were experiencing something special, or out of the ordinary. To this day, I mentally kick myself daily for that.

Which had led me to, over the years, formulating a plan for a long-term sasquatch research project. I won't go into detail here, for fear of someone with better resources than I have at my disposal swiping the idea, and running with it themselves. Suffice to say that the project would take months, or, better still, even years, to run. If I'm ever able to do this project, I hope to get not only the raw data from it, but also turn the project into a documentary on the project as it plays out over time, as well as a book to that same effect—at least three projects from the expenditure of resources.

Luckily for me, Desirée is almost as enthusiastic about the research plan as I am. She would like to be part of it, and part of any other projects that come out of it. Yes, I know—I have the greatest wife ever!

Also interested in joining this project, should it ever happen, is my good friend Thomas Lee Curtin Jr. Thomas is an experienced fortean researcher. He is a member of several high-profile groups dealing with several areas of the unknown. He has a solid background in criminal investigation, and security/law enforcement, too. Thomas is also the creator, and driving force, behind the Facebook-based paranormal, and cryptozoology news, and discussion group "Eerie Ohio".

So, please allow me to close with a plea for assistance on this research project. If any sasquatch researchers, research groups, or anyone with money, and interest to fund a long-term sasquatch research project is reading this, and would like to help, please get in touch with me. The best way to reach me on-line is by using the "Contact" page on my website: www.scottharper.net. If you'd prefer to use good old snail-mail, please write to me at:

Scott Harper
C/O Umbral Press
P.O. Box 671
Dorris, CA 96023-0671

There will be a non-disclosure agreement that we'll need to sign before I spill details about my idea for the research project. This is, again, to ensure that no one with better resources than I currently have access to simply takes the ideas that I've developed over time, and runs with them. Sadly, in our modern world, such protective measures are often needed.

Thank you for reading.

DESIRÉE'S SASQUATCH EXPERIENCES

While Scott's experiences have been more extensive than mine, I've had two potential sightings, as well, plus some possible evidence sightings.

The first occurred in the spring of 2014. We were returning home late one evening. It was a cold, rainy night. I turned the corner toward our street, and saw something standing next to a dumpster a few houses in. I glanced around, double-checking to make sure there was no cross traffic I might have missed when I looked the first time. When I looked back to the dumpster, mere seconds later, it was gone. It's possible, it could've been a person, but when we drove past the house, there was no sign of a person going into the house. It was unlikely a human could've made it from the dumpster, back to the house, and gone inside in the few seconds between the time I saw it, and when I finally drove by. It stood about 5-6 feet tall.

Even I doubted at first whether I saw something or if my eyes were playing tricks upon me in the darkness. Then Scott, who was in the passenger seat, asked me if I saw it, too. We believe it may have been a juvenile, scavenging in the dumpster.

The second sighting was actually when we were on our way to the Bigfoot Days festival in Willow Creek, CA. We'd got a late start on the drive down there. Plus, our daughter's carsickness forced us to make a few unanticipated stops, so it was very dark, and we still weren't even in Willow Creek.

Along the side of Highway 299, somewhere in a remote stretch of windy road not too far out of Weaverville, I saw something moving in the trees alongside the highway. Before I could get a better look (as much as I could in the dark at least), we'd rounded a corner, and it was out of sight. Perhaps it was a deer, but it seemed much taller than that.

I've seen some X formations in trees in Oregon, between Chiloquin, and Chemult. Those were seen during the day, though. I wouldn't expect to have a full sighting at that time.

Scott holds the dual hope that I do see one as definitively as he has, and that I never do. Who knows what the future may hold? I've lived in several haunted houses, and seen more ghosts than I care to count. Maybe a positive sasquatch sighting is in the cards for me someday as well.

ABOUT THE AUTHORS

Scott Harper is the bestselling, award-winning author of more than 30 published short stories, and several novels. There has been talk, from several fronts, about turning his fourth novel, "Predators or Prey?", the first book in his Wendy Markland series, into a live-action project. Interest from a movie producer has also been voiced about turning his bestselling, award-winning eighth novel, "Quintana Roo, Yucatan", into a film.

Harper grew up in Ohio, and graduated from Marysville High School in 1993, and began screenwriting in 2007, after the publication of several short stories and novels. He has worked on projects for James Tucker Productions, and 11th Dimension Films. He is currently involved with several projects, covering literature, film, and comic books. He was also a contributing writer for "Nuclear Winter Entertainment" for several months before that site shut down.

Scott is very happily married to bestselling paranormal author Desirée Lee. Together, they have a wonderful little girl, and are working jointly on several projects. Those projects include multiple books, as well as the hit webcomic "MoonWraith".

More information about his work can be found on his website: www.scottharper.net

Critically acclaimed, best-selling author Desirée Lee is an amalgam wrapped inside of an enigma: a book junkie, vampire, and self-proclaimed geek with a fascination bent toward the dark and macabre. When not writing or reading, she feeds her gaming addiction. Des loves the dark, evil characters. If word ever got out that she was secretly a level 15 paladin, her reputation would be ruined.

Des currently lives in a hole-in-the-wall town in Northern California, further away from civilization than she'd sometimes like to be.

Check out Des' website at http://www.desireelee.com and find her on Twitter: http://twitter.com/authordeslee or Facebook: http://www.facebook.com/authordeslee.

Coming soon from Umbral Press

Brothers at Arms

By Desirée Lee

For 250 years, the Arcée brothers have been in conflict. The vendetta between these two powerful vampires has shown no signs of resolve or waning. The concession made between the two is that the location of their ongoing war is moved every five decades to help prevent hapless mortals from discovering them. It was determined that the new locations would be chosen by a delegated Keeper, symbolized by a custom-made tarot card. Where the card goes, so do the Houses and also the war.

When the card changes hands, each House sends out Seekers, specially trained vampires who race against each other to be the first to discover the card's new location. The first one to find the card and take control of the new keeper has the upper hand in the battle for that duration as they gain first foothold in the new city.

This year is a turning year. Julio Mendoza receives the card in the mail, unaware of its meaning. When he learns of the history of the card, he realizes he has been thrust in to a war that holds nothing for him, yet he cannot escape his fate. Still he will not accept his role meekly.

Michelle Bryson is a Seeker for the House of François Arcée. She is pitted against a rival from the House of Pierre Arcée to get to Julio first. Michelle is a young Seeker and if she fails to capture the Keeper, her life may be forfeited. What Michelle did not plan on was to find the Keeper to be a sexy, rebellious man who has a spirit in him unlike any Keeper she has seen in the past.

Julio knows the vampires are coming for him. He knows that he cannot hide forever. When the Seekers find him though, he cannot deny his attraction toward Michelle – an attraction that they will both pay dearly for if the Seeker from the House of Pierre Arcée has anything to do about it.

www.ingramcontent.com/pod-product-compliance
Lightning Source LLC
Chambersburg PA
CBHW061608170626
46811CB00001B/362